THE BOY MADE OF
SHINING HAPPINESS

The Boy Made of Shining Happiness

Geoffrey Riddell

Copyright © 2014 Geoffrey Riddell

ISBN: 978-0-9874978-9-5

Adventure science fiction, young adult

Published by Geoffrey Riddell 1378 Old Tolmie Rd Tolmie 3723 Victoria Australia

Recommended reader age: 13+
If you are twelve or younger, read this book with the help of a mature adult available.

Cover art by the author. The painting of the boy was inspired by a Neil Selkirk photograph of Nicky Rozar Brooklyn NY, in the powerHouse Books publication, 1000 on 42nd Street. Thankyou Neil, Nicky, and powerHouse Books.

First published in 2014, this book echoes the political reality in Australia at that time – a government elected on a promise of "no surprises", who then canvassed the lowering of the minimum wage and reduced access to healthcare, victimised people on welfare, actively encouraged a coal economy knowing it was contributing to catastrophic climate change, bullied the state media, increased surveillance of the civilian population, cut support for scientific research, underfunded education, and spent up big on weapons.

Books by Geoffrey Riddell –
The Gift of Destruction, The Fly-ahead Boy, The Boy Made of Shining Happiness

READER: if you sometimes need an asthma puffer have it ready
– there is shortness of breath in the first five pages of this book.
After that is clear reading for you.

THE BOY MADE OF SHINING HAPPINESS

A WORLD ENDS

John was running late. It would have to be toast for breakfast,
with nut paste, and fruit jelly on top.

He had the knife loaded with jelly when the whole house
suddenly wrenched sideways, knocking him off his feet. The
toast plate and his mug of drink went onto the floor.

He lay on his side ready to leap up, wondering what was going
on.

The house's stilt legs were breaking. It tilted more, slid, and came
to rest one side down in the garden.

Everything was cascading out of the kitchen cupboards, rolling,
tumbling, clattering.

He slid down the sloping floor to the door. It fell open, and he fell
out, down onto the ground.

Outside, trees were crooked in the garden, in all the gardens, not
just his. In the distance, the towers of the main power backbone
wire were twisted and tangled messes, and the huge wire was
sparking where it was too near the ground. It wasn't just his
house. Something had gone horribly wrong. Something huge had
slammed into the planet.

There was new technology. A voice was everywhere, because the
air was being made to do it. All the air – the air in his nose, and
the air in the hollow area inside his mouth even.

'Your government has surrendered. You are no longer a member
of the Star Alliance. You have agreed to join the Freedom
Collective. You have agreed that all assets resources and produce
of this world are now available for the common good of that
collective. In the peace initiative you signed last year, you listed
as a reason this planet should remain self determining its asset of
five billion people. Under this agreement we now claim that

asset. People who do not move towards designated areas will not be able to breathe.'

John realised he wasn't facing in the right direction, because his chest muscles clamped up, really tight, and he couldn't get any air.

He turned around, and then he could breathe, for a moment. He gasped air in, but when he went to breathe again, he couldn't. A step forward, a breath, and then no air. Another step forward, another breath. One step for every breath, or his chest would clamp up, and he would be starved of air, until his eyes felt like they were going to pop out.

CORT

Cort was at the edge of a huge crowd. This was the strangest school day he'd ever had. A monster sized white sausage shaped thing was being lowered down from the sky. It had no windows. He didn't like the idea of being taken somewhere in that. In the distance he could see another one, and far away on the horizon, three more monster size white sausage things.

A speed hopper appeared, its crew jumping out and setting up a little box shaped room, like an outside toilet at a concert. Cort could tell the box shape was a room, because it had a door.

Now they were raising it, and wheeling a piece of machinery in underneath.

A long dangling pipe was coming down from the sky, from the huge white sausage. It got plugged in, and then another pipe too, short this time, going from the side of the machine under the box room, to a large bag sitting on the ground. There were more bags, empty, folded up and stacked in a big pile, waiting to be filled with something.

Steps were dragged in, steps that led up to the door. One of the workers blew a whistle, like a signal that everything was ready.

The people near the steps suddenly couldn't breathe, not without stepping closer, then closer, then closer, to get each desperate new breath of air.

The first person went up the steps, and in the door.

There was a soft grinding, whizzing noise.

Dusty fluff came blowing out the side pipe, going mostly in the big bag.

Nobody came out.

The next person nearest the steps suddenly couldn't breathe, until they began climbing, unwillingly, step by step.

In the door they went, eyes bulging, desperate for air. Again the weak grinding whizzing noise, a puff of dust, and again nobody came out.

It wouldn't be very big in there, inside that little room. Soon it would be crowded.

Cort decided he wanted to go home. He turned, to begin quietly walking away between the people, but as he took his first step, his lungs clamped up tight. He had to stay where he was, or walk towards the steps. He sat down on the ground.

WEAPONS AND MONEY

The crowd was smaller now. There was a gap of open car park between him and them. A man in yellow work overalls, with Capitalisto Wins! written on them in big red letters like a sports team logo, was rolling one of the huge bags of dust past Cort, to a big stack.

'Kid, just get it over with. This is democracy at work – the Freedom Collective have voted. What was your planet is now Feedlot 431. The powder in this bag is protein we will add to the animals' food, and all that water, that huge tank full up there – home planet seven has been having short showers, no water for their gardens, and hardly enough to wash their cars, for a whole month now. They are going to be very grateful of you.'

A machine had the bag now, for stacking up high. The man was coming back to talk more.

'You know why we'll never lose? It's a big secret, but it will be safe with you – dust and water can't talk. We will never lose, because every single thing we make has the same material, and all that material is linked. Those steps over there, and our most powerful battle cruiser, they are one. Everything Democratzia Capitalisto is one big thing among the countless little building blocks of everything else in the universe. Even the Indestructible

Being is a gnat compared to us, to be trapped one day, slaughtered, then taken apart for copying. If you built the most humungous weapon ever, and aimed it right at my belt buckle here, nothing would happen. It would be like a speck of dust blowing past in the wind, because to break my belt buckle, you would also have to break everything else we have ever made, and we have grown so great it's too late for that now – it would be physically impossible to build a weapon powerful enough to make more than a tiny hole, which would only last the quickest moment anyway. So use your legs for one last time, go over there, and become one minute of hot shower for someone. Just think of it as your destiny. I've seen thousands and thousands of sitting kids just like you, all hoping this will stop happening to them. It won't, because our first right of freedom is our right to have weapons, and the second is our right to make money. We do a world a week. Nobody cares kid. You can do me a favour though – don't make me shove you down the hole.'

Cort couldn't understand exactly what he was being told. His brain didn't seem to want to, and then he saw Uncle John. Uncle John! Everything would be all right.

UNCLE JOHN'S LAST DAY

John watched, and thought about what was happening around him – shocked and frightened people, with no-one to save them. People who would soon be dead, turned into water and dust. He wasn't the strongest, or the fastest person, but he was here, and someone had to do something? He could move forward through the crowd, and then at the last moment, there would a tiny chance he could grab one of those workers, take them hostage, and demand that the process be stopped, in exchange for that worker's life. Get an arm lock stranglehold around their neck or something. Then he could ask for at least the children to be saved.

John was feeling awful, his legs shivering with fear, but it was now or never. He took a deep breath, but right then, just as he was about to spring forward, several men bigger than him had a similar idea, and made a sudden rush to capture a worker, and drag him into the box room.

4

They grabbed hold and lifted the Capitalisto worker forward onto the steps, but then they stumbled, let go, and crumpled to the ground. What looked like work lights on top of the visitors' work vehicles were little targeting superlight weapons, that would boil your brain inside your head, in less time than it took to have a thought. Nothing had been achieved by the men. Nothing could stop this.

The workers picked up the bodies, dragged them up the steps, and dumped them in through the door. A grinding whizz, a puff of dust, and they were gone.

People kept clutching at their air starved throats and necks, and climbing those steps.

John saw the boy coming. His sister's boy Cort. That child had survived the life of a fly-ahead boy out in space, only to come back to this. To end his life like this. The young face was full of relief.

'Uncle John, Uncle John, now we can go home,' said the boy.

John grabbed the light body, lifted and held it, hugged it tight. He was so sad he was beyond tears, beyond saying anything. All he could do was hold Cort close to him.

There were hardly any people left. A small group at the steps, trying hard not to go up, and Uncle John and Cort, sitting on the ground, because it was easier to breathe down there.

One of the workers was looking across, and talking into his headset.

'You want one child, male this time, and an accompanying adult for the trip. I have them. You two, with me.'

They were being walked towards a speed hopper.

'You, the child, you will be a worker on The Great Karoshi. It is the largest moving thing ever built. It is in exospace. That is a kind of nowhere, that things are in if they travel faster than light. It is looping around and around out there, unseen and unfelt by anything in this universe, even though it is the shape of a cuttlefish and the size of a small planet. We, the Democratzia

Capitalisto, have been building the Karoshi in exospace for one hundred and sixty years, roughly. Everything it needs – food, water, hull plates, internal machinery, has to be got ready in small pieces, and brought to near light speed, so it can be collected invisibly, on the way past, by the hulk of the Karoshi. Now they need a small person to disassemble the nose cone, so huge robotic grippers can be got ready, to catch a little ship we are after. For you, it is not so much a job as an honour to serve, and, I'm just guessing here, better than being turned into car wash and garden mulch.'

Cort had a good feeling as he climbed up into the speed hopper – they were going somewhere strange with nasty people, but he was with Uncle John, an adult who cared about him, so he would be safe.

THE DEATH OF UNCLE JOHN

A man in Capitalisto Wins! overalls was coming back through the speed hopper, to talk to him and Uncle John. The man had a tool, or a weapon, in his hand.

'Thirsty yet, kid?'

'Yes please?'

An electric spark, like miniature lightning, went into Uncle John, followed by a thin flexible tube that shot out and speared into him. There was fright in Uncle John's eyes, and pain, and then his body crumpled, smaller and smaller, until it looked like a dried, lightweight, funny shaped shopping bag. The man pushed a tap into a large clear bag of water that seemed to have appeared from nowhere. Screwed the tap in. Held out a straw, and a little cup.

'Help yourself. Make it last. That's your water for the trip.'

The man kicked Uncle John like he was litter on the ground, towards a chute. Shoved him with the toe of one boot until he crumpled more, and was mostly in the chute entrance. Pressed a button. There was a quick sucking noise, and Uncle John was gone. Forever.

'Don't feel bad kid. It's unwinnable. The politicians and the really rich people have impregnated themselves with the armour plate stuff. It's all through them in tiny little particles. They can't be stabbed, shot, or blown up, so we just have to be grateful for whatever life they let us lead. Seems it's always a life that gets them richer.'

The crewman pointed to the rubbish chute.

'About that – I don't let myself feel at all, not any more. If I did, I couldn't go on living.'

Cort sat in shock.

The man began walking to the cockpit, but now he was turning around, coming back.

'Look son, if that technique doesn't work for you, try this – "equal opportunity, not equal outcome" – it means everyone gets born equal, and after that, if someone decides to be a loser, that's their fault. That means there's no reason to feel guilty if you make yourself the winner. So, an example: your dad just before, you say to yourself "He was a loser", and you'll be amazed, you won't feel half so bad. Take away respect for someone, and you can do anything to them, and not feel rotten. You might even feel a bit superior. Hmm?'

"Yes, but then you'd be a mentally ill piece of shit", Cort wanted to say back, but Uncle John wouldn't have wanted him to poison himself by speaking those words, so out of respect for John's memory, Cort kept his mouth shut. Memories were all he had now, so he needed to live each moment true to them.

Those words might be off limits, but Cort felt his lips silently saying "Paybacks are double", and by double, he meant the largest amount of "to the power of" that was ever invented.

He wiped tear water away from his eyes and stared at nothing, so his feelings wouldn't tear his heart apart.

This morning his world was a happy planet, with living things all over it getting on with being themselves. Now it had all turned sad, with everything good destroyed, because there was no-one there any more, no-one to enjoy games, music, films, books, holidays, friends, pets, the list of all the things Cort had lost seemed to stretch away into forever.

A tiny bitter wish was calling from the bottom of his heart – someone, please save me?

THREE YEARS EARLIER, FAR AWAY FROM JOHN AND CORT

It looked so peaceful, just darkness. Stars, with nothing between them. Up there were all sorts of ships, including big armed cruisers, like the one that had turned his family ship into a space wreck when he was little, and tiny scout ships that were watching out for them, like the stingray scout ship that had saved him. Somewhere up there were Mark's family. He might never see them again.

He needed to be out among those stars, in a ship going somewhere.

THE END OF JUNIOR SCHOOL

This school felt small. Some parts of the buildings Mark knew so well that when he was somewhere else, he could see them in his mind, like they would be there forever. Last day today.

'Come in lad.'

The School Director's office was empty. Just Mr Arthurs. The college people had left. No college scholarship then. Mark wasn't going to be a Navigator. A horrible realisation soaked icy-cold through him – he would never leave this planet.

Mr Arthurs was talking on, about subjects Mark had eventually done okay in. Mark had to look away. This hurt. He didn't want anyone to see, not even Mr Arthurs.

Outside the window there were leaves, new green leaves, fluttering in a breeze. Life on this world would go on as if nothing had changed, but for Mark this was the end. He had no idea where to go, or what to do with himself for the rest of his life, because always his goal had been to get back to his family, somewhere out there in space. He had waited on this planet for all these years. Now for the first time he understood – he had lost his family forever. He was only twelve, but he would stay here and grow old, and they would live and die out there in space, never knowing what happened to him.

Mr Arthurs was turning over a piece of paper, and talking like he was finally coming to the end.

'Getting an education is hard enough for children with families to help them on their way. For a space orphan, getting a fair start in life is near impossible. They know that, and I am very sorry the High College did not see fit to do the right thing by you. But these days they are run as a business, so one could say this isn't their fault.'

It was strange – Mr Arthurs didn't look upset that Mark's whole life was ruined. He was chatting on like he did in class. I'm going to miss you thought Mark. In a world full of unreliable self-important adults, Mr Arthurs had been a solid rock.

'But phooey to that – we have come up with our own solution. Congratulations Lefty – the Parents Association and the Junior School staff have clubbed together, to make a scholarship of our own. High college is just the first hurdle lad. Kind-hearted people won't get you into the Academy… but, well done. I'm glad I had the…the experience, of teaching you… Now, where is it?... You all came good in the end. Here we are. Shake hands, and here's your certificate.'

Mark held the piece of paper tight. Suddenly all his tomorrows were looking bright again. A shuddering sigh went through him. He should feel good right now, but he nearly felt like crying. Life was hard. He just knew navigating space would be heaps easier than this. That fly-ahead pilot boy, the one who came crashing down out of space, he had been doing it when he was only nine.

CREW DAY AT THE ACADEMY – MARK GOES TO SEE HOW IT'S DONE

They marched awkwardly, some of them out of step. They were shorter than the rest of the marchers, younger, in their school uniforms, not yet Academy trained. The crowd weren't interested, but those boys were what Mark had come to see. College students, on the tail end of the Academy Parade. That little straggly group were hoping some huge company would sponsor their Academy education, or apprentice them aboard a ship, as boy trainees. You had to march in that group to get considered, so boys did it and hoped.

Those marching boys weren't much bigger than he was.

He waited, watching. Finally, a boy was chosen. One boy. Marching out of the ranks to the clapping of the crowd. One boy out of fifteen, and he was the tallest one. Mark knew when his time came his chances wouldn't be good. Twelve, thirteen, fourteen... He had three years to get himself ready. Miss Shandy already had him marching better than that at cadet club.

'Thanks Miss Shandy. For bringing me. Getting me in.'

'No thanks necessary Lefty. Some years they choose more than one you know.'

She knew it would be his only chance.

CADET CLUB ENDS, TEENAGE LIFE IS COMING

Cadet Club was over for all of them when they turned thirteen. Thirteen year olds were too big for the littlies, Miss Shandy said, and Cadet Club was there to give the little ones a place to go, a start in life.

There was a party in the hall, and one last muck around on everything, and after that, evenings were just homework, more homework, and no-where else to be. He really missed cadet club. Why did this planet have to be so boring?

He started to think again about going home. Where-ever home was. Somewhere out there among the stars. Things were happening out there, while he was stuck here, on a small lifeworld at the back end of nowhere.

Lying in his top bunk, listening to Shane's mum and dad talking contentedly in their living room, and to Shane's sleeping breathing coming from the bunk below, he felt glad to have this much of a family, but it also made him long for his own, before it was too late. He wondered when you became too old to be part of a family, and became just another grown-up person, alone in the middle of everything.

HIGH COLLEGE, AND NOW THE STORY REALLY BEGINS

High College was unexpected fun. Some days he would feel guilty, as if his family knew that while they were somewhere far away, feeling bad wondering about what happened to their little boy, he wasn't little any more, he was fourteen, and he was having a good time. Today he was definitely having a good time.

People were cheering him on. Everything the girls said he wasn't allowed to do, he would do. Sprung bad though – the teacher just walked in. He would have to lower himself down from here, as quietly as he could.

'All right all right. CLASS… Thankyou. Some order. Planetti, get down off the lighting bar, this isn't a zoo.'

'Mr Noonan, we told him not to,' said the girls.

'Show some skin Planetti,' yelled the boys, cheering and whistling.

He was stretched right out, reaching down with a foot for the bench. They were laughing at his skin showing between his shirt and the top of his school shorts. He stretched out further, dangling down as slinky long as he could. He could feel eyes liking looking. His clothes felt loose around him. He felt great. He wasn't in a hurry to find the benchtop to jump down onto. He was liking the feeling of looking good.

'Planetti. This is High College, not Primary school. We've all got over giggling at naked ribs and belly-buttons.'

'Sorry Mr Noonan.'

The girls were facing the front now, ignoring him.

The boys laughed at his apology – he obviously didn't mean it.

Reaching down with a foot. Where was the benchtop? Retro (Samuel Retreaux) had a hold of his foot steering it, pretending to help, but Retro was moving Mark's foot around so Mark couldn't put it down anywhere.

'Piss off Retro.'

Sammy did a wet laugh, and a wide happy smiling face, like all the fun was on his side of what was happening.

'Say that again and you'll regret it…' he said.

'Piss OFF!'

'Okay… you asked for it.'

One swift yank by Sammy and Mark's shorts were around his ankles.

He could feel air around his nuts. He dropped quickly to the bench top, grabbing at his shorts to get them back up, but he lost his balance because they were tangled around his legs, and while he was trying not to fall over the edge of the bench onto his head, his shorts and a shoe were left behind, wrenched off by a wickedly chuckling Sammy.

His shoe clattered down to the floor, arriving there the same time he did, head first, legs in the air, sandwiched between the bench and the chairs in front. He got back up vertical really fast, to see his shorts being thrown from boy to boy across the classroom.

'Retreaux. Right. You wait outside. Can I have some staff help in here. Yes now – I've got half-dressed boys hanging off light fittings, teenage girls going hysterical, and... Thankyou. Now. You lot, Burton, give him his pants. Try acting your age, and I mean all fourteen years of it, not just the first four... Grrrrr. You little buggers are really trying me out. Burton, hand over the pants, and sit. No, Planetti is not going to punch you.'

Yes I am thought Mark, as Burton dangled his shorts just out of reach.

He would have liked to punch Burton, but he couldn't, because Mr Noonan had hold of Mark (and the shorts), and was dragging Mark away. Mark got busy getting his school shorts up his legs and back on him.

'Burton, you've got detention. You, Samuel Retreaux, I said outside. And don't try happy grinning me – that doesn't work on me. Planetti, dress yourself properly. Right, back to the matter in hand – let's see what Planetti's put himself down for this time... Scout.'

Silence in the classroom. Nr Noonan was staring, like he couldn't understand something.

'Planetti,' he said finally, sounding flustered, 'sometimes I really think you have no idea. Lad, people read these career path applications. One day the wind will change direction, and you'll end up a... what was it?...a deep space navigator... a rescue ship crewman...and now a scout. Why can't you just write fighter pilot, or Ship of The Line crew, or... prototype flight speed tester, like everyone else? You might as well add fly-ahead boy to your daydream list while you're at it, because it's not happening.

'While we're waiting for today's guest, we will see a little piece on being a scout. You can thank Lefty – Master Planetti…and if I have to say your name one more time Planetti, you'll be outside with Retreaux… For Pete's sake lad! Do the zip up properly, do the button up, tuck your tee shirt in, tuck your school shirt in…on second thoughts, just sit down. You can look like a loose pile of un-ironed laundry with a boy halfway out of it, I really am past caring.'

HALF A LECTURE ON BEING A SCOUT

"…Being a Scout in today's Universe is an out of this world career. We can't show you the current scout ships, because they are top secret, but here's a guided tour of one we can show you. Note there is room for only one crew. This little ship has no metallic parts. Water, air, food and fuel are all stored as solid materials. A tiny ship like this one can stay off-world for years. It can hitch a ride on most cross-galaxy size vessels, without them ever knowing it is there. Scouts are sent out into space to get a better picture of what's really going on. A first hand view. They go anywhere, and everywhere, on the will and whim of the scout pilot. Who can be a scout? You can! Scouts are chosen from our best and brightest. You must serve in the Open Fleet for a minimum of…"

'Enough of that. Desk screens off. There's been a change. Any minute now a very important person will enter this classroom. He has come all the way from Blue Skies One. Why we get someone so grand for our careers afternoon I do not know, but let's make the most of it.'

The classroom door began to open.

'It gives me great pleasure to introduce our guest for today, Commander Warnock.'

SHIPS OF THE LINE

'Scouts – a very appropriate start to our afternoon. I am here to talk to you about our place in the universe, and in particular, how we take responsibility for our safe and secure existence, and the part you can all play in that. Who here is going on to your Academy?... Who here hopes to go on to the Academy? I see.

The League Of Stars Territory home worlds are a loose association of planets, from five galaxies, that have agreed to form an Open Fleet, for trade and protection. Blue Skies One is the key world, and supplies most of the military muscle, the weaponry that is an integral part of today's vessels. Terra builds our most powerful ships, fast and strong. Very fast, with very strong hulls. Greencloud 13 is the havey cavey world of intelligence gathering. This world, Outer 17, would have little to contribute, if not for its training facilities. You are very lucky to be here. There are other Academies on other worlds, but the Academy on Outer 17 has a reputation for producing young men and women second to none. Now, what comes after the Academy? That is the question I am here to answer, today. A line has been drawn across Space. We let the rest of the universe do as it wishes, on the other side of that line. On our side, the Open Fleet goes about its business in safety. Who holds the line? The Ships of The Line do. Massive powerful vessels, armed to the teeth, and manned by people like you. Lieutenant Andrews has career path brochures, and we will both be available for questions… Yes?'

'Does the Open Fleet have weapons? Or only Ships of The Line.'

'Yes, the Open Fleet has every sort of vessel you can imagine, and then some, but the power and glory is in the mighty Ships of The Line… Yes?'

'Can you get sponsored for the Academy, by putting your name down for Open Fleet service?' asked Mark, 'I heard that, and I just want to know if it's true?'

'What's that boy's name? Planetti?...Planetti…hmmm. Career path card?... I see.'

The commander's fingers were tapping the side of the lecture stand. Something about the career path card interested Commander Warnock. His eyes were hard, different from when he was lecturing.

'I'll take that question up with you during the break. A quick answer is – there are many ways to gain access to financial assistance for your education.'

Not quite a yes, but a thousand times better than a no thought Mark.

'We will take that break now. After the break, Lieutenant Andrews will discuss the darker aspects of defending the League Of Stars Territory, and why we are keen to get well-trained young people like you on board our Ships of The Line. You and your families might feel safe here, but there are dark days ahead. I'll see that boy now.'

CRONO-REGRESSIVE BIOSTRUCTURE TRAUMA

Commander Warnock lost that jolly charm the moment he was outside the classroom.

'I think you are the boy we've been looking for. Here will do. Look at my hand screen. What's this?...Come on lad. I've been through two Spaceports, an airport, five hospitals, and fifty-three schools, all in ninety-six hours, and I'm tired, very tired, of this lousy dry empty little planet.'

'Stingray scout ship?' said Mark.

He knew it was, because it was the same as the one he was rescued in when he was five.

'Cockpit view. Name me one internal fitting.'

'There? Loose rubbish tube?'

'Yes. Got you. You're coming with me.'

The Commander had hold of his arm, and was walking him away from the school building to the car park. Something was wrong. Mark yelled, as loud as he could.

'Mr Hedgedon, anybody? Help?'

'Good on you Brat. Make it hard why don't you.'

Now they were walking back towards the school buildings, still with the grip on his arm. Teachers were running from all directions.

'This boy has biostructure damage caused by an irradiating weapon. He is going for treatment. You will have him back when we are finished.'

About turn.

Shoved into a car.

Away towards the city the car went, smooth and fast. Cars didn't do that often on Outer 17. Most people travelled by the breeze tubes, and the cars that there were were old and slow. Outer 17 didn't make cars, so the cars that got brought in had to last, and last. This car was shaped like a slippery slug, and it smelt strange, new inside.

'Cool car?'

'Yes. I had it brought in, down the tube tower. This lifeworld doesn't have a good reputation for personal transport. Most of the good things about this car I can't use here though, because I don't trust it to do the driving, not on your roads.'

The commander held his hand screen out.

'Remember this man?'

'Yes.'

The pilot of the little Stingray Scout vessel that had rescued him. It seemed a long time ago now, that day he had become a space orphan, and ended up on this planet. The pilot looked younger than then, at least his image did, on the little screen.

'He is ill son, and so are you. When he rescued you his scout ship was irradiated, placing you both, for the rest of your lives, in danger of crono-regressive biostructure trauma.'

Commander Warnock was looking across at Mark.

'I would like to be able to say we're doing this for you because we care. I do care boy, even about one roughnut badly dressed mouthy young teenager, on a back of nowhere lifeworld, but nobody else does. They want to know military B4 ray victims can be cured and returned to fight, so they are experimenting on you. But it's win win, because you get free treatment.'

Nice one thought Mark – what if the experimental free treatment didn't turn out good?

LOTS OF BLOOD, AND SURGERY SKIN PATCHES

There was a line. A long line, outside the window of Mark's hospital ward. So long it went past the wide windows, and he couldn't see where it ended. They were all boys his age, looking in to see who was getting their blood. His blood had been sucked out of him, until he felt dizzy and threw up. Commander Warnock was standing beside the blood machine.

'Thirty-six more times, and also, they don't know it yet, but between each blood swap we are going to graft a little circle of skin from the boy onto you. They will be in a line like little buttons down your upper arm, and that's the best we can do for you,' said the commander, 'I'm off now lad. Your blood will be tested back on Blue Skies One. You will get the results.'

The waiting boys were every shape, colour, and size of fourteen-year-old. Black hair, yellow hair, brown hair, red hair. Curly, spiked, straight. Did they have to be so ugly? The red hair one had freckle spots, like a thousand times too many. His name was Crackers, from school, and he was an idiot. Fun to hang around with, but you always got in trouble for it. There was one of those freaky thin bones kids, with white eyelashes, and a dopey looking kid with buck rabbit teeth, even bigger than Cracker's. They were so bad the lips folded out and away from the teeth, like the boy was some rare creature. Thirty-six different colours of skin! Well, at least of the boys he could see every one was a different skin colour. Sammy Retro was waving, and doing his silly-happy goggly-eyes grin. Sammy's skin was an excellent chocolate brown, and his hair turned his head into a huge black fuzzball if it wasn't cut. Sammy was a great kid, but Mark had an idea that his blood and skin wouldn't be a good match. Mark began wondering what getting their blood inside him would do, to him. He didn't have to wonder for long – the answer was – make him feel really sick.

Mark felt tingly strangeness all through him, but it was over. Thirty-six dizzy spells, chucks, and new lots of blood. His arm stung. The little circles of skin weren't that little, but once they had healed around the edges, he could tell they would be hard to see, all except for Sammy's circle. It was a golden brown smooth patch, like a repair on a tyre.

HOSPITAL
Two weeks rest here they said, and then he would be back at school.

This was boring.

He wasn't allowed near anyone with germs. If he got germs now, that was supposed to leave a marker, a marker that linked all the diverse genetic material they'd just gone to so much trouble to get into him, and then he would be more vulnerable, in future attacks. Future attacks…as if – Outer 17 was the most boring, attack free planet in the universe, and to get to him with a B4 cannon weapon, they'd probably have to like attack the whole planet? Mark didn't think that was likely.

His hospital bed was inside a soft, floppy bubble thing, so thin and light that it floated in the air. He couldn't touch it. When he reached out it moved away, even from just the warmth of his hand. He wondered what was going on out there, in the rest of the hospital.

'Can I have the curtain things open again… Please?'

Better. He wasn't allowed more than one hour a day of coloured light, in case he got a marker from too much of one colour. Now he could see his room, the leaving nurse, and the window along the empty corridor.

'Thanks.'

MARK GETS VISITED

Footsteps coming. Lots of them. It sounded like a herd of little kids?

Visitors! Cadet Club, like an army of mini people, all in their uniforms. And older kids too, friends from school.

Shane couldn't wait to get into the room. He fell in the door before it even opened properly.

'You were all over the news! Outer Seventeen's first B4 victim, shot like heaps of times, by a HUGE ray cannon, from an evil stealth cruiser.'

'You said your family ship fell to pieces, but it got zapped! By the Democratzia Capitalisto maybe even the news said. They can like blast whole planets to pieces.'

The crowd around the bed were excited and expectant. It felt good that just being him was interesting and fun for them.

'Yeah. I was only small, but I know where it got me – my poo's glowed gold ever since.'

'Has not!'

He listened to the littlies talking eagerly. They were holding hands up, and watching the bubble skin around his bed floating away from their warm outstretched fingers, wonder in their eyes. He saw Miss Shandy standing behind them, proud of her flock. These people were family. Almost. He didn't want them to go.

THE DIAGNOSIS

The results came back. He had B4 radiation sickness. In his blood, before the blood changes and skin grafting, and after. It wasn't really a sickness. It was a deliberate signal, embedded in radiation, that put a marker bar in your genetic code, then imprinted instructions over it. Your body would attempt to follow the instructions, and die a horrible death, unless you surrendered your body to your attackers, immediately, for decoding. The marker bar had got through the Stingray's hull, but the little scout ship had protected him and the pilot from the imprinting. He was okay, so long as he never came across B4 radiation again. If he did, he was half safe – his body would attempt to return to its nearest genetic instructions to that original marker. Nobody knew what that would be, but if it happened to him before the end of high college, he would be fourteen growing down fast to be a five year old again, and that couldn't be good. Commander Warnock was on the wall screen explaining.

'We've done our best for you son. The goal was to get you clear of childhood. We've pumped you full of so much wildly varied adolescent material, that if you ever get 'triggered', you won't know if you're Arthur or Martha, so to speak. Chances of your body seeing its way clear through that lot, to misshape itself back to childhood are, I would guess, highly unlikely. Your pilot friend hit eighteen, and steadied. Any younger, and it would have killed him. Bodies are not designed to grow young. That's when he told us about you. If you see changes in yourself, any time – straight to hospital. Any questions?'

Yes, Mark had a really important question.

'Do you know who did it?'

'Did what, lad?'

'Fired the B4 ray? What ship it was? Where it came from? The news said maybe the Democratzia Capitalisto?'

'No. Don't pay any attention to the news: they are just pumping out rubbish they think people will be excited to hear. I can't tell you anything more reliable either. It might surprise you lad, but commanders are not leaders of the universe. Most of my questions go unanswered too. Why would you want to know?'

'They took…they took my family.'

He had to rush the words out. After all the years that had passed they still hurt, and he was ashamed of how weak they sounded, how childishly simple. Commander Warnock wasn't finding them simple. He was taking time answering.

'…I know very little more than you… But, I can tell you that our little stingray's departure from that unknown ship's grappling gear would have caused major damage. They aren't called stingrays for nothing. They have a very nasty sting in the tail. If the ship did make it home, it would have been in a serious, newsworthy mess. I'd start looking in those picture collections – you know the sort – mysterious disasters, and great wrecks. That's it then, for you and me. You've cost us as much as a small space ship. Hope you appreciate it. Make your life count.'

Outer 17's picture books of Space disasters were older than before Mark was born – they would be no help at all.

The screen was blank. Commander Warnock was gone.

THAT DODGY LECTURE

Still not up in space, but closer? Maybe? Somehow life felt more exciting. They were all at Bernard's place. They didn't hang around there often, because Bernard's dad was loud and full of himself. He had to be the one being funny, and he would always want to interfere, decide what "the boys" should be doing. But Bernard's parents, and his little brother and sister, were out.

They'd wrestled each other, had races on broken old scooters around and around the house, dacked James and thrown his pants up on the house roof for the whole street to see, until he said "give them back or I'm telling", and now they had Bernard's kid brother and sister's little floppy wader pool out. It was too small to be a swimming pool. Even so it used a lot of water.

Retro was spinning in the air to do a back first landing on top of everyone else, and doing a wild cross between a giggle and a yell as he came down on them. Shane was standing watching.

'We should empty it and put it back, before your family gets home,' said Shane.

'Never knew you were a sneak,' said Bernard.

'You've done it already, you and Lefty, so no point saying don't, so making it go away so they don't know it happened will hurt their feelings the least,' said Shane.

'Get over it and have some fun,' said Mark, stripping off his shirt and pants and belly flopping onto the shallow water.

Soon there were boys wearing underpants for bathers running around shoving and laughing, throwing each other into the small pool, and dragging each other out. Mark felt great, sort of strong, young neat muscles, and good looking. It felt ace to be the person inside the shape he was. He stood back for a second, watching his gang of friends. James was skinny hips and wimpy sweet looking, Shane looked tough, in an "I'm skinny because I'm fourteen, but don't push it, I've still got muscles" way, and Bernard and Philip were both a bit…Mark considered the point – they had like a smooth thin layer of fat over their fourteen-year-oldness, because their families ate more crap, and they got away with being couch potatoes, because their parents were. But we look good decided Mark, all of us. He was backing up to take a run-up for the pool when Bernard's dad appeared behind him, at the back door.

Fun over.

'I think it's time we had a little talk boys, don't you.'
Not a question, a statement, a bullying statement.

'Nah…not really,' said Mark.
Bernard's dad had him by the back of the neck, hard.

'Sit, boys, or I will make you. On the grass will be fine. Not you Lefty – you're my example.'

Bernard's dad weighed like half a ton, and had a grip like the jaws on a building wrecking machine. Mark hung from the hand awkwardly, not liking the pain it was causing in his neck.

'Now boys, see this? Lefty here? This revolting skinny useless mouthy little creature? It's a boy, and worse, it's an adolescent boy. No use to anyone. In fact, he's what I would call a fucking pest. Thinks he's funny, thinks he looks good, thinks he's the best thing since sliced bread. Well have a little think now, all of you, right now, about why anybody else would care. Do we get thrills out of you being fourteen? No. So here's my point – no-one else, no-one else at all, gets kicks out of you being a silly little self-loving wanker, so how about you just get your clothes back on, and keep your runty little stick bodies, and your sickly-pretty bloated faces to yourselves? Aye? And tidy up this mess.'

He let go of Mark's neck, and was going back in the back door, but he turned around for another go.

'You think you are just the ant's pants when it comes to sex, because you are all you need – hey, I know, I've been there, been fourteen myself – isn't that a surprise, a man who was fourteen once, and I can tell you what you are going through is just to get you ready for the main game – women. Big dopey eyes skinny legs and pretty hair don't cut it with them, so hurry up and grow out of it, into something useful.'

Door slam.

James giggled awkwardly. Big dopey eyes, skinny legs and pretty hair definitely applied to him.

'Big prick,' said Bernard, about his dad.

'He's just jealous,' said Philip, 'coz like he said – we are the most fun, and we don't need anyone.'

Shane pulled the plug out of the pool.

'My dad did a better sex lecture than that. For me and Lefty, and it didn't have strange stuff in it about how we look. My dad says being our age is our private thing, our business only, and anyone not our age has no business noticing.'

'Yeah well, my dad loves himself so much everything's his business,' said Bernard, not happy.

Mark lay in his bunk bed that night thinking, mostly about
Bernard's dad's words. Surely everyone can see how good we
look? His thoughts wandered. Older boys at school had been
pretending, or not, that one of the teachers looked good, that the
teacher was sexy. Sexy? She looked like a grown-up, a full size
all the bits out everywhere in big roundnesses type female grown-
up. How could that be sexy? If it was him and Miss Haymaker, it
would be like a rat hanging out with a big hairy talking bag full
of luke warm water. And then there was that other thing
Bernard's dad said – what use was a fourteen-year-old boy to
anyone? Not much really, Mark decided, but it was fun being it,
most of the time, and on that thought he went to sleep.

FREAKY FOURTEEN, OR B4 RAY VICTIM

B4 rays. Mark had a scare. His hair started changing colour –
only blonder highlights, like a good hairdresser had had a go
when no-one had, but it curled too, around the edges, like the
curls liked his ears so much they were thinking about licking
them. Also, his eyes changed shape. Bigger. People noticed.
Treated him like he was becoming some-one different. He got the
breeze tube to the city, and reported to the hospital.

No, they said, not B4 ray contamination, just normal fourteen –
pretty hair and dopey big eyes – make the most of it kid, because
after this comes fifteen, with awkward hips and pimples.

He let B4 fade, into just one more wild experience in his past. It
had company – his family losing him, the children's home, his
first days of Outer 17 school, nearly being frozen to death,
rescuing Cort the Star Alliance fly-ahead boy as he crashed down
out of space, they were all there in Mark's memories.

And then, the day came – finally, he was old enough for his
chance at the Early Entry Exam. Being out there in space, going
somewhere new, was really close.

THE EXAM THAT MEANT EVERYTHING

He thought back to those fifteen marching boys, that day Miss
Shandy took him to a passing out parade. Fifteen, out of all these
people. There were so many students sitting the exam that it was
held in the old zoo biosphere. He thought he could see Shane,

about thirty rows in front, and a fair few rows of desks off to the right. Some-one with a jacket on like Shane's, anyway. There was no roof above them all, just glass, thousands of odd shaped facets of it, all melted together, into a high, long, domed hall. Daylight all around.

Do the question, check it once, and move on. Next question, and next, and next. His heart was in his mouth. This was worse than any High College exam, by far. No-one here to say 'Planetti, stop mucking around, and get on with what's in front of you'. No-one here cared less. The exam observers where just paid workers. It was up to him. Fail, and he would go nowhere. Scrape a pass, and he could get an on-ground job as a flight-deck worker. Then he could talk to people coming from Space. Ask them to find things out for him. A good pass meant he could be hired as a crewman – you got no say in where you went, or what happened to you, but at least you were up off this planet. What he really needed was a commendation, so he had a chance of getting a scholarship, or being sponsored onto a ship. To get a commendation he had to really surprise the examiners. Do everything perfect, or one thing so well that it made up for everything else. He'd never done things 'perfect'. Plenty of people would get high marks. All the James's of this world, the "Please Mummy may I?" boys. It had to be in the extra questions.

Extra questions…where were they? What was this? Page twelve. Practical stuff. Really weird practical stuff. Why did they want to know what toys, home appliances or machinery he had taken apart? Especially since they weren't asking if it got back together again. He laughed, remembering Shane's Planetman doll that now had its right leg for an arm, and the arm for a head. Not so funny what happened to that ancient mantel clock. James's dad had been really cross about that.

Next question said to sketch the inside workings of an item from your last answer. Couldn't do Planetman's insides, or the propeller plane, because they both had almost no bits. It would have to be that clock, and it had far too many. Better get started. Maybe do just the parts that were why the hands went around, even that would be hard. Hmmm, hmmm, don't stick my tongue half out while I'm drawing – it's daggy. Hmm? Sort of right, but some of the cogs were a bit oval shaped, nah, get over it, and call it…finished! Back to writing stuff. Concentrate. He had to get to 'extra questions' with some time left. Nearly finished. Can you wash your own clothes? Well derr, of course. Explain the process. Easy. Sketch a basic layout for a small interplanetary vessel's flight controls. He wondered how many kids who didn't go to Cadet Club could do that. Only the rich kids that the Academy gave pre-exam coaching to. Yeah – so it was just like he thought – the exam was rigged. Don't go sooky, this is going really well so far he told himself.

Okay, all finished and checked. Now for extra questions. Focus, focus. Scrolling down… No point in doing do-able ones. He might as well take the biggest risk, and just do his best. Like Mr Arthurs used to say, 'A valiant attempt at the impossible is all I ask', meaning stop handing in easy assignments done impressively, and have a serious go at something worthwhile. Let's hope the examining board thought like that.

Yes. This. This section – 'Current, unsolved'. The whole League of Stars was looking at these questions, and no-one had the answers. Yet.

No… No… This? No… Problem 9.

"The Soft Cargo vessel Nordecia 2 is lost, far out in Space, beyond The Line."

This was a question very close to his heart.

"After a minor space trash collision, a major fault state occurred in the navigation system, causing an emergency fallout from a hypertravel corridor. The vessel flew blind, dodging and weaving as it slowed, possibly fishtail drifting across most of a galaxy. Continual panic avoidance actions caused many changes of direction, one so severe that the internal motion sensor was thrown out of its cradle. There are now no external sensor systems operating. The crew are trapped within the hull. A message packet has come through deep space, giving all on board data. Your task is to propose a use of that information that will enable the ship's crew to get their bearings, and return home. Your task is not to do the math – you do not have time. You are in the control room of the Nordecia 2. All Nav. systems are down. Propulsion systems logged data is erratic. You must realise a utilisation of what reliable on board information there is, to get your ship home. You are reminded that this is a current, real time problem, that may not have a solution. The depth and intelligence of your enquiry into the problem is what will be judged. This is a timed question. The clock will start when you tap the screen to begin your answer. Stop the clock the moment you have done your best.'

He felt a cold chill sweep through him. He knew the answer, and this question mattered – there were real people out there, waiting, helpless in Space. Thankyou Miss Shandy. She'd taught him all he needed to know for this, when he was 'too small to give cheek to a fly', as she would say. He was sitting still, holding his breath, and not doing anything. He realised it was the fear of doing something wrong, and wasting this one chance at his future working out, that was stopping him. He told himself not to be a wimp, and tapped the screen.

Now his clock was running, the numbers flickering through tenths of seconds too fast to read, like this was a race, not an exam question. He began writing.

'The most accurate, sensitive monitoring equipment on board is life support. Begin the shipboard computer at last reliable known position. Navigation through to the current position will be done by the adjustments the life support system had to make, to correct internal temperatures in the different hull sections, as stars were passed. Note temperature changes in all hull sections. Cross check with gas pressure records of the sealed outer hull voids, and adjustments to heating and cooling. As each star is passed, system figures will fluctuate. Make sure that data from all 'sides' of the vessel is used, to maximise data input - cross reference all assumptions. Walk the computer forward, from each set of stars to the next. The life support system will have adjusted. The information is there.'

It seemed an easy solution, but he was sure of it. He looked quickly into the ship's data. He didn't have to do the maths, just show them how. There, one example, and he was finished. He rose from his seat, knowing he had done his best. He felt a strong fondness go through him, for Mr Arthurs, and Miss Shandy.

They'd prepared him for this. Prepared him for Life, like the armorer had done for the little prince in that folk story, 'Alito, The Indestructible Child'. He owed Mrs Benson from the children's home some credit too. He felt glad about everyone in his life.

As he waited for Shane and James outside the exam hall, he felt happiness soak through him. For the first time he felt in control of his future. Next was space ships and being up there, with the whole universe to explore. His journey had finally begun.

CADET CLUB ONE LAST TIME

The hall looked small. The yard around it looked small. The kids were all inside, sitting cross-legged on the floor, looking up at Miss Shandy. Mark felt like laughing, they were such simple, trusting little beings.

'What's funny?' asked Shane softly.

'Not funny – I just love them being like that,' said Mark.

'We were like that once.'

'Yep,' said James, 'I'm going to have kids.'

Miss Shandy still had a big voice.

'Time for talking's over. Into your ship.'

The kids were scrambling madly to the ladder. Miss Shandy was coming to the door.

'Come in. I want to hear how you went.'

YOUR DEATH, AND WHO DECIDES

She had asked them to stay, until after the kids went home. She was very earnest. She was looking old. It might be the weather. There was a sharp wind outside.

'Lefty, you know where the kettle is. I never told you boys. I didn't want to spoil things for you.'

She sat herself down onto a chair, thump, without any of her usual bounce.

'I had three brothers. I don't have them any more. They're dead. Died before your time at cadet club... It was at a time like this. Little bits of unsettling news, from places far away, and full steam ahead at the Academy. Did you ever wonder where all the students go? Year after year of them, in their fine uniforms?'

'Ships of The Line?' said Shane, because he thought she was waiting for an answer.

'They all leave this planet, and most of them never come back. Not because they don't want to, but because they can't. The League Of Stars Territory is a very small player in space. That's why the Home Worlds banded together… I'm not saying we shouldn't have ships of The Line – that we shouldn't defend ourselves. I just want you boys to know how things really are, before you find yourselves out there, far away from those of us who care about you.'

She was watching the drinks being made.

'I'm not allowed sugar now Lefty.

'My brothers went to the Academy. They did well, and all got 'Line' postings. Very proud we were – pictures on the mantelpiece, big going away party. A few months later, we got a picturecall from Jean. His ship was going to somewhere we'd never heard of, and never heard of again. He was distressed. He said goodbye like he wanted us to hold him… Sorry boys. I get a bit teary sometimes… He was my favourite person, in all my life… What I'm trying to tell you is, children's lives are treated like money – and people put themselves in charge of spending it. Of course the Home Worlds need defending, but the people who decide whether to take a risk with you, do it at no cost to themselves. They are sitting in comfortable chairs, in grand offices. There is a reason we, a training world, don't get news from beyond the line. Things are dirty out there, so horrible that whole planets are being destroyed, with many many ordinary everyday people like us dying before their time. They don't tell us about that, because they don't want to put off all their young recruits. I'm not saying don't go. I just want you to go knowing that your life is more important to us, to me, to your friends, to your teachers, and your parents, than anything they come up with, that so 'has to be done'.

Silence. Passing the drinks around.

'Father said, if the people who decided to send Jean, and Robert, and John, to their deaths, so far away from their home, so far from the people who love them, if those people were to lose a toe, or a finger, for each life they decided was expendable, they would decide nobody needed to go. Can you imagine the Planets Union President holding up his right hand, with three fingers missing, because you three were dead? Only a finger, one finger, in exchange for your whole life. They'd need over a million fingers for all the boys and girls since our family, and those 'wars' were too unimportant to rate more than a passing mention on the news. They make decisions that kill, not just 'enemies', they kill you, and for that they get fat, and old, and huge pensions. While me, I earn just enough to get by, cleaning at the academy, and now Father has died, the only family I have is you boys.'

Miss Shandy's voice was going wobbly tearful.

'If one of you, if only one, even one of you, makes it back alive, I will be so grateful.'

Shane was making her stand up. Giving her a hug. This was why she did Cadet Club. Because the little kids kept her going. They were all she had left.

WALKING BACK

It was dark, and cold. Mark and Shane were walking home.

'Did you do that music box thing? In the exam? The one we took to bits.'

'Nah – I did James's dad's clock.'

'Thought you would. James did Alan's pressure rocket. He reckoned he was trying to guess what we'd do, so he could do different. So was I. We are so going to ace that bit. Everyone around me was groaning when they got to it, but all I could think of was Mr Arthurs in grade five going "Draw draw draw – I've never had such pests for drawing".'

Walking on in the dark. The smear of light above the distant city looked weak, reminding Mark of his first days looking out the window of the Children's Home. He thought of Mrs Benson. Miss Shandy had made him realise tomorrow's Crew Day Parade was a bigger goodbye than any of them had been thinking.

'I'm going to see Mrs Benson.'

'What, now?…'

There was more. Shane was looking like he used to, like some-one was ripping him off, right when it really counted.

'Come home first?'

It wasn't much to ask.

THE PARTY, AND BEING THE LEFTY

Their names were on a home-made banner, hanging limp in the cold air over the back yard. People were there to congratulate them on good marks, and to say goodbye, if tomorrow turned out to be goodbye.

It was a surprise party, and it was supposed to be happy, but Miss Shandy had spoilt it for Mark. He was glad of that – her words had been a warning to make goodbyes count. James's family came, and James embarrassed everyone by being sooky. He would stay really close to his parents, or really close to the rest of the boys, like he was afraid he would get lost. He looked panicked just crossing the grass by himself.

'Lefty, you do it – Wimpy's your friend.'

How come James was suddenly 'his' friend? This again. He realised the other boys had just consigned James to the loser's brigade, and he, Mark, had always been the champion of social outcasts, because he was a Lefty – a child left at the children's home.

'James, Matey, what's the problem?' he asked.

James's eyes looked around. He was in some sort of internal misery.

'I don't know if I'm supposed to want to go, or want to stay,' he said.

'I don't know if I want to, either of them, I don't know?'

The grown ups had been waiting for this. They rounded like an army flank. James's mum had him, arm around his shoulders.

'Sweetheart, a little of both.'

And now his dad was crouching down in front of James, like the parents used to do when they were all in little school together.

'There are opportunities, excitement and adventure out there, new opportunities, to get you to a better life than this. We don't want you to miss out. We will be very worried about you, and longing for you to come home, but we'll all be glad our boys are making a go of it in bigger space. Imagine all the places out there you can go. Places us old stay-at-homes only dream about.'

'A celebratory drink, for our lads and girls doing so well in their exam,' shouted Mr Arthurs, raising his glass, and the party was starting again.

Shane's dad had something to say now.

'Boys, tonight is just a practice, really. We're not ready to lose any of you just yet. At the end of the academy, when you're all a bit older, we'll do this again.'

'If putting in good words, and miracles have anything to do with it, Lefty will be on his way tomorrow, but we'll have to wait and see,' added Mr Arthurs.

Mark felt his own insides unwind. Nobody would get chosen. We are still school kids he thought sadly. Small, sillier, not wanted. If he didn't get chosen tomorrow, that would be his private disaster. No, I have to believe he thought. He calmed his mind, his thoughts hiding from the growing doubts.

MRS BENSON, AND THE CHILDREN'S HOME

The alarm clock went off. The air hadn't got any warmer. Shane rolled over on his mattress.

'Are you really going? You haven't been back for like years.'

'That's why. She's the first person on this planet that was kind to me. I should have gone heaps of times. Parade's not 'til ten. I'm definitely going, now.'

As Mark got dressed his breath made steam, even inside the house.

Softly opening the back door.

The lawn was frozen. It wouldn't matter. Five minutes of fast walking and he'd be hot. He was going to run for as much of the way as he could, anyway.

The turns in the path seemed closer together, and the hills and hollows smaller, shallower, flatter – he was older now. Much sooner than he expected he was rounding the last turn, and there was the old building. Looking even worse than before.

Poor kids. The windows were nearly all broken now, and there was no good paint left on the walls. Why weren't the lights on? Mrs Benson was usually bustling around by dawn, getting her chores done before little people got in the way.

This door never did lock.

The kitchen in the children's home was strangely cold, but there was furniture-wood set ready in the fireplace – some splintery broken chair parts. Spiderwebs on it. Spiderwebs old with dust, and a dead spider shell. Nobody had lit this fire for a while. Oh well, a sad homecoming, but he might as well remember it looking warm and cheery. Top shelf? Yes, the lighter was still where Mrs Benson used to keep it, out of little people's reach.

He filled the kettle. He would like to hear it whistle, in memory of her. He wondered where she'd gone in the world. He would have to go soon.

He felt eyes on him. Some-one was in the doorway.

'Mrs Benson!'

'Mark! Oh…Mark. They took them all away!'

She needed some-one to talk too. He wished he'd come last study break. Any study break.

Volunteers weren't good enough to look after children these days. Companies had come to make money, bid for the contract, and the children were rounded up, and taken away. The children used to escape, and come home to her, but not any more. This was the shape of the world he would be risking his life to defend. They could stick their Ships of The Line. He wasn't going to volunteer for that, not after this. He would just hope that tomorrow, today, he got an Open Fleet posting. He would have to go soon.

'I'm all right young Mark. Rebecca, and Greg, and Shirley, you remember them? They're coming tomorrow, with paint for my walls, and so many other things. I've set the fire.'

'I'll just have a quick look at my old bed.'

'No?' she said, like a questioning wail as he bounded up the stairs.

There was nothing in the dusty rooms. No beds, no cots for the littlies. No neat piles of clean clothes near the windows to be sun fresh. Nothing. Empty floors and dust. They'd made sure she couldn't do her job. How brutally efficient, clever, and unpleasantly official.

He looked out his old window. There was a sign out there, standing large among the flat, dirty, rubbly nothing. A sign, with a picture of a grand holiday resort. Palm trees, and an artificial beachfront. They were going to build a beach. Wouldn't the kids have loved that. This world couldn't afford a decent children's home, but they could afford a holiday resort. She was climbing the stairs. Coming to stand beside him.

'Sorry about going loopy, about the fire, and about people coming. There's nobody coming. Today's the last day for this old building,' she said, her voice quiet.

'I didn't want you to see, because I wanted you to remember it always like it was. I'm glad you came, of all my children...my own little Alito the Unbreakable Child, if there ever was such a boy. I will never forget the day you showed up.

'I'm going in to town this afternoon, to look for somewhere to stay. Then I'll find your Miss Shandy, to see if I can't be of use. I've been saving that chair wood for one last fire, but...this morning, I just didn't feel like lighting it.'

She was silent crying. He held her awkwardly. He couldn't go now. Not for a while.

He heard the sound of wrecking equipment in the distance, grinding its way closer on its heavy metal tracks.

THE BIG DAY – SPACE IS REALLY CLOSE

Crew Day. He and James and Shane went with their school packs on their backs, just in case. Dad's old broken ship's watch, his other pair of socks, his second pair of underpants, and a tee shirt and old around-home long pants. Shane's mum said if he was that sure, he'd better take his toothbrush too, so he did.

'Parade isn't 'til this afternoon. Wonder why we have to be here at ten?' said Shane.

'Practice?'

The parade ground was empty. They could see the main Hall at the Academy was full of people. Shane began walking across the parade ground to the Academy's main entrance, James following.

'Hey wait up,' said Mark, 'This is a big moment for us. Cadet club conference huddle?'

They were arms interlocked in a small circle of three boys. In his mind Mark was chuckling wickedly.

'First, a song,' he said, and then he began singing softly, silly, and badly, an old song, but with words he had just made up.

'Now how can I bend, this smokin' fart, how can a loser suck it in, how can…'

Shane was struggling to get his arms unlocked. James was cranky.

'You stink. And it's not funny. My mother says boys who think farting is funny have a lot to learn.'

Mark chuckled wickedly. It really did smell bad, in an almost solid, foggy warm, laughing gas sort of way.

'Thanks for sharing,' said Shane sarcastically.

'He's a farting machine,' he added, like it was an explanation to the whole world,

'Mum gave him boiled eggs for breakfast. I told her not to, but do mothers ever listen?'

James giggled.

'No. Not you too. NO, no you don't,' said Shane grabbing hold of him, but a tight squeak noise came out of James's pants, followed by a groaning sigh of disgust from Shane as he pushed him away.

'Nice one Wimpy,' said Mark.

There was something special in the moment for Mark – it was maybe the last time they would be boys together, in all of forever.

INSIDE THE ACADEMY'S MAIN HALL

A doorman was waiting for them, the moment they stepped inside the building.

'Take your packs out and leave them in front of a number on the wall. Remember the number. Then come back here and touchscreen yourselves off the list. Then you can go in and help yourselves, boys.'

There were tables and tables of food and drinks, and noise. Lots of noise. Displays of things that moved, and stands with huge screens showing films, all with P.A. systems barking out sound effects, music, and voice-overs. Big models of space ships were hanging from the ceiling, up among the lights.

'Look, a Fly-ahead,' said James pointing up, 'That little one, with only room for a kid pilot inside. We rescued one of those. Lefty and me.'

'Right now Cort's probably doing exactly what we're doing,' said Shane, 'Finished his exams, and he's somewhere on his home world checking out the local academy.'

'He stayed alive because of us,' said James, pleased with the thought.

Because of us, but more because, even when things were as rotten desperate as they could possibly get, Cort hadn't given up thought Mark. But Cort had missed years of school being a fly-ahead boy out in space, so most likely, wherever he was, he was still in junior school. Mark turned his thoughts back to everything around him.

There were people in strange uniforms, lots of different uniforms, standing in front of displays of their ships, their companies, or their home planet. Others were moving amongst the crowd of Academy pass outs, handing out free things and brochures. A lot of fake cheeriness was going on. There were men shouting rehearsed jokes to each other to attract attention, and women with their uniform tops too far undone, stinking of perfume, grabbing students by the arm, and taking them over to displays. The three boys stuck close to each other, and began eating the food, and testing the drinks.

'Alcohol!' said James, giggling as he sipped, but he was joking.

'That's okay, just don't drink the lemonade – you're not man enough for that yet,' said Mark.

They all laughed at the stupidity of the words.

'It's you that goes hypo on lime cordial,' pointed out Shane.

Then they heard a man saying he was giving away free comics. That was more their speed. Boys were already there, crowding around.

'Hello boys.'

He was big. Slimy eyes. James stepped back into Shane, as the man leant forward.

'Here to give smart boys like you a warning,' the man said, like he didn't want other people to notice him doing it.

The party-like din went on around them.

'You boys mightn't know this: The best crew for a Death Ship are brave young men like yourselves. You are smaller, lighter – less live meat weight – don't take up as much space as a grown man, just like in a Fly-ahead. Cheap to cart across Space. Don't know where you're going, don't know what's going to happen to you, then – oops, gone forever. Is that why you're here today? Think carefully my fine friends. Think carefully. Death is out there waiting. Don't sign anything. When you're on that parade ground this afternoon, and you feel eyes inspecting you, choosing you, just remember, crews for Death Ships have to come from somewhere. No-one will ever know what happened to you. Remember my words. Be wary of signing. Be very wary.'

They got their comics, but the pages were full of adverts. Only the cover picture was any good. Some of the other boys were white faced, and whispering among themselves. The man had moved on, with film star posters this time, further down the hall, talking to older boys.

'What do you think Lefty?'

'He's just scaring us.'

'Why?' asked James.

'His idea of fun.'

'Pretty nasty idea of fun,' commented Shane.

'Forget him,' said Mark, shoving his comic into a bin, 'Let's eat more.'

They couldn't. There was one of those women standing in the way.

THE HIGHLINERS CRUISE SHIPS LADY

'No tags on you. Open market,' she said, like someone had done something very wrong.

She adjusted the zip in her top down, and eyed them.

'Come over and see me on the Highliners stand.'

There was makeup all over her face, hiding her feelings and what she was thinking. She wanted something from them, but what? Mark looked across at Shane. Yes, he thought there was something suss too.

'We could come later?' said James, being polite.

'Don't leave it too late,' she said, and then she walked away into the crowd.

'What was that about?'

'Dunno James. Let's check out some stands.'

They couldn't get near most of the stands, because the Academy students were all bigger than them, and in the way.

'Hey, an empty one,' said Shane, pointing.

They ran over. No one serving. There were only two things on display – a wall poster, and an odd looking model of a bubble shaped small brown space ship. There was a pad for signatures on the bench, with a pile of light brown tags next to it, in a bowl.

'Quarantined Disposals,' read James from the poster, 'For ships unable to leave space dock due to suspected disease or contamination, we offer the finest, most cost effective, fully legal service for disposal of human waste and medical contaminants… err yuck!'

'If they have to say those things, like "fully legal" and stuff, something's wrong,' said Shane.

They stood there staring at the poster.

'Why do they even bother having a stall?'

'Dad says "cost effective" means a company cheat their staff with crappy pay and mean conditions,' commented James, and then they heard a voice from behind the stall.

'Counted the tags again – no fools yet, but I might have scared a few into going out on parade unchosen. We could still catch a few there.'

'Comic man,' whispered James, his eyes looking frightened.

'No one's catching me,' said Shane, sounding serious and determined.

'Got ya!'

'Piss off Planetti,' said Shane half laughing.

'It's too noisy in here,' said James.

'And too crowded,' added Shane, 'let's go outside.'
They turned to go, but that woman was back again, standing in the way. She shrugged her shoulders, as if they'd been having a conversation with her.

'Can't let you go without you sign for something, so how about you three come with me?'

'No,' said Shane under his breath, 'No, James.'
She was walking away, expecting them to follow? She was coming back.

'I know you feel like young men, but you are really nothing more than three dear little boys. I can't let you throw yourselves away. How about you come over to our stand – Highliners Holiday Ships, and our recruiting ladies will sign you up. No obligation after. No catches.'

'If there's no obligation, why do we have to do it,' muttered Shane.
She wobbled her oversize breasts at them again, jokingly.
Mark knew what to do – joke back – stop things from getting serious.

'No thanks – had my milk at breakfast,' said Mark, and ducked away as she tried to grab him.

She was quick. She had both James and Shane by their shirt fronts, and was almost carrying them, making them walk backwards through the crowd.

'Sorry, but we're in a hurry,' she said, 'You three have only got a minute or two left.'

Shane stumbled, and fell under her feet. She trod on his pants trying to keep her balance, and then dragged them down his legs without knowing it as she pulled him upright.

'Walk. Don't make this hard. You don't know how big a favour I'm doing you. Move.'

One of Shane's shoes had come off. Mark picked it up. He had never seen Shane so panicky, and then, (when Shane couldn't reach down to his pants because his shirt and coat were pulled up tight under his arms), so mad angry. He was shuffling backwards unwillingly, with his pants tangled around his legs. They were falling down, almost off, only just tangled around his remaining shoe, and then they were left behind on the floor. For a moment he was still, hanging from her arm, then he did a sob, not crying – rage, and angled his knuckly little fist around, to dead-arm punch, as hard as he could. Shane was right to be mad Mark thought as he watched – half undressed, underpants in full public view, shirt and jacket up around his neck, he looked strung out and dangling skinny like a kitten about to be thrown outside. He was beginning to make a noise like an angry cat too.

Punch.

'Ouw!,' she exclaimed, dropping Shane.

James saw his chance, and slithered out of the top half of his clothes. He ran backwards, to stand in the middle of all the people, bare chested, his dreamy head for once wide awake and paying attention. Shane ran straight to his pants.

'Bloody child!' she said rubbing her arm, 'I'm not giving up. You'll thank me for this later.'

The woman waved the top half of James's clothes at him. Mark almost ran in to snatch them from her, but he had a nasty feeling, just as his legs were about to spring him forwards. She knew he was the hardest to catch. It was him she really wanted to get hold of. He could tell from the way her eyes were pretending not to watch him. James's eyes were on his clothes, held up in her left hand. Shane was pulling his pants back on, at a safe distance from her. A waiter, removing a large plate from the tables, stopped to watch.

'Look at yourself,' said Shane, cranky, 'Anyway, why don't you help us get our clothes back?' He added accusingly, as he sat on the floor to get his shoe on properly.

'Boys your age like showing themselves off,' said the waiter.

'I'm not boys my age,' growled Shane, swivelling quickly back up onto his feet while he kept his eyes on the woman.

'Aren't you just,' said the waiter laughing, and then he walked away into the crowd.

'I'm not either?' said James.

'Yes you are,' answered Shane, 'you're almost as bad as Lefty.'

A bell rang, and a voice announced over the noise in the hall,

'Parade, fall in.'

The woman had been thinking.

'Look… I can't let you three go out on parade without at least one tag,' she said, sounding like a mum making you wear a raincoat to school.

She held a piece of James's clothes out, dangling. She was going to do the carrot in front of the donkeys thing. Mark had had enough. This was like a Children's Home battle, and he was going in.

'Here James, have mine. I'll see you out there… Just do it. I'll catch you up – I can run faster.'

'Boy germs,' said James, giggling like a six year old, and holding Mark's top half clothes awkwardly in front of him.

Bloody hell James, just put the clothes on. Now Mark was cold, his naked shoulders and ribs out in the open. He spread his arms, tensed his muscles, watching her. Shane was trying to get around behind, trying to rush, and to sneak, through the crowd, both at the same time. Just as James was pulling Mark's clothes over his head, she lunged forward, reached out, and grabbed him.

Now she was dragging him, clothes tangled around his head. James! You dopey freak! Shane was running in, crouching down, wrapping his arms around her ankles, and holding tight. She was going down, over backwards. Mark pulled James out of the way, but her other hand had flown up, trying to get her balance, and the clothes in it went flying. Another announcement was happening.

'Parade ground doors closing in one minute... fifty seconds... forty-nine seconds... No one wants a tardy crew.' Everyone was leaving. A whole herd of Academy students trampled past on their way towards the main doors. The clothes were flattened, dirty, and spread out across the floor. They weren't going to be neat for parade any more. James looked like he was going to cry. She was getting back to her feet. He couldn't see for the makeup what she was thinking. I can do this, thought Mark, I just have to watch carefully, and be quick. He ducked, snatched James's clothes from the floor on the way and ran for the doors. He heard her voice behind them as they ran.

'Boys?'
She sounded desperate, and sad.
So weird.
'Please?'
Shane turned back, watching her. Now wasn't the time for his "be fair to everyone" habit. She was holding out three little badges of a cruise ship company.
'You don't have to wear them. Just put them in your pockets, for if you find you need them. Please?'
Shane snatched them, and stuffed them in his pocket as he turned and ran.
As Mark slid the white undervest on he could feel scratchy floor dust, and the remains of James's body warmth in it. Today had become strange, horrible.
James was trying to swap back.
'Not now Dopey! Tuck yourself in.'
'That's a first, you saying that to James,' sniggered Shane, 'Here, wear my jacket over the top, and no-one will see the shoe prints all over,' he offered Mark as they ran.

Someone was yelling across the parade ground for college students. They went towards the voice, and arrived at three wobbly lines of boys.

MARK GETS CHOSEN

It was taking a long while for all the different squads to form up properly. Parades were boring to be part of. Mark could hear the crowd of friends and families murmuring, somewhere behind him. They were bored too. He looked along his line. The other boys all had coloured tags pinned on them.

'What are those for?' he asked of the boy next to him.

'Didn't you get any? They're like insurance… if you don't choose some companies for yourself, or a fleet or military Arm… If you don't have these on, then anyone can pick you, and you can't say no.'

'You should have got at least one, you and your friends,' said the next boy, 'just for safety. In case something real horrible picks you, like Extreme Personal Prejudice Chemicals Delivery.'

'Only prisoners get to do that,' said a voice further back in the squad.

'You should've still got at least one,' repeated the boy, 'I've got Highliners Holiday Ships… Nobody ever gets to go on that, not that I heard, but it means if something crap picks you, you can say sorry, you chose Highliners … um, this one's Open Fleet… Home Planet Shuttle Service um… Ships of The Line lower deck,'

'Everyone gets Highliners, dopey. The girls make sure.'

'Those three didn't.'

'None of us will get picked for anything anyway.'

'Maybe,' said another boy.

Mark could feel the mood in the squad was worry, not hope. It made even him feel scared, just from being in the middle of them, and he was the boy who wanted to go, any way he could.

'Silence in the squad. Standing with your friends is not an option, because a neat orderly squad is our priority. Reorganise yourselves, tallest on the right. Straighten yourselves up. Better.

Prepare to march. Rrrr-right, turn. Left leg steps out first, left leg, looking to your left to keep a straight line, quick… March.'

Shane was getting something out of his pocket in a hurry. Trying to pass Mark a Highliners badge, but it flicked off another boy's jacket and fell to the ground. Mark couldn't get to it because the squad had begun to move. Too late. This was it.

Like Miss Shandy said they should, he Shane and James called the step out quietly to the rest of the squad.

'Left,… ,left,… ,left.'

'Watch the boy in front of you. Keep in line, and when I give the order, turn your heads right, towards the dais,' shouted the man in uniform herding them.

'Look-ing good!' He added in surprise, for them to hear.

As a squad they weren't marching too bad.

The march past ended. The squad had arrived back almost where it started. The loudspeaker was calling out the young Academy men for their postings, and they were marching across the tarmac, one by one, into the building.

Less and less people on parade. The crowd was thinning too, families leaving as their boys were chosen, and marched away.

Mark looked along the row of boys in their little squad. Shane was up the end pinning a Highliners badge on his shirt pocket. He said quietly he didn't care if he wasn't chosen, he had decided he would be happier at home.

'If you go Lefty, keep my jacket,' he said a little louder.

A boy they didn't know started crying, and ran for his family in the crowd.

'Me too,' said the big boy next to Mark.

He sounded satisfied, like he had reached a good decision. He unpinned a tag from his chest, and pinned it on James.

'Just in case, okay?' he said.

He took a step forwards, turned smartly to the right, and marched off towards the spectators.

'I'm happy with whatever happens,' said James softly, but he sounded unsure.

The loudspeaker cleared its throat again.

'Mark Planetti. A special commendation goes to young Mark for his solution in the unsolved problems category. Open fleet ensign. Ship undisclosed.'

'Bye?' said James in a scratchy urgent whisper, his eyes big and his face white.

One step forwards, turn to the right, marching, marching.

Left right left right went Mark's legs. The tarmac was bigger than he thought. The distance further. The clapping of the crowd so far away.

WHAT SHIP, GOING WHERE?

The Parade was over. He was back in the Hall. All the good stuff was being taken down – the model space ships and the picture displays. Now there were lots of desks, and queues of young men and women waiting to sign their lives away.

'Come on son, people are waiting.'

He looked down at his enlistment paper. Open Fleet ensign. That was like a very junior trainee officer. For ship's name it just said 'unrecorded', for primary destination it said 'not stated', and world of origin was 'undisclosed'. He thought that was all a bit shonky, but there was a really official looking stamp at the bottom, and a fancy scrawl blue ink hand-written signature. Some-one important, someone so old they used liquid ink in a nib pen – that person thought the details were okay.

'Excuse me?'

'Yes? What's your problem?'

'Is it okay that it doesn't say which ship or anything?'

He held the form out for the desk attendant to see.

'I mean, is that from an important person?' he added, pointing at the signature.

'Two reasons for hidden details boy – either you are a secret agent signing to crew on an awesomely powerful megafast stealth ship...' Laughter from the line behind him, 'or, they've got several ships needing crew, and don't know which one you're going to end up on yet.'

'Okay.'

He took the form back.

They were still laughing at him.

'I've always wanted to be a secret agent,' he said, trying to sound like James day-dreaming.

Silence. Now the people in the line behind him thought he was a simple kid. He turned around and gave them the one finger up gesture, like 'sit on it'.

'Oy! Enough of that. Get your form signed and your smart little arse out of everyone's way.'

Oh well. He didn't care what ship – only that it was going away from here. He signed his name.

'Wait...for your boarding card, and kid? Just a warning: out in space some people can't take a joke.'

'Thanks.'

He had his card. He was going.

I've done it. I've done it! he thought. Fourteen, and I'm getting off this planet, back out into space. There were answers out there, and he was on his way to find them. On a ship. It might be important big, or happy small, slow and comfortable, or very very fast, might be anything, but one thing it would be was flying across space, away from here.

There was a large set of stairs on one side of the Hall. An old man in a grand uniform was standing on the first landing, watching everything happening below him. He had a child hanging onto his leg, his hand, then his coat, as it looked around. Mark glanced up at them as he left the signing desk. Its large eyes were staring straight back at him.

'That one,' it said.

'Don't point. Yes, I know you chose him.'

Mark had a thought that it might have been wise after all, to find out what sort of ship. What type. Well maybe not that, but more what they actually did in space, before he signed. Surely there weren't like school ships, full of snotty brats he would be expected to clean up after. Nah. Not likely. It cost a heap of money to have a ship up in space. Nobody would muck around trying to have a school, would they? It didn't matter – he'd signed already, and he had to go anyway. If a child chose him, for whatever, then, well, he could just be glad he got chosen at all.

NO LAST GOODBYE

He couldn't see Shane or James among all the people in the hall. It was hard to see anything in here other than the people right next to him, because the Academy pass outs were all taller than him. James and Shane might be outside already?

Outside there were busses. Still no Shane or James. Mark went to get himself a seat.

The bus shuddered to a stop. He knew this building. The tube tower. It went up and up and up, almost to space itself. He was back here, after all those years in between. This really was happening.

Excitement zinged his insides, and then he thought of a day years ago, a day in a local library, when everything had been going so right, and then his application to use the computers was taken from him, ripped up and thrown in a bin, because he was a lefty. Don't get too happy yet, he cautioned himself. Not yet. Not yet.

A large crowd of Academy pass-outs were waiting out the front, looking up at the huge tower. He didn't want to wait around out here. Something would go wrong. Men were moving through the crowd now, picking boys out one by one, taking them off to the side. He thought he heard a yell, 'Planetti?' but he couldn't be sure, in all the noise. He went into the lobby, and walked fast towards the lift.

He reached the lift doors, but a man in a uniform was standing in the way. Lift attendant, not security, Mark thought with relief. He held out his shipping card. He heard running feet behind him. Was this when everything went bad? He couldn't turn around. He hoped. His heart hurt. His ears ached from avoiding hearing imagined words – 'not that one, he's a lefty. Knew he was here somewhere. Caught you just in time'.

'Level One!' said the lift attendant, breaking into his thoughts, 'and you no more than a nipper.'

'Can I go up now?' Mark asked, trying to hurry things. The running footsteps were close.

'I was going to tell you to wait outside. I'm supposed to do you all in orderly lots, load after load, from when it starts until supper time… But how about I sneak you up early.'

'Wait, wait! Please?'

James, out of breath, holding his card out.

'Level One only,' said the attendant.

James's hand stayed up, holding out his card, but it began to shake, and his face went white.

'Please?' he managed to say.

The attendant was inspecting James's card. Goodbyes had been easy when they were all together last night, Bernard, Dennis, Philip, Joanne, Shane, James. This is rough thought Mark, to be here by ourselves, and then to go in different directions. The lift doors were going to close, and… then nothing. James would be on the other side, with no-one. He's got a family and yet he needs, more than me. I've got no-one, and I'm doing okay. Why didn't they let families come here for a last goodbye?

Mark knew what he had to do – keep James company until they both had to go. Why did life do this? This was an echo of the escape pod, another time in his life when things really mattered for him, and yet he had to come second. Brave – he really disliked that word. Everything was getting screwed up.

'I'll wait,' he said unwillingly.

'I'm going with him?' asked James over the top of Mark's words, panic rising in his voice, as if he was in the middle of a nightmare he couldn't escape from.

'All right, I hear you. Yes. Level one for you too,' said the attendant, handing the card back.

'Come on then.'

The lift doors shut. Colour was coming back into James's face. Mark realised his own breathing had gone a bit weird too, from panic. Panic that, in the last minutes on this planet, while he was waiting around because of James, something would happen, and he would be stuck here forever.

'Rich families?' asked the lift man, as the lift began to move.

'No,' said Mark, 'space orphan.'

'Me neither, but I've got Mum and Dad, and a big brother called Alan.'

'Just thought some-one probably bought you a cushy berth. Level one shuttle dock is for the mega rich and the frighteningly powerful. Life is strange, isn't it – all my life I've been hoping to go. Not level one. Any level. Out there. In Space. Across galaxies. To see what's out there. Here I am, still working this lift. Closest I can get. What do you boys think did it for you?'

'Cadet club,' said James, crouching over like he was getting his breath back.

'Damn. I knew it,' said the lift attendant, 'I wanted to, but, you know, it was the most uncool thing anyone could do at school – admit to wanting to wear a silly uniform and play games on a pretend space ship in a local hall.'

The lift was rising, and rising.

'Are there clouds up at the top today?' asked James, looking around inside the lift.

He's pretending things didn't go a bit strange before, thought Mark.

'No, don't think so,' answered the lift attendant.

'The sky's going to be a bit see through, out into the dark of space, like that time we went up in that extreme altitude plane,' said Mark.

The lift attendant looked down.

'Space orphan? I remember now. Rescued from a space wreck by a scout ship. Lost among the stars you were. From that, to this. Well done lad.'

The man shook his head.

'Well done…well done.'

The man sniffed, and looked away at the lift wall.

'Well done,' he said again, to himself.

Strange things grown-ups cried about, Mark decided.

JAMES BEING JAMES

There were Academy pass-outs aboard this shuttle. They were older than him and James. Loud. Bully hero joking amongst themselves. They were too big to be children, and too excitable and full of themselves to be grown-ups. Mark went back to looking out the window. The planet was huge below them.

'Sorry,' said James.

'Nothing to be sorry for,' answered Mark.

'There was no-one I knew, in all those people. I thought I caught a glimpse of Shane, and then he was gone. It wouldn't have been him. I know he's probably not coming, not with us. I felt real rotten all of a sudden. I ran, but I lost him in the crowd. I...I couldn't believe how bad it felt. When I saw you, I just knew, whatever I did, I mustn't, I couldn't... I called out, but it was like you couldn't hear. It was weird, like it was the only thing that mattered – to stay with some-one I knew. I know it doesn't make sense. I nearly chucked in the lift, from relief. I know it wouldn't really have been Shane. Just some-one...'

'Don't sweat on it, James. My whole family just flew off into space one day. Show us your card thing again?'

It did look like they were going to the same ship. He wanted to warn James that that mightn't happen. Get him ready, so he didn't go loopy again. Mark turned to speak. No, everything had gone too far – it was too late to turn back now. Say nothing. James was looking out at the planet. The dry grass yellow light of Outer 17 was reflecting on his face.

'Goodbye,' he said softly.

He looked away from the window, sideways at Mark.

'I'm with you,' he added, gently happy.

'We're with us,' said Mark back, and they did a cadet club fist to fist, just like old times.

'Now I feel tough again,' said James.

ON BOARD THE SHIP

There was so much to take in. Lights, people, uniforms, strange equipment.

Mark and James kept to themselves, kept their voices down, and followed the bigger ensigns wherever they went.

They were walking through the passageways, and up and down ladder tubes, getting ticks on their familiarisation sheets, so they would learn where different departments, and places things happened were, inside the ship. Since they were all doing it together, they were all getting the same boxes ticked, but a lot of brainless, trying to be intelligent, trying to be funny, trying to sound tough type talk was going on, up the front of the straggly group. Thats the difference between being eighteen and fourteen thought Mark. Bernard's dad would have gone mental, if he'd had to listen to that.

The ship was on a different world's time. It was early morning on board, even though it was late afternoon down on the surface of Outer 17. The ship's crew didn't alter their on-board routine to match each planet they visited.

THE SOFT CARGO AND THE HELPOD

'Good morning Ensigns. Welcome aboard. I am Commander Pecker, and I am your gunnery officer. This vessel is divided into two sections, so much so that it is actually two separate ships. My half is called a what?… Yes, an Aggressive Helpod. Help pod. This vessel is a?… Soft Cargo. Why is that? Because it contains a permanent non-combatant crew, which both makes it need, and causes it to have, at all times, atmosphere, temperature, and moisture content appropriate to the maintenance of healthy life, throughout the ship. On board my half, the 1418, we have many destructors – chemical, gas, wavelength modifiers, superlights, etc etc, right down to good old fashioned hurling a lump of matter at the perceived threat, and that, my fine young ladies and young men, is where the term 'Gunnery' comes from, the firing of a projectile. So, what is all this about? I am aware you did not complete your orientation…'

They looked down their lists. Captain's private deck, the bridge, the communications centre, Internal Disasters Containment, External Disasters Recovery, the Honesty Verification office, ship's stores, the loading bay crew, ship's laundry, dining hall, galley, and the Polite Helpers – people whose job was to provide assistance to anyone who needed it. The ensigns had visited all those people and places on the Soft Cargo. Only one thing remained undone. It was the next thing under the polite helpers, and it simply said, 'Litmus (ask around for a small boy)'. What sort of joke was that?

'No excuses? I think you will all serve me well. But, pay attention – the first line of defence for these two vessels is on your list, and you have treated it with contempt. Two more questions from me, and then you can go and complete your task. With a little more integrity this time I hope.'

Commander Pecker sounded Uncle-like, but Mark could just tell – if any of them gave Commander Pecker the slightest reason for displeasure during this voyage, it would be the long journey home for them.

'What is the greatest threat to ships like these?... No, not pirates... Not newly declared areas of conflict... Asteroids! I don't think so... No, not the design. Lad! What made you say such a disloyalty? Wash your mouth out. Humorous, perhaps... No, not taking on board diseased water or supplies, though that is a good one. The crew, and the passengers. Ninety-nine times out of a hundred, the crew and passengers where what brought the ship undone. So how do you defend a vessel pair against that? Look to your lists, and go and find out.'

STRANGE DEFENCE

Since when was a small boy a weapon, and how do you find one small boy, aboard a ship pair with over one hundred crew, and a fair few passengers? The midshipmen were sitting in their quarters, discussing possibilities noisily.

'Well, there's like, only going to be one of him, or not many, anyway. You don't see children off planets.'

'What about our two mascots here?'

'Good one. We're not children,' said Mark, speaking up for himself and James.

'Fair enough. Whatever you reckon.'

'No, it's got to be a trick, you know, like a trick question
– first line of defence. It's going to be something else, and that's
like the pet name…'

'Yeah – they call it "Little Boy", because it's a
humungous great bomb or something, and they think that's
funny.'

'A humungous great bomb isn't going to defend a ship
from its own passengers.'

'Just an example…just saying.'

'There was this man at the refreshments station, he was
telling me how there's this ancient ship hidden on board, that
hasn't flown for hundreds of years, because they're keeping it
hidden, so enemies can't find it and destroy it before it flies one
last time.'

'Yeah, and what would that one last time be for, exactly?'

'To save the Universe! Derr. It's a seeder, and it can
destroy whole stars, just by passing through them.'

'Damien, shut up!'

'You watched too much Planetman as a kid.'

'Yeah well, sitting around here is only going to get us into
trouble. Let's try asking one of the Polites.'
And there was Litmus, waiting outside the door.

YOU HAVE TO COME SEE
'I'm Litmus,' said the boy looking shy, and suspicious of the new
ensigns, both at the same time.

'Wait up, something's going on. I've seen this kid
before.'

'What are the chances of meeting a kid you've seen
before, out here, on the back side of a mooring satellite?'

'High - he was at the Academy.'

'Good one. Like when?'

'Derr, today, Crew Day?'

'Enjoy the parade little mate?'

'It was very good, thank you.'

Litmus leaked all the flavours of being a child, the simple happiness, the frustration, the wanting, and all while he was just standing there, doing nothing. Awkward, uncomfortable when the ensigns first looked at him, but cheeky friendly the moment the critical stares stopped.

'Well Litmus, you little runt, you can call me Sir now. See these? They signify rank.'

'Damien, shut up! Kid, what is it you do on board?'

'You have to come see.'

The ensigns crowded onto a balcony that looked out over the gangway area. There were people queued up to come on board. Mark could see the front few, like toothpaste about to squeeze out of a tube.

'I thought we were crowded, when we were in that transfer lock thing.'

'We were,' said Ensign Geets, pushing forward to see what was going on below the balcony.

'You aren't allowed in front of me, or you get in trouble.'

'Good one kid.'

'You, up there, junior officer, stand clear of Litmus while he's working... Bloody fool.'

'Working! He's just standing here, looking cu... Looking around, and talking to us!'

'Yes, looking cute. That's his job. Stand clear of him while he's doing it, so I can start passenger ingress.'
The gangway supervisor's attention went back to the name scroller in his hand, but he was still talking.
'You ensigns have held us up enough already. When you keep Litmus waiting, you're keeping the whole ship waiting.'
He was looking up at them again.
'Learn who's important on this ship. Just as a clue – it isn't trainee junior officers.'
Litmus looked up at the ensign.

'I don't lie, much, and Captain Thomas is my ship pal, for most things, so I tell him, if you're not nice to me.'

'Oooo, scary. Where's your big Captain Thomas now?'

'He, being me, is standing behind you.'

He was tall, old, and wearing a uniform straight out of the movie, 'They Died For Us', only he wasn't dead. Captain's bars on his shoulders, and a stern face, with eyes that seemed not to care. Like they said at the end of the movie, the survivors weren't heroes, they were people who carried the terror and sadness of what they'd seen in their hearts, for all their days.

Mark looked at the old man and wondered – if there was an ancient ship hidden on board, then this grand old man would have to be its captain.

The captain stood with one hand resting on Litmus's head, watching the ensigns' clumsy attempt at forming themselves into a parade row.

'I am not the commanding officer of these ships. The rank I hold is for other reasons. I do not require a salute, but when you see this uniform, you will always make the mark of respect, for those who are not here today – Look up, both hands over your heart…now stand easy. Well Litmus, how's work this morning? Haven't got a spare laugh in you today? Then make sure your eyes…good boy.'

Litmus was crying. The new crew and passengers were passing right underneath, and all looking above them, at the old man in the grand uniform, and the small crying boy.

'Last one's in, Captain Thomas,' said Litmus, hanging himself out over the railing to see.

'Are you having lunch with me?'

'No child, lunch with the 'important' passengers, today. Why don't you lunch with the ensigns? They can tell you a few stories.'

'Yes please. Can I?'

'We have to fill out this, first, and we still don't know what you do.'

'I'll see you at bed time Litmus, and the rest of you in the wardroom, at dinner this evening. Carry on with the lesson Litmus.'

'See that over there? And that other one? They sort of aim at the line of people. They look through the air, and they record the chemical content of the surface gasses, that are on the skins of all the people. It's called the SOB test. No stupid, not coz I cried! It means 'state of being'. They record what happens when people see me, and sometimes Captain Thomas helps too, as a double check, if it's important.'

'Yeah well… how?'

'If I sound recorded, it's coz I've done this lots before. Ready?… The humanoidian is a finely tuned, complex chemical device. At all times, adjustments are being made, and when these adjustments are occurring, hormones, acids, alkali and minerals give off gaseous indications of their presence,… or don't, if they're not there… I can tell you my version? All right. It's like you baked a cake. You knowed already what went in, but just to make sure, you show it some icing, or a knife, in the oven window. The cake can't help farting with love, or fright, and you analyse the fart, and go, yep, that one is that sort of cake… Only it's not a fart – it comes out their skin.'

Litmus still thought it was a bit funny, a machine for watching people farting out their skins. The ensigns standing around didn't think it was funny.

'How accurate is this? I mean, is it really worth doing, just to see if some-one likes children?'

'Yeah, and what's seeing the old man supposed to do?'

'People can get trained for things. You bigger ones, you passed your detector tests to get in your Academy – like the girly picture, don't like the hand picture doing stealing. But what are you supposed to feel, when you see me, and a old man? Didn't practice them, did you.'

'All right, but that doesn't tell you much though.'

'Does too. Bad people learn to hide all sorts of stuff, but only nice people like Captain Thomas and me, just because we're alive too. That big battleship, the one on the other end of our mooring pontoon, the, umm… the Mandelthing, it uses a nasty man in a secret police uniform, and a woman, with big boozies and yellow hair. Crew day, we were both screening for new crew

– them, and Captain Thomas and me. We picked you. They got four murderers, a rapist, two men who wanted to do bad things, a woman who wanted to keep me as a pet, a spy, and a woman coated in hormone cream, dressed as a man. She had chemicals in her cream making her gas like a man who was seeing a nice girl. She didn't have any chemicals for seeing small boys. We had to tell them after, because it's a security thing.'

The passenger bay supervisor wolf-whistled for attention.

'Litmus, lockdown time. Move your boys along please.'

LITMUS'S PRIVATE SADNESS

'Soon as she pulls away from the mooring, promotions all 'round. Midshipman Mark. I like the sound of that,' said Mark.

Litmus could tell the ensign was being silly for him. Two of the ensigns were still boys – that one Mark, that he'd picked on Crew Day, and another one Captain Thomas had chosen, so the Mark one wouldn't be alone among bigger boys. The Mark ensign was being silly: no-one used their first name with their rank. Litmus concentrated on what mattered – food this good wouldn't be happening soon, once the voyage really got under way. Around the back of the last world, and pudding would be well and truly off the menu. The ensigns were still on about becoming midshipmen.

'Yeah, and then we can wear our uniforms for real, with the collar flags.'

'Midshipman Mark! You're a wanker Planetti. You two stay ensigns, anyway. Hey, look at junior here.'

'More pudding? Gees you can eat.'

Litmus looked up from his plate.

'I don't get much lollies or pudding. What time is it please?'

'Litmus! You're wearing a watch.'

'I only asked.'

Litmus looked down at it. He'd never figured it out. He would have to pretend, and go now, even if it was too early.

'You can't read that, can you. How old are you Litmus?'

'Old,' said Litmus, looking at them warily.

'All right, how long have you been on board?'

'I don't know.'

'Something's not right here. Litmus, kids aren't allowed on ships like this. What are you doing here?'

'I showed you. I'm the test for coming on board. They're kids anyway. What are they doing here?''

'You're not like some incredibly well made robot or something?'

'Damien! Dope. Serious Litmus, you shouldn't be here. You should be having a life, going to school, getting ready for college… growing up and having your own Crew Day. Ship's life support systems aren't good for growing children.'

'Where's your mum and dad?'

'I have to go now.'

'Gees. Did you see his little face. We nearly made him cry. For real this time.'

'Yeah, well, but what is he doing on board?'

'Crew testing.'

'Other ship pairs don't need that. Not like that. There's something else going on.'

'Makes you wonder where we're going.'

'And what we're doing when we get there. Did you see, not out the main view glass, but in the little entry tube check window, that hell pod thing? They had it hidden in the shadow of one of the mooring pontoons, and it ain't no help pod. I did my special field of study on helpods. They're neat little ships, usually, not lumpy and bumpy all over, like they've been doing exercises. Someone's been doing something to that one.'

'It does look wonky strange, like you'd want it on your side, if bad stuff started happening.'

SOMETHING REAL FOUL

Mark and James were listening, and staying quiet to keep themselves out of trouble. Mark hadn't seen the helpod, because out the other side of the entry tube had been a nasty looking battleship. A really foul powerful looking thing. He didn't like it. He didn't even like knowing it existed. Not one thing about it, not its dirty dark grey colour, not its nobbly armoured skin, not its big brutal rounded wedge shape, said happiness. Happiness and it, thought Mark, could not exist in time and space together. He wanted the soft cargo and the helpod to start their journey, so he could be somewhere that battleship wasn't.

LITMUS AND THE CAPTAIN

'Shhh. Come on now. You spoke very well today. Bed time for tired boys,' said Captain Thomas, pulling Litmus's suit off, 'Ensigns are just very young men. They don't know much, about anything really, yet.'

'Grandpa?'

'Yes?'

'Can I have the story? Please?… The one about the boy who lives forever, but he has friends?'

'I really don't like telling you that story Litmus, it breaks my heart.'

Captain Thomas was swapping the dirty one piece suit for a clean one. They were both worn out.

'We need a new pair of these. Zip at the front or the back this time?'

'Front! I mean, back. Then I can go floor surfing again… Story, Grandpa.'

'Litmus, anybody can be a friend. It doesn't have to be some-one nearly the same as you. We're friends.'

'But you've forgot how to play.'

'Yes, I've forgotten how to play. Up on your bunk.'

'I'm too old for jump suit pyjamas? I'm seven,' said Litmus climbing up.

Seven, going on seven, and about to turn seven, thought Captain Thomas sadly. All Litmus needed was a little flying friend, and he was the story. The orb-like eyes were watching, concerned about whether the story was going to happen.

'Tomorrow Litmus, I promise.'

'Story?'

'Story.'

Litmus would dream bits of it to himself tonight. And cry a little, because he couldn't make it come real enough. Captain Thomas walked slowly towards the wardroom. What healed the boy's heart, tore his apart. There wasn't much story left. Litmus had decreed, 'no pirates', and, 'NO crocodile'. The boy just liked hearing about escaping to another place, where bad things couldn't happen. A place where friends would always be waiting for him. Too old for jump suit pyjamas, yes, but the boy practically lived in them. Not even getting the bunny tail sewn back on, each time he removed it, gave him the hint. The fact that he was aware of that again meant a reversion was close. On the bright side, that meant the pirates and the crocodile could go back into the story. For a while.

Bulkhead door already. On the other side were bright lights and laughter. Another crowd of people, being noisy about who they thought they were at the start of a voyage. They began their lives with food, and warmth, and caring, and they all ended up dust. As he lifted his hand towards the door lever Captain Thomas heard an idiotic boisterous laugh, coming from the passages behind him. Some-one who hadn't forgotten how to play. Found you at last thought the captain, but which one are you?

Now some-one was objecting to people having fun.

'Planetti, stop pissing about.'

Planetti. The boy rescued from the stars when he was little. Litmus had chosen well.

THREE OF US

'No. I don't want that… You… you just, it's like that time you found me a mother person. You said choose someone for on board? He's just for on board.'

Litmus was looking up, thinking 'don't do this to me, don't do this to me'. Captain Thomas was looking down, thinking please don't make this hard. Litmus wrapped his arms around the leg in front of him.

'I don't want some-one else. It's our special story. You have to read it to me.'

A snivelling whining noise started coming out of him, but he hurt too much inside to care.

'Litmus, I'll still be here. There'll just be three of us sometimes, instead of two.'

'No. I don't want three.'

'What about those other stories you like? "The Three Mice Get Ears". They wouldn't be much fun with only two meece. They'd be a bit lonely then, wouldn't they?'

'They're mices Grandpa, not meece – I'm not a baby.'

THE REASON MARK WAS CHOSEN

Mark looked at himself in the long mirror. These were the best uniforms: Ensign. Not gold-crusty overdone like the senior officers, not trashy showy like the midshipmen, and not plain cheap like the crew, but simple and good looking. The blue was darker, but it still reminded him of the Cadet club play uniforms. Dinky little cadet club. Small. Simple. Back street poor suburb cheap, but it was what got him here. She was a good old chook, Miss Shandy.

He looked around him. The Captain had nice quarters. This little entry chamber, a sitting room, a private café setting, and off that would be the standard senior officer's shower and toilet, and a tiny cupboard-like sleeping and dressing area. More space here for one man than the eight midshipmen had to share between all of them, but where did the boy sleep? That boy had problems. The Captain was trying to talk him into something. Why am I here, Mark wondered. The Captain was back, looking into the entry chamber.

'Sorry lad, we're not doing too well this evening.'

'That's all right Sir, I can come back at a better time?'

He wanted to leave, but the Captain wasn't saying anything that would allow him to go. Just standing there with that look in his eyes – I'm too old, and I've seen too much in my life to care, about anything that happens now.

'This is the time we have. Come in – I want you to sit with him, so he gets used to you. I'll be here if you need me.'

Captain Thomas sat, stretched his legs out and crossed them, folded his arms, leant back and closed his eyes.

Mark looked into the sleeping/dressing cupboard. There was only one bunk, and it was empty. That boy was in here, but where? Above the desk opposite the Captain's bunk was an equipment shelf, and on the shelf was a bundle, a bundle that was sniffing every now and then.

'Go away,' said Litmus.

He was curled up in his small bunk, with his face to the bulkhead.

'Captain Thomas Sir, I think I've found your problem… A serious infestation of bookshelf squirrels. Whole family I'd say, from all the sniffing and carrying on going on in here…'

Nothing from either of them. This was a tough gig.

'Tell you what though, the little buggers smell something awful, don't they?'

Still nothing. Mark looked around the corner of the door, back into the sitting room. Captain Thomas was deeply asleep.

'Sir? You're not going to eat all those lollies are you?…It's just that we've had an attack of the bookshelf squirrels too, at the midshipmen's rooms, and one huge fat one ate us out of our entire pudding supplies… Sir, if I could just help you with those red ones?'

Gees that kid was quiet. The head just appeared under his arm, to look around the corner too.

'I knew you were pretending. Grandpa doesn't like lollies any more.'

'Kid, come on. Don't go back in your hole.'

'Why?'

'Because … who am I going to muck around with?'

Litmus was climbing back up, into his bunk. Mark couldn't help sniggering. Seven-year-olds didn't belong in bunny suit pyjamas. Now Litmus was climbing back down… coming over… punch.

'Well gees, thanks a lot for that, Bunny Bum.'

Litmus began pushing and shoving, and grunting with the effort. He was trying to be angry, but he kept nearly laughing.

'I can do real pushing,' he said, 'You don't know how good. Want to see?'

'Stop for a sec first,' said Mark.

'Why should I?' said Litmus.

'Because I have to do something.'

'What?'

'Turn you upside down.'

This kid could really scream. Incredibly loud and pure, like an emergency siren.

'Oy! The pair of you. Outside with that racket. Let an old man have some peace.'

'It's my cabin too.'

Mark was surprised – apart from anything else, the kid was quite happy talking upside down.

'Other way up, or the food comes out,' said Captain Thomas, as if he was giving instructions on how to operate a piece of equipment.

'And don't think you are in charge of the position of his body. He is letting you do that, the same way he is letting this ship move him. Now we've all met, let's talk business.'

'Thankyou lad. This evening was beyond the call of duty. There are a couple of other minor details you need to be aware of, but overall, I think we can consider you trained. I'll have the duty roster amended.'

'I like red lollies,' said Litmus, as if it was an important add-on to the Captain's words.

'Yes,' said Captain Thomas, 'that is one of the details, but not put quite like that. His stomach works more like a furnace, and he uses sugar like it's rocket fuel, don't you.'

'Sometimes?'

'All the time. We'll see you back here tomorrow morning, eight o'clock sharp ensign.'

'Yes Sir.'

The cabin door shut. On the other side were the captain, and the boy. On Mark's side were the lights of the empty passage.

The Soft Cargo seemed big, but it didn't take long to get anywhere inside it. Along a couple of passageways, and down a few laddertubes, and he would be back at the trainee officers' quarters. Half-way there he ran into James.
'News is on.'
'Okay. Where?'
'Main cafeteria.'
He could tell James about his new job later.

THE NEWS

There was standing room only, just inside the doorway. The picturewall was blank. Waiting. Suddenly there was loud tinny music.
"Ship's News Service. Bulletin eight."
There were images of an off-planet shipbuilding dock, with some new class of cruiser being completed in rows. The Soft Cargo's crew were excited, the general opinion being that these new ships would 'show them', who-ever 'them' was.
"Quicker and cheaper to build, these ships have the advantage of less fuel and stores loading, making them faster to manoeuvre in action".
The news camera was panning across the docks, to show how extensive they were. Just before it cut to another news item, Mark saw, in the very last dock, a damaged battleship. Larger and more powerful looking than the new ones. There were hull breach rescue units limpeted onto its sides. People were dead and dying in it – that was the only reason why they did that. There was a war going on, and back on Outer 17, nobody knew. All those new ships. The Academy was going to be a very busy place. It would be hard to fail from now on.

'Mole, that,' said an old crewman standing in the doorway, 'The battleship at the back. Supposed to be unstoppable. That crew are lucky to be on her – they got to come home. The new ones are called Super Lights. They go in fast, and cause as much damage as they can.'

'Quicker to manoeuvre in action,' said a young crewman.

'They have a perfect record,' said the older man, as he turned to walk away down the passage, 'None of them make it home.'

'James? I'm going back to quarters. Nah. I don't want to watch any more,' said Mark.

He lay awake that night, thinking of Miss Shandy and her brothers. Jean, his name was, once. He had been the most precious person in her life. If there was a way to put a stop to this, the battles, the wars, the heaps of ordinary people losing the ones they loved, then some-one should find it.

JAMES LEARNS HOW TO MARCH LIKE A ROBOT

'Form a line... LINE... you two boys come up the front for once. The meat heads can wait. What's your name? Fargo? You're first – top off, arms up, and tongue out.'

Sick Bay was interesting. When it was his turn Mark was trying to figure out what all the equipment did to people, but his head kept getting pulled back around while the staff measured and poked and looked in his ears, mouth, eyes, and into his arm-pits.

'Full of genetic misfits, that planet. Don't know why we recruit from there.'

'I don't come from there.'

'Oh, so you're the space orphan. Tough little runt aren't you. Been in hospital before kid?'

'Yep, B4 radiation.'

'We don't have time for jokes here.'

'No, really, I was!'

'I see. And what was the treatment?'

'They like drained blood out of lots of other kids from school, and pumped it all into me.'

'I heard you were a bit of a funny bugger Star Boy. Get your top back on, and on your way.'

So that was it? For a joining the ship medical it seemed a bit rushed, like their main aim was to finish everyone before lunch.

Now he needed to catch up with James. These passageways were crowded. It was still the start of the voyage, and things hadn't settled down.

'Oy! You lad, come here… Are you a man or a boy? Well? Here's a clue: men don't run down ship's passageways half dressed.'

The man was large, big stomach, and gold on his collar flags: someone important on board.

'Son, during daywatch hours, behave like an adult, and you'll get adult privileges. Behave like a child, and you'll get treated as one – smaller rations, always put at the end of the line, and always the last to be told anything important. I've already had to tell your friend off for giggling. Now tuck yourself in, and start behaving yourself. And book yourself in for a haircut; your head looks like a haystack. All right lad: on your way.'

How about adding a few other things while you're at it thought Mark. Here came James, back down the passage, marching like a robot.

'James!'

'Just doing what Commander Burnett told me to. Coming to lunch?'

'Not if you're going to do that all the way.'

'Okay. It's not as much fun as it looks anyway.'

SOMETHING DISGUSTING, AND, LESS THAN FAMILY

Mark had discovered something he didn't like about shipboard life. Sharing quarters wasn't hard, but this he really disliked. He didn't have to watch, but if they didn't turn it down he would have to go walking the passageways again, until it was over.

'Planetti, it's started. You're missing out.'

'No thanks… and can you turn it down a bit.'

'Nah mate – we like it loud. Turn it down and we miss out on all the wet slippery in-out sound effects.'

'He wants the men for men version…joking. Planetti! I was joking.'

'I don't care who's doing it, or who they're doing it to. It's ugly, and it's gross – "Ooo, ooo, ahh, aaah, aaaah, I'm carming". It's total crap,' said Mark.

'Yeah well shut up. We like it.'

I don't, thought Mark, shutting the sleeping quarters door behind him. I'd rather be playing with Litmus. He realised with surprise that that was true. It was fun, mucking around with the kid. Fun like he hadn't had since the great pillow fight. The one Mrs Benson had called the pillow fight to end all pillow fights, and then she'd confiscated all the pillows. It hadn't seemed much of a punishment at first, but after a while…his pillow was, in the silence of those nights at the Children's Home, the closest thing to family that he had. But the fight was high fun. How was it, he thought, that the midshipmen only seemed to remember recent events in their lives, yet he remembered the times that were good in his childhood, one by one, almost as if they'd only just happened.

While he was thinking that, and walking the passageways, he arrived outside the door to the captain and Litmus's cabin.

For other people on the soft cargo, their "cabin" was a communal sleeping area, with toilets and showers along a passageway, somewhere near. Straight after each change of watch, the offgoing crew would be wandering the passageways, wearing towels. For Litmus and Captain Thomas, their "cabin" was like their own little town house – a tiny entry hall, a living room, a dining space off that with a little cafe´ style food ordering bench, their small sleeping room that was more like a deep cupboard, and their bathroom. Behind the door in front of Mark they had everything they needed to feel at home.

This wasn't right. Working hours were over. It felt like coming back when a shop or the library was shut, and saying 'Hello, surprise, it's me'. He wasn't sure he was supposed to be here, unasked, by himself. If he knocked, maybe Litmus would answer. Knock kno…

'Ensign. You surprise me.'

The captain didn't look surprised.

'Litmus is out, irritating Commander Burnett. They both enjoy it. I believe the pair of you went exploring today? When he was supposed to be tidying up. Come in. We will take this opportunity to more clearly define your duties. Be seated.'

There was something strange about this living room behind a cabin door. Not the unexpected feeling of space, inside a cramped ship. It lacked something. Show. Nothing was on show. There were cushions, and books, scattered around. Books could be showy, because they were trad. Old old family. But these books were well worn from regular use. Threadbare on the edges, the books, and the cushions. And, thought Mark, with an involuntary laugh, there are toys, all over the floor. That would have to be a first, for a senior officer's cabin.

'Yes, but I don't laugh any more. I trip over them,' said Captain Thomas from the cafe´ area.

Mark could see the captain was ordering himself a drink with the hand panel. It was at times like these that distance came between people, Mark thought sadly. They invited you into their lives, and then they ate and drank in front of you, and wondered why you asked to go back to the children's home. It was because you knew, right then, that they considered you less than family. The longer you stayed, the less you became, until you were a nobody, in the way of their lives. Mark looked up at the picture panel. No smutty movies here. Not even a painting. The screen was just a dull gentle fog grey.

'The screen is my choosing. Litmus can be so…noisy, in the way he moves, the things he does, that when he's not here I gather some quiet around me.'

The captain was standing at the cafe´ bench, waiting for his drink to be sent from the wardroom galley. There was a tiny little bell sound. Captain Thomas's order had arrived.

'I observe the rules, Ensign Planetti, because they keep order in our lives. They keep a ship safe, and a happy place to be. A healthy chain of command is a fragile thing. Captains cannot ask ensigns what they would like.'

No. But apparently this captain could carry mugs over, and put one in front of you. It looked like kai, the shipboard version of hot chocolate. It is, thought Mark as he sipped.

'Thankyou Sir.'

'There are ways of making people come first, without doing damage to the system. You will learn them from Litmus. If you look to his toys here on the deck, he wanted to play with that green one, so he put this blue one next to my chair, to say – "You can play, if you want to". He knew I wouldn't – it was a simple courtesy. That is how we handle food and drinks within this cabin. If you would like something for yourself, order it, and also order what you think the other people present might like. It is easy, does not interrupt people's thoughts, and, more importantly, does not cause inappropriate behaviour. Now lad, let's get this over with – ask me some questions.'

Do what? Ask questions? Of a captain?

'Sir, is it true that people from a warship were there, on Crew Day, drafting, and they couldn't even tell they were getting murderers? Litmus said something like that, when he was showing us his duties.'

Captain Thomas smiled slightly at his thoughts, just a shadow of remembered happiness, passing lightly over his face. Mark wished he would never get that old. So old his life felt like that. The captain was talking.

'This time you have surprised me. I meant I would answer the usual questions people want to ask about Litmus. To answer your question first – a ship of the line has the right, if it finds, during a deployment, that its crew are unsatisfactory, to exchange them for crew from other passing ships – this is because the defence of the home worlds is seen as the first consideration. Bad crew are cheap. Good crew cost money. That particular ship has a reputation for taking on crew they know will prove unsatisfactory. Now, as we speak, they will be hiding behind a moon somewhere, waiting to ambush a ship with a happy, healthy, well-trained crew. We've done our best to stop it happening – posted warnings on all communications channels, and Captain Murray has agreed to go to the assistance of any vessel that signals for help.'

Mark wondered what the little helpod and the Soft Cargo could do, against a Ship of The Line.

'I understand your thoughts, ensign. It is more likely that we will not hear of them again – they know we are watching. But just in case, I have informed them that we have privileged crew members aboard that they cannot take. Now, about…'

Litmus bounced into the cabin.

'He called me a noisy, mouthy… um, goggle eyed, snot faced brat, so I said… Oh, hello… Did you start already?'

'No, the ensign is just leaving.'

'You didn't give him his collar flags, Grandpa.'

'Get them for me then.'

No wonder the captain liked his picture dull fog grey. Litmus was loud, rough, and over-excited about his day. His voice was coming out of the bunk cupboard, happily saying, 'everything fell out again'.

He was back already, with two sets of collar flags scrunched up in his not clean hand.

'I've been looking after them, for YOU,' he said proudly, the "you" almost a shout as he held them out.

I can tell, Mark wanted to say, but he said 'Thankyou', instead.

As he stepped out into the passageway, he heard a little speaker in the Captain and Litmus's cabin make an announcement.

"Mandelbrot off the port bow, holding position".

Captain Thomas was coming to the cabin door.

'Ensign, back here a moment. I want you to…to…to do an hour's watch on the bridge. Report there now. And, Ensign? You are to wear those collar flags, at all times.'

'Yes Sir.'

MADE FOR DOING

The bridge was a busy place. Information and updates were coming from everywhere within the ship. After a while Mark realised most of it was sections reporting that everything was stowed, sealed, or stored after leaving Outer 17. Huge images of the Mandelbrot would drift across the wall screens every now and then. It was big and brutal looking. Not with weapons sticking out all over the place, but like a heavy blob of dark coloured uneven rock, with rounded bumps and slight dish-ins in its surface. The weapons on the Mandelbrot were mounted like a fish's eyes, swivelling around inside the hull, leaving nothing sticking out on the surface to be damaged. It also meant, thought Mark considering it, that you couldn't tell what it had aimed at you. He'd once seen a picture of a Demacratzia Capitalisto battle cruiser – they had a great big turret mounted front and centre, letting the whole world know they believed the person with the biggest weapon was the most important, and got to be right. The Mandelbrot wasn't made to show anything. It was made for doing, and whatever it did, thought Mark, would not be nice for the people it did it to.

Soon his hour on the bridge was up, and they didn't want a very junior untrained officer hanging around.

THOSE COLLAR FLAGS

Back at the trainee officers' quarters, life was going on like normal. They were noisy, smelly, and full of themselves. When I'm their age, I'm going to be more like the Captain decided Mark – aware other people needed space, not showy shallow muscly, and using my dick for brains. Then again, if they were all doing it, maybe that was what being their age was about. Like poo and wee being funny when he was four, and the grossness of snot being pretty clever funny when he was six. Some-one threw a pillow. It hit Mark in the head.

'Planetti, come in, or go out, but shut the freakin door!'

'Pretty cool hey, meeting up with the Mandelbrot. Thought we saw the last of it on Crew Day,' said Bransen.

'Yeah, it's like huge. Wish they'd picked us.'

'Midshipman Geets, Ship of The Line. None of this 'open fleet' crap.'

'And weapons! Did you see the weapons! They're like all over it.'

Mark stood watching, listening to the bigger trainee officers. They were behaving like the Mandelbrot was the most amazing thing they'd ever seen. He couldn't get excited about it. It was a huge, foul, misshapen thing, and he knew, rather than 'pretty cool hey meeting up', the Mandelbrot had been waiting for the little helpod and its soft cargo ship. Who would they call to, for assistance? The helpod would lose the best of its crew, and the midshipmen would suddenly find themselves promoted, into dangerous jobs they couldn't handle, with no-one left on board to teach them. With perhaps a murderer or two for company, from the Mandelbrot. The conversation had moved on to food.

'We're not even around the back of the last world, and the pudding's run out!' said a midshipman, as if it was outrageous. 'Yeah well, I wouldn't be complaining about the food. This room is way too small for eight people. Bransen farts when he wakes up, Geets picks his nose when he reads, and Lloyd, you bloody snore.'

'Hey Planetti, what's with the new collar flags?'

'Don't know. Captain Thomas said I have to wear them, "At all times".'
So they'd seen what he was hiding in his hand. They did notice things, if you didn't want them to.

'He wasn't joking. It's been like action stations here. Go check your laundry.'
What? What were they talking about?

'We thought you were dead or something.'

'They came and emptied out your locker. But then, like not even half an hour later, they brought it all back, and we're watching, thinking what is going on.'
Emptied out his locker? How come nobody said anything about this until now?

'Right then our laundry came back, still all mixed up, a-gain, and, well, couldn't help noticing when I was untangling little boy undies out of my socks... Didn't you know?'

'No. Thanks a lot guys. Good one. Real nice.'
Little boy undies ha ha. The midshipmen had this fixation about making sure he and James wouldn't forget they were smaller. It's like a grinding need they have, to share being our age with us thought Mark. To get upset only made them keener, but one more pat on the head from that Damien, and Mark was going to hit him as hard as he could, with whatever would hurt the most. There would be no more patting of James's head or his. Now some-one had interfered with all his possessions. It was time for paybacks.

Definitely paybacks, and if that didn't work, James would dob.
All Mark owned was in this locker. Not much, but it was
everything. His heart was in his mouth as his finger registered for
the lock to open. Dad's old ship's watch…still here. For a
moment, until he held it in his hand again, he'd felt like crying. If
you only had one small thing left from your family, one tiny little
old broken thing, then that thing was what your heart needed
most to keep, in the whole universe.

The socks! His socks had little flags sewn on them…oh come on!
– the pyjama collars!, – little flags… and even his underpants,
like the big dope said, little flags sewn on. Any time of night or
day, even if he was stripped near naked, it would still be clear
which branch of service he belonged to now. What was wrong
with a simple tag on a string around your neck, like the
midshipmen wore? This had to be a prank.

'Who's trying to be funny?' he asked, his voice hard.
They'd really gone overboard this time. And broken into his
locker to do it.

'Nobody Planetti, calm down. They just came in here, all
high and mighty, two polites and an armed guard, and collected
your stuff.'

'I've got it, I've got it. Should have thought of this
before… Flags and insignia… But?… no, yours hasn't got the
red stripe for blood…'

'There, Geets.'

'Oh yeah… Member of Survivor Staff. What the fuck's
that? I mean like who are they when they're at home? What's in
our handbook, Bransen?'

'Entitled to privileges above his or her rank. A wise
midshipman will steer clear of these rare onboard gods. Oh, far-
nee. See that Planetti, first you're the amazing orphaned Star
Boy, and now you're a god.'

He didn't feel like a god, and as for privileges, Captain Thomas
had said 'Helping Litmus entitles you to privileges, but we won't
ask for them. I will take them for you, if the need arises.' Then
the Captain had thought for a while, and said, as if it was
weighing on his mind – 'The need will arise. I have informed

them I am deadly serious, and they have failed to reply'. Who 'they' were, Mark had no idea.

Minding Litmus wasn't just an easy time waster, it was a career path change, and it looked like that career path was going to have its own problems.

THE CHOCOLATE RUN

'Planetti, it wasn't us, okay?'

Geets, standing next to him, at his locker. All right, he'd said it – why didn't he go away now?

'Looks pretty cute but? The flag labels? Tough cute I mean. Yeah? We were wondering… if… you two, like, I mean, the ensigns, could do that trick again – go up to stores and get extra chocolate rations? For us to share out?'

'Why don't you do it yourself?' said Mark, although he knew why.

'No, I mean how you two do it – look sort of hopeful, and disappointed, at the same time, like life is new and big for you, and you need a hug from your mum to charge you up, but you'll settle for chocolate. We do stuff for you?'

'Oh yeah, like what?'

'We'll punch Damien stupid, if he keeps on with the puppy treatment?'

'Stupider?' asked Mark hopefully.

Geets turned around to the mess.

'We're getting chocolate. All we have to do is punch Damien stupid.'

They enjoyed a good pretend fight. They were too big for James to join in, but Mark leapt on top of the stack of rumbling bodies, and started deadarm punching. Payback time.

'Hey hey hey, get him off. Little bastard. That's going to bruise.'

'We need to get them ready for the chocolate run anyway,'

'Yeah… stand still James.'

'Tuck him in.'

'I am.'

'No, not like a wedgy, with his undies hanging out up the back of him. Do it tidy, like if his mother's done it.'

That did not look right to Mark – James's pants being unzipped and pulled down him while his clothes were rearranged on him. That did not look right at all. James didn't seem to mind, but it made Mark feel uncomfortable, just watching it happen to another boy.

'Bit of hair combing… yeah… nice… and now for…'

'Touch me and you're dead,' said Mark backing away, arms up ready to fight.

'No point on him. He looks better rough. Do us proud kids… I mean messmates.'

'Go James 'n' Mark.'

Now they were yelling down the passage.

'Hey? You two won't eat it all on the way back, will you?'

'Might,' yelled Mark back.

James laughed.

'It's going to be okay, isn't it. I mean I can stop feeling scared of them. I realised last night they are just a whole lot of Alans, going a bit silly because they've got no Dad here to threaten to box their ears.'

'Yep.'

'I bet Shane wishes he was here.'

No, thought Mark, after Miss Shandy's speech, Shane would be glad to be staying home. He was a family boy, and Outer 17 was his home.

HIGH COMMAND MEETS

Next morning there was a meeting going on in the cabin. Captain Thomas, the helpod's commander, the gunnery officer, and the Soft Cargo's captain, all sitting among Litmus's toys.

'Come in Ensign. Litmus is tidying up, then the pair of you can choose breakfast. Don't forget Floppy Bunny, and Happy the hoppy frog,' added Captain Thomas to Litmus.

'HOPPY the HAPPY frog,' growled Litmus, as he tugged it out from under Captain Murray's shoe.

Captain Thomas turned back to his meeting.

'Seal the gangway at the first line of containment, and follow my lead. The Emprino is on attack. I know I've said this before, but – never try to help, or get between him and the aggressor. The Emprino can be simplistic, and brutal. I am on defence. We need everyone on all ships, so hopefully there will be no crushing of heads, or ripping off of limbs, but I can't know that, so I ask you to remember the advice of the Magnificci – "Tread carefully around a Giant of Death, or your life may be mistaken for a small thing".'

'Yes Lord.'

Mark looked and listened from the doorway. They scared him. They weren't their usual selves. Quietly serious, agreeing carefully, their words showing their respect for each other's abilities. They kept addressing Captain Thomas as Lord, as if he was separate from them, and had some amazing power over everything.

'We are finished here Lord?' asked Captain Murray finally, 'to our places then, and wait. Don't forget we are silly old duffers.'

They strode past Mark to the door like warriors on a mission, and then ambled away down the passage outside like midde-aged holiday friends.

'Was that all as you would wish?' asked Captain Thomas of Litmus.

'Yes Grandpa. We will breakfast now.'

WHERE IS THE EMPRINO?

The captain of the Mandelbrot came aboard with an assault team, armed, in full battle gear, as her honour guard. Also there was a group of mistreated looking people, dressed in old uniforms that didn't fit them, being herded along at the back of her entourage. She seemed to have all the power, and the Soft Cargo none. Mark couldn't see 'The Emprino' attack warrior anywhere. He could be semi-invisible? How could you keep out of the way of a killing machine you couldn't see?

Mark was glancing around nervously, when he realised with shock that the Mandelbrot's staff lieutenant was holding a program, the program, from the Academy passing out parade. Mark was getting a real bad feeling about this. The Soft Cargo officers were standing on the other side of the gangway area, looking like nice old duffers from a gentlemen's club.

'They can't just take them,' said the gunnery officer from the helpod, 'We have an obligation to the lads' families to look after them. We don't even know what rank they will be given.'

'Probably ordinary crewman,' said Commander Burnett, 'Don't doubt me – look at the uniforms on the "exchange". And, on a vessel like that, the life of an ordinary crewman is very ordinary, and sometimes short.'

'Grandpa, they didn't "look up",' said Litmus.

'Leave a clear space around me,' said Captain Thomas softly, 'Only Litmus is to stand near me'.

Now there were three groups.

'You know why we're here. Names. Let's get this over with. Read, Lieutenant,' said the Mandelbrot's captain.

'By right and in need, as decreed in the articles of peace, we...'

'Names, Lieutenant, we haven't got all day.'

'...Bransen, Fargo, Geets, Planetti,...'

Captain Thomas took a huge lung full of air, and yelled, 'Withhold your reading,' like it was both an order, and a warning.

He was white with anger.

Silence for a moment, with the commander of the Mandelbrot looking at Captain Thomas.

'I'm sorry old timer, this is how we do things these days,' she said finally.

'Team leader, pass me your weapon, in case we have any more outbursts... Now, I am entitled to use this weapon... any more advice?'

'Yes, if you're going to shoot yourself, do it now, coz you've had it.'

'Litmus, let me do the talking. Aim carefully Commander Yorker. Your career depends on it.'

'I have no time for hollow threats. Read, Lieutenant. I am setting this to stun, and hoping you won't make me use it.'

'Bransen, Fargo, Geets, Pla...'

It was hard to hear the names, because Captain Thomas was announcing a sermon over the top, as he walked across the gangway area, Litmus shadowing him.

'No man may put himself above me. No law shall fail to recognise me. Observance will be made. This will always be my right, as a Sur... as The Last Survivor.'

His hand reached towards the Lieutenant's list.

'I'm sorry old timer, your surviving days are over,' said the Mandelbrot's captain.

She aimed the weapon, and fired.

'All right, get that fixed team leader. Pass me another one...'

Again she fired, point blank, at Captain Thomas. This time, he was sparkling and glinting all over, like he was a black ice statue.

'Finished?' he asked, 'Keep on your current course of action, and you will die.'

'We all die one day,' said the Mandelbrot's captain, while she held the weapon between her knees, so she could adjust the power output up.

'No, we don't,' said Captain Thomas.

As she lifted the weapon back up, he took hold of its aiming tube, and squeezed, steadily, until it shattered, as if his fingers were powerful robotic jaws. His hand moved further up the weapon, and crumpled it. The commanding officer of the Mandelbrot was still holding it in her hand, but now it looked more like a rough bunch of flowers than a weapon you could aim.

'We will discuss this in the privacy of my cabin, along with other things that displease me... You may bring your lieutenant. My personal staff will be present. Gunnery officer, Commander Yorker's honour guard might like some tea and cake.'

'Yes Sir.'

Tea and cake. They were in full battle gear. Not funny, but very strange. Mark realised he was light headed, from shock, and relief.

Litmus was pushing at him.

'That's you, Stupid. We are the 'Personal Staff'. Walked yourself, or they will be leaved us behind.'

They were in the gangway lift. The doors shut. Captain Thomas had his hand hovering over the up button.

'Commander Yorker, what happens from here on is up to you. You have a ship to command. I have faith in your ability to do that. I am only asking that you recruit your crew with more honesty. There is no point in secure home planets, if they are corrupt at their core. Our officers of the fleet are our front line, in many ways - people who show by example that we are a just, fair, powerful and caring star league. As you are, so shall you use your ship. Let that be as it was when you took your oath, for your first command. I am a little rusty…if you could repeat the words?'

Silence in the lift.

'Commander, the oath is many things to many people. I would like to hear only the words that made you proud to take command.'

She did a sigh of resignation, and began.

'With this vessel to fly the Heavens, above all, with shining honesty, that every world will know we sail for no flag, but for everyone.'

'I love that bit,' said Litmus quietly to himself.

'So do I,' said Commander Yorker, her voice sounding tired, and then she brushed a hand across Litmus's hair like a loving mother.

Mark realised he had never heard it before, not with its meaning intact. It was the tail sentence that never got noticed, after all the other grand words of the oath, all the posturing about wealth, and might, and pride.

'If you are ready, we will suggest to Captain Murray that a compromise can be reached,' said Captain Thomas.

'Thankyou Sir,' said Commander Yorker.

As Captain Thomas pushed the button to open the doors again, he added,

'Any agreement is not to include your "exchange". We are not equipped to rehabilitate them.'

Mark whispered to Litmus as they followed the Captain, the Commander and the Lieutenant out of the lift.

'Where's that Emprino thing?'

Litmus giggled. His eyes looked up cheeky happy.

'You don't know much secrets,' was all he replied.

ON BOARD A SHIP OF THE LINE

It might be huge from the outside, but every space inside it was small. The crew scurried along the narrow passageways like rats, the pipes and wire looms above them making them bow their heads. Half way along a passageway, Mark realised the passageway was a pipe too, with the midshipmen inside. The lighting was weak, dull fuzzy red, and, after a while, hurt his eyes. They'd done a lot of walking, but they hadn't seen much. The crew slept in holes in the walls, in rows of passageways that were like honeycomb. To sleep, you got in feet first, and the walls blew up around you, to hold you, so the ship could manoeuvre at any time, without worrying about the safety of sleeping crew. The others were going to see the galley, and the sick bay, and the crew recreation areas. Mark's guided tour was over. The Mandelbrot commanding officer's personal Lieutenant had come to collect him.

'Commander Yorker would like a word Planetti, with you'.

The commanding officer of the Mandelbrot had a tiny cabin, like a narrow box, with everything visible. Including the toilet.

'Tough life, a ship of the line. Even for me. Good crew are very hard to get, but everyone wants to live on protected planets. I command this ship to enforce safe and secure skies. If, sometimes, I need to take a shortcut or two, to make that possible… But I have made a solemn promise to myself – they are the ones that count – that I will be doing some serious straight flying from now on. You're new to your job, staffer. You were my first pick. I ran my eyes over that parade and thought, still a kid, but I'm having that one. Two types of junior officer we get here – pudgy muscled up rich boys, with high opinions of themselves, and pale, weedy, dark-eyed boys from aristocratic families, with even higher opinions of themselves. It was easy to see you were neither. I was prepared to part with good money, but…Life has some nasty tricks. I could have you, but you could never be an officer – you have no provenance. I'm no snob, but no family, at all? Not done, on a ship of the line. I nearly took you for deck crew, but I'm just not that much of a bitch. You don't realise how angry your Captain Thomas made me, him and that wretched boy, standing next to us, and going, "That one, grandpa, have that one," and the old bugger going, "Well, let's have a look… He's a space orphan, rescued from the stars…definitely our kind of boy". I had to watch, while out of two hundred cadets, they snapped up the eight worth taking. I was so stinking mad. One thousand I get, to buy my junior officers. Thirty-eight thousand your Captain Thomas spent. I counted every greedy penny. Some dirty old bugger with a cruise ship wanted you, and one other, and he's boasting how he always gets the 'boys' he's after. "No, you don't", says the old goat, and that weird boy adds, "Quit while you're behind". If you'd been honest about your family staffer, you'd be my gun midshipman now. You've met me – would I have cared that your folks were back planet poor? Space orphan is a weak lie – nobody has ever survived a civilian shipwreck in space that I've heard of, and, with a name like Planetti – so cliché – it was a dead giveaway. Ah well, you raised your cannon, and fired your shot – no point crying over which hole you tried. Now – your Captain Thomas is no captain. One hypermessage, and I'm on suspended promotion and five years good behaviour, just from being in the same galaxy as him and not falling to my knees. One more slight indiscretion, and I become a bitter old hag, who used to be an officer of the fleet, growing daisies in balcony pots. That's me, and my ship. What about you and your dinky little pair? What are you up to, I wonder?

'I believe your Lord Thomas is on board because you are carrying dangerous cargo. I am almost sure of that. My guess is some filthy rich political family, with arms of power reaching right across space. They have two ways to travel – with a whole fleet of ships of The Line, or sneaking quietly past, with a souped up helpod for company. And let me tell you, now we've had more time to observe it, that is one hell of a helpod. You haven't noticed... any unexplained people on board, with very high opinions of themselves?... I would shadow your pair out of curiosity, but I have orders to open next orbit, that I suspect will take me to the other side of the galaxy. No point in having the number one battlewagon in The Line this far from the action. Soon you lot will be the last thing on our minds. Well, glad we had this chat. Tell your friends I look after my crew, when I've got one. The lieutenant will show you to the gangway. Thankyou staffer. You are dismissed.'

Mark hadn't said one word, just stood inside the doorway while she talked sitting at her desk, nibbling a biscuit, sipping something from a cup, and dropping her ideas into his thoughts.

'Oh, and staffer, back here a moment... I am sure you won't know, but I have to ask. What the hell sort of body armour was that? All right, it's official – nobody knows. Lieutenant, take him back to the gangway.'

Lord Thomas, she had said in jest, without realising the truth of it thought Mark, as he walked.

They arrived at the gangway. The shuttle was waiting, full of the other midshipmen. The lieutenant turned to him.

'Well staffer, that was a first. The commander didn't say "Don't fly so straight, you make me nervous", when she'd finished talking. I think we're all going to be grateful to your Captain Thomas. Hey, you lads, what do you think? She's a bit rough on her crew, but she's a fine ship. None more powerful. If you join us, you'll be in with us lieutenants. Hope we see you back here soon. Okay, safe journeys.'

JAMES THROWS UP
'Did you see that 3D fire control thing? Oh gees Planetti, you don't know what you missed. They strapped Fargo in, and

cranked it up – he's just like floating up there, like a little doll, then the bloke on the simulator controls goes, "Battle at Needle's Eye, ships and ground fire," and Fargo's jerking around all over the place.'

'Yeah, yeah – they got him down, and his eyes are going like flick flick, and he keeps falling over.'

'Gees it was funny.'

'And the pilot fella goes, like, how was it, and Fargo just barfs, all over the place. So cool.'

Mark looked sideways at James, sitting next to him. Not cool at all.

'You've got this great big weapon that's going to crack their ship open. You know when you do it, they're all going to die. Forever,' said James.

'That's what dying is, Jamesey boy, you dope.'

'You know nothing,' said James, 'It was real, from when it happened. They just add extra effects, for when you shoot somewhere different. People were looking at me. Ordinary everyday people like us, who knew they were going to die. Just scared people. The cannon thing kept going off. I couldn't make it stop. I wish I never joined the fleet. It's wrong. It's all wrong.'

'Ensign, report to sick bay when we get back,' said the shuttle coxswain without turning around, 'No big deal, you're entitled to some medication, and a de-briefing. I'm going to log you in for it, so make sure you turn up.'

'Medication? Do you reckon it's like…'

'Sshh.'

'I was just…'

'Damien, joke's over.'

NO MORE MIDSHIPMEN

The midshipmen's room was very quiet. Only two bunks occupied now.

'Do you think I should have gone? Lefty? Do you?'

'No. Just because you're the only one who stayed, that doesn't make it wrong.'

'They said we could choose. I liked it here.'

'Yep. I still like it here. It's better even without the farts, and the nose picking, and the not-funny practical jokes. Also, we shouldn't forget what Miss Shandy said.'

'I hope they're alright... want to do a movie?'

'No, thanks. I'm on night duty. Have to be up and ready, in...oh crap. Like in five minutes. James, don't just dag around here all the time. Go to the canteen or something... Litmus! Can you stop hanging around outside doors?'

'I'm coming here to play. I'm going to bring my floor fliers. You've got more room than anybody now. Hello? Is your name Fargo? That girl with orange hair who does long range navigation, the one still doing school – she's called Phoebe, and she wants to navigate you. With... her... tongue.'

Litmus pressed the words home, like he was cramming James's personality into a tight sock. Mark saw James's freckles stand out as his face whitened. He was sitting awkwardly on the edge of his bunk, his breathing going funny, as if his brain didn't know what to deal with first. Another shock to his system thought Mark. In his own small boy way Litmus could be a real bully.

LITMUS IS LOST

Mark and Litmus began walking away down the passage. It was evening, so doors were open all along it, doors into cabins, with people inside them feeling sociable. Between people calling out 'Hi Litmus', as Mark and Litmus went past, Mark said,

'Litmus, why did you have to go and say that? He's really upset at the moment.'

'Grandpa told me to. He said, "It's what the boy needs to distract him". Are you going to wear your toy soldier suit tonight?'

'What else would I wear?'

'Oh. I didn't know you were allowed to wear that flying.'

Flying?, thought Mark.

'Litmus, I told you, I don't do that. Ensigns don't take a run up, dive, and skid down passageways on their bellies, little bunny bums poking up in the air, squealing "Weeeeee".'

83

'Don't call me Bunny Bum. I don't keep sewing that stupid thing back on. It's not what I meant, anyway.'

It was quiet in these passageways, on this side of the Soft Cargo. The starboard gangway that went right along the side of the ship wasn't full of stores after all. It was sealed, but Captain Thomas had the codes. The primary hatch would only open a couple of hand widths, because there was something parked close to the other side. They squeezed in, between the bulkhead, and the edge of the large bulkhead door. Mark was last. He could hear Captain Thomas beyond the door.

'She's moved a little. No harm done.'

No harm done? Mark could see a huge gash-like dint, along the inside wall of the Soft Cargo. Apparently that didn't count.

'What is this?' he whispered.

'This is our ship,' said Litmus proudly, 'and it's the best ship in all of everythingness.'

Large, dark, and smooth skinned, like a giant sea creature. No. There were no sticking out fins. It looked like a huge plum coloured shiny pip. It took up all of the starboard gangway. Mark realised with surprise that that meant, in the scheme of things, this vessel was tiny, even compared to a Helpod. It looked so monstrous because of where it was parked. Captain Thomas and Litmus were standing with him, waiting.

Litmus was cradling something in his hand. Water?

'Son, I'm sorry, there is no bottle any more, and it mustn't leave its storage container until the moment before it is administered, or it won't work. To join us on board you must join us – bio security. You must drink from Litmus's hand.'

It wasn't clean fresh tasting like water, but then, thought Mark, anything that had come into contact with Litmus's grubby little hands would be disgusting, even if it was the most pure bio-security essence ever made. He swallowed, wondering what was in it to make it warm, sticky feeling on his tongue, and slightly slippery.

'See? My spit doesn't taste so bad,' said Litmus, wiping his hand off on his bunny suit.

Mark wanted to vomit. He tried, but he couldn't. He realised they were watching him, so sticking his finger down his throat wasn't going to be acceptable. He put his hand back down. For the first time ever, he heard Captain Thomas laugh.

'No son, I didn't. There used to be a bottle, once, and the contents hadn't been inside the boy yet. Swallow it well, or we'll have to do it again.'

We!, thought Mark with indignation. He felt hard done by, and he swallowed again very unwillingly. They were watching him.

'I think it's in him now Grandpa… Do you feel alright?'

'No. That was disgusting!'

'I wiped my hand?'

After, thought Mark.

'Stand close… Up us,' commanded Captain Thomas.

They were sucked in so fast Mark didn't see it happen.

Dim soft light everywhere, on all surfaces, just the softest whitey-blue glow. Whitey-yellow in a few places, like really early morning. Gentle on his eyes.

'The Mandelbrot is red inside, but a bit like this.'

'Yes. Red is the impure version. Harder on the eyes. With a vessel this small, there is no need to think of economies. She is the best of many worlds, and many peoples.'

'Grandpa, are we flying tonight?'

'Perhaps. We'll see,' said the captain, but his headed nodded a no at Mark, when Litmus wasn't looking.

Litmus was standing looking at the blank forward vision wall. For once he was still. Too still, as if he was sleeping standing up. The three of them stood in silence. The captain was waiting for something, and then, finally,

'Alito?' he called, softly.

'Father!'

Litmus spun around. His face was full of joy, then the joy turned to cold fear. In a lightning flash of micro-moments he had remembered his distant past – all the people and places he had lost. As Mark watched, Litmus was rising to total panic, with nowhere nothing and no-one left for him to turn to. A howl of unhappiness escaped him.

'I'm here. Grandpa's here.'

The captain, on his knees, hugged, tight. Mark had never seen people hug each other so tight. Their hands were white with pressure, and they were locked together, head against head, as hard as a struggle to the death.

Colour was coming back into Litmus's face. His normal wondering child happiness seemed to be rising into him, until he was full of himself again. Captain Thomas looked just as careworn as ever.

'This is what we came here for tonight. It's called a reversion. It is the moment when Litmus dumps all the daily thoughts and memories he has no real need of. For a tiny moment he is lost, until he hears his name, and then we're back in working order, aren't we Litmus. Except he won't remember you yet. When you are important to him, he'll remember you through a reversion.'

'Look Grandpa, I've got a tail!'

'Yes, I can see that.'

'I like it.'

'Yes, I know.'

Mark woke next morning still thinking about what happened in the strange craft. If anyone needed a reversion it was the captain, he thought. The captain could do with getting a few years of daily cares off his mind. Alito… Alito. Mark knew where he'd heard that before. Nah, not true, couldn't be… but he would ask Litmus this morning about his other name. Kids often got named after people from stories.

'Alito is ME. I am the only Alito. No-one else is allowed.'

'Okay okay. Keep your hair on.'

What would a kid know anyway? The little snot was like only seven.

86

THE WISDOM OF COMMANDER BURNETT

Mark was looking for James. He needed someone to tell Litmus's sillinesses to. It wasn't likely James would be there, but Mark stuck his head in the door of the officer's reading room. James was more likely to be down some storage passageway these days, groping and being groped by that orange haired Phoebe.

'Come in ensign,' said Commander Burnett, 'We'll have a game of Places.'

'Sorry Sir, I don't know how it's played.'

'I'll teach you.'

Oh bugger, thought Mark. He did know how it was played. There was a box of miniature pillars, in the style of a very very old Blue Skies One building. You chose your twelve pillars, and then for no reason, and in no particular order, each player would make, turn by turn, a line of pillars on their side of the table. Slowly a collection of faint images, disjointed 3D sections of pictures of places long ago and far away, would begin to shimmer between the two rows of pillars, as light from the room refracted through them. Then the pillars had to be swapped around, and turned carefully, little by little, until there was just one larger clear sharp image, of one place. There wasn't a winner, as far as Mark knew the game. Old people liked it, because the pillars were full of places they'd forgotten about, and liked to remember again.

Mark had his twelve pillars. He was trying to see up inside them, to see if there were any parts that moved. Commander Burnet chuckled.

'There's not a lot of difference, is there,' he said happily.

'Sir?'

'Between you and Litmus. That's exactly what he did.'

Mark didn't have an answer. Some standing up of pillars happened.

'No need to rush it,' said Commander Burnett, 'growing up. It will happen when it's ready. Young Fargo is on the cusp of leaving childhood. You never get it back you know. I remember standing in a bathroom of a house we lived in at the time, cleaning my teeth, and I glanced up at the mirror, and saw this amazing thing. It was me. I should have lingered in that moment for a year or two, enjoying what I had, but I was a silly boy, in such a hurry to grow up that I got all fired up and into girls before I needed to, and once that started, girls would cause this huge exciting need in me, and then suddenly I had three daughters and four sons, and now it's grand children, popping out all over the place, and that first year or two of just liking being me is gone, lost forever. So don't rush it, right lad?'

'Yes Sir. I get a rotten feeling, every now and then, that I don't get to choose anyway,' said Mark tweaking a pillar, 'how fast it happens.'

'I see you cruising around, that little wedge of tough-kid hair sticking out at the back of your neck, and your young eyes looking excited hopeful that your day will go well, and my heart goes softer than the evening dusk on a lifeworld. I knew, when I took this posting, that I would most likely never see my wife, my children, or my grand children, ever again. I took it because if we don't succeed, one year soon a great dirty-orange pile-driving ray will appear out of the sky, smash our planet, and turn them all into death soup. Often, Litmus's behaviour causes memory echoes of my family in me. I love him for that, even though he can drive me to distraction with his annoying little kid-ness. Ah – we have an image. Terra. I can tell by the small gnarled trees, the pebbly beach, and the windswept sky. A planet covered in bridges. Perhaps that's why Captain Thomas is so good at building them between people. Game over. Thankyou for your time Ensign Planetti.'

CAPTAIN THOMAS'S WARNING

Another day of Litmus. Mark was tired. Watching the little brat just coping with his seven-year-old existence would cause a deep fondness in Mark, and then, like even the very next minute, the little shit could be so irritating that Mark just wanted to strangle it.

'Sir, I think he's asleep?' said Mark, meaning "I'd like to go now".

The captain was taking a look into the sleeping cabin, at Litmus curled up on his shelf. And now he was closing that door quietly.

'Sit for a while ensign. We are running out of time. By that I mean I haven't any time left. Soon, very soon, whether or not I am ready, regardless of what wars are being waged, or what time of the day it is even, I will cease to be aware, of you, this ship, Litmus, of everything. My memories will start rewinding, all the way back to the start of this. There is no way of knowing if that state will be permanent, by that I mean there is no way of knowing if I will ever wake from it. Litmus needs only familiar surroundings, a short moment of silence, and then a voice like his father's calling his name softly to him, and he is back with us. But I have a horrible feeling I have put this off too long, and there may not be such a simple rescue technique, not for me. This is too early for you – you haven't had a chance to get to know us – but I can't be so close to the edge of time running out without briefing someone. Please boy, watch all I do with Litmus, with great care, because my duties may fall to you. On a lighter note, don't worry if he starts to be obnoxious, asking inappropriate questions and thinking he's being funny. Each time he nearly has the whole sex situation sussed out he has a reversion, and is back where he started, with no idea at all. That is it for now. Thankyou for today, I know it was long. Sometimes one day with Litmus can feel like a lifetime.'

Mark walked slowly back towards the trainee officers' quarters, thinking, and hoping the captain wouldn't have a reversion any time soon.

PRIVATE AND PERSONAL

'We're winning! Look!... Well don't look then. It says "Mess with the lowest power consumption: trainee officer's quarters", and then about how good that is, because it's the first time a Soft Cargo mess has beaten the helpod.'

'Yeah, good one James. Stop reading that stuff and go to sleep.'

Mark was lying on his bunk realising that mess, something he had always been good at, was getting a bit out of control around here, even for him. That power thing, they'd won it for two reasons – there were only two of them left in the mess, and they were doing their own laundry. That was wearing a bit thin. He rolled over on his bunk to look across the mess, and a pile of mostly clean clothes near his feet that he hadn't got around to putting away yet fell off, to land on the deck down below with a thump, in a heap.

'Wimpy? If anyone comes in here we're stuffed. This isn't how it's supposed to be.'

'Don't call me Wimpy.'

Drying their clothes on bits of wire stretched across between the top bunks did work. Mark lay there, considering why it was bothering him. His eyes ran across the clothes lines. When they were strung up like that, without his or James's teenage bodies in them, the drying clothes looked pathetically junior, dinky small, particularly James's socks. This ship was full of men and women. This wasn't the way to get treated as one of the crew – hanging out a line full of children's clothes, for anyone to see.

'James, when this lot dries, we're not doing it again, okay?'

'Okay. I saw, but I was too embarrassed to say.'

'What? What are you talking about?'

'Dried stuff that didn't wash out, in the front of your undies, from doing you know...'

'Shut up shut up shut up shut up shut up,' said Mark. James was giggling.

'I did already,' he said, 'Shut up shut up you go, when I did already, for like ages.'

Mark realised he wanted to grab this little nerd by the neck too, and do some squeezing. The one thing that was really personal, and off goes James, 'yap yap yap'.

'You do it too,' pointed out Mark.

'Private,' said James forcefully.

'You do it over that… .'

'Don't say, or you'll get hit. Hard.'

'Good one Fargo, try it, and see how far you get.'

James was sitting on the edge of his bunk, looking around.

'Yeah well, they need to get washed better, but I like the rest – it's sort of like there are people here still.'

'All right. If you need it. But we don't talk about…that other stuff, okay?'

'Okay,' said James, doing another awkward giggle, 'got you stroppy though, hey.'

James was giggling again – kid size socks weren't the only problem.

'Shut up Wimpy. Go to sleep,' said Mark.

JAMES'S NIGHTMARE

Something had woken Mark. He lay there, on edge. The dim night time safety lighting was normal. The bunks all around were empty… but that was how they were now. The dried clothes on the lines were hanging motionless, like sentries asleep on duty. That shadow… it looked…humanoid. Standing in the dark corner, over at the lockers. Towel. It was just a hung up towel. He could feel his heart thumping hard in his chest, like it didn't have enough room in there, and wanted to burst out, spraying blood all over the place. Scared of a towel? But…then, what had made him come awake? He couldn't see around the corner into the wash area. Was there someone, some Thing, waiting there? His ears were listening hard, so hard they could hear themselves doing it. The ship was making that underlying everything dull hum, and then he nearly jumped out of his skin: a voice was yelling into the silence, and finishing with a terrified questioning whine on the end.

'Shane, Shane, come back. We have to stay with Mark. We have to stay together?'

Mark swung down from his bunk. James was still asleep, and still talking, but in a determined murmur now.

'No. No. I'm not indestructible, you can ask Mark. I'm not, I'm not, look – things hurt me. No, no…'

James was tearing his pyjamas away from his body, wrenching them apart with determined arms, like someone was trying to tie him up, and he wasn't going to let that happen.

'No. No. Somebody help me. Shane? Shane.'

For a weakling, James's muscles could tense up pretty tough. There was a ripping sound, and a button hit Mark in the eye.

'Oh, good shot Wimpy! James, wake up. Wake up.'

'What? What? What's happening?'

'You were. You nearly scared me to death, and then you hit me in the eye with a button.'

'Hey! These are my best jarmies,' accused James.

'Don't look at me! You were doing that. Only kids wear jarmies anyway.'

Mark was climbing back into his bunk when he remembered childhood sleepovers, with James and Shane. Once James got scared, he would keep waking everyone up, all night.

'James? Let's go to the nightwatch café – we can have a midnight kai, and then you can spill what's screwing with your brain.'

They were sitting at a café table, mugs in front of them. Mark looked at James. Skinny kid's neck sticking up out of crumpled pyjama collar. Dopey head. Night mess hair. Mark laughed.

'What?' asked James.

'Nothing. You are such a dick.'

'So you're all grown up all of a sudden? Who made you so big and tough?'

The Children's Home, and not having any family to look after him in life – Mark knew that was the truth of it.

'Nobody. You're just looking a bit rough.'

'Oh. Thanks,' said James, pleased.

'James? What's with the "I'm not indestructible" nightmare thing?'

James wouldn't answer. Wouldn't meet Mark's eyes.

'Come on. Can't be that big a deal.'

'Promise you won't get mean,' began James, like he'd already decided that was going to happen, and he didn't like it. Mark waited.

'I was worried about Shane. I didn't tell you because you're going to not like me for it. I should have been listening.'

Silence. James just sitting there, holding his mug.

'Spit it out Wimpy.'

'You know on Crew Day parade, when we were getting chosen, well, you went Open Fleet, and I was thinking how good it would be, us three together, flying across space, and the announcing voice was like droning on, and then I realised Shane was walking away across the parade ground, into the building. I didn't even hear where he was going, or if... if...'

'Who got him, you mean... No big deal, okay? First home messages run, we'll ask.'

'Sorry,' said James.

'We'll find him. If we have to we'll put out a search query on spacenet, and he'll answer. He will,' said Mark, starting to feel scared.

He knew what it was like to be forgotten, lost in Space. It happened to him when he was five. He was fourteen now, and his family still hadn't found him. James was talking again.

'I did that already, and I typed in LOST, after, and this whole new screen bubble opened, and that's where the other thing came from.'

'What other thing?'

Sometimes, getting information out of James was like listening to a little kid owning up to something.

'Well, it went: "Do you mean L.O.S.T., League of Stars Territory?" Since that's where we come from, I said yes, to see what it said...and, and, it said the LOST worlds were a small player in Space, whose main claim to fame was inventing the Line Listener.'

'I hope there's an 'indestructible' somewhere in this,' said Mark.

James just gave him a dirty look, and went on.

'That sounded interesting, so I was checking it out – it's a thing where they aim at the minutest bits of what makes up everything, all at exactly the same angle, and they record them, how they are like shivering in Space, from the bits beyond them affecting them. Then they give the recording to a huge computer, that takes like forever to analyse it, and then they know what happened to every other bit that affected those bits, in that direct line across Space. The first time they turned it on, they aimed it out into nothing as a background noise check, but there was something there – a planet, three whole galaxies away, and they just fluked aiming right at people talking.'

'James, I'm going to sleep,' complained Mark, and then pretended he was.

'It was a big politician and a military boss, planning how to catch "the I.B". Their plans were really horrible, and sneaky, and cruel, and they were going to build a monster ship to do it. I didn't even know what an I.B. was. You know how I do good homework, well, I date checked the story – it was like really old, like one hundred and eighty Blue Skies One years at least, so it wouldn't matter any more, and although everyone kept looking, no monster ship was being built anywhere they could see. I looked up I.B. anyway, Mark?'

The sound in James's voice had changed. So it wasn't just the Shane issue.

Mark eased an eye open a tiny bit, to watch Wimpy through the slit between his lashes.

'I know you're looking at me… It stands for Indestructible Being, and then they had a picture of the only known one.'

'Yeah? Then what?'

'It's on this ship, our ship. He's small, he's got big eyes, and he plays with his floor fliers in our mess.'

'Yeah. I sort of knew anyway. You know that kids' story – Alito the Unbreakable kid? Well that's him. His real name's Alito, Alito Magnificus, and Litmus is like his baby slang for himself. The "Lit" part comes from Alito, and the "mus" from Magnificus, but I didn't think it was for real. I thought maybe he was just named after the story.'

'They said that it had to be destroyed or trapped forever, because it was unnatural, a foul obscenity against the fabric of the Universe, and then they were telling each other that they couldn't build their monster ship fast enough, so while they were building it, they had to invade some great stable old worlds Empire to capture the scientists, so they could build their own I.B.s. That's wrong.'

'Enough, enough James, okay? Nothing we can do about any of it, so let's just sleep on it. No more nightmares but, all right? Nothing's going to happen. They've had like nearly two hundred years to catch him, and they haven't yet, and, if he was so bad for the Universe, I reckon we would have seen evidence by now.'

'I always get the best marks in tests, but you have like proper answers to real stuff,' said James, as they stood up to leave the Nightwatch Café.

'Yeah well, sometimes it takes both, hey,' answered Mark.

A SPY COMES IN THE NIGHT

As Mark climbed back up into his bunk, he realised he hadn't really believed the Alito thing, not until now, not totally. It was one of those times when you thought you'd found something out, when you heard a word or saw something, but then you realised it was a bit too amazing a coincidence to be true, so you just went 'yeah yeah, as if', and let it wander around in the back of your thoughts for the rest of your life. So Litmus really was Alito the Indestructible Boy. Well, he was only a kid still, right? He couldn't be dangerous.

Mark was drifting into sleep when James started being James, again.

This time he was standing next to Mark's bunk in the dark, pulling on his shoulder, and spit whispering.

'Mark? Mark.'

'What? Can't you just go to sleep?'

'There's someone knocking at the door, real quiet?'

'And? Who is it?'

'I don't know. I didn't see yet.'

There was a quiet tapping, almost like scratching, on the mess door. James was standing in the dark in his pyjamas, waiting for something to happen.

'Wimpy, you're hopeless,' said Mark, jumping down from his bunk, walking over, and yanking the door open.

It was one of the Polites.

'Sorry to bother you. Polite helper Jayman. May I come in?'

Now the door was closed again, Polite Jayman was squirting something into the door crack, all the way around.

'It will come off. I will take it with me when I go. It will just be a rubbery dry string by then. Now, where to begin?'

He was looking at Mark, then at Wimpy.

'Who accessed the ship's library?'

James held up his hand, like back in Junior School.

'I thought it was a child, from the search technique. We need the light to stay off, because it is another way to be overheard.

'Now, when you ask questions about indestructible beings, people get interested in you, in who you are, where you are, and where you are going. There are lots of ship pairs going on journeys at the moment, to make it harder for this ship pair to be found. One way a spy on board can send a message about us, to say we are the ship pair to be hunted, is to make enquiries about a certain subject, from Central Knowledge. You made that type of enquiry. Now I can see you are not a spy, but you need to know your interest is dangerous, for you, and for everyone on board. I am a spy. I am here to be one extra secret layer of defence, guarding our interest in the Emprino and his craft, while they are on board our ships. I know more about the Emprino than anyone else here, including even him and his companion. Right now is your one opportunity to find things out. After tonight, there will be no more dangerous questions. Shall we sit?'

The dim night lighting was making James's, and Polite Jayman's, faces look odd. The stripes in Wimpy's pyjamas were standing out strangely in the semi dark.

'I have to keep this short,' said Polite Jayman, 'but even the short version will take a while.'

Mark dragged his bedding off his bunk, to wrap around himself.

'Now you know about Alito. Alito was the royal child of The Magnificci. The Magnificci were fighting a war. It had reached a point where the Magnificci had to use their most powerful weapon – their ability to destroy stars, or they would lose everything. But destroy their enemies' stars, and all life on the worlds around those stars would be gone, forever. Not just the army generals and politicians, and not even just the everyday people and their children, but all life, the trees, the life in the seas, everything. Alito's father decided to move his whole empire to another, far away part of space instead. It was a great sacrifice, done to save his enemies, but it was to get worse. Much worse. His only son, Alito, had to be left behind, because he was the very first Indestructible Being, and there were two unexpected complications. The first one – if he became unsure of his surroundings, or upset about what was happening to him, or to people and things he cared about, he would stop, rock solid still, in the middle of everything, and howl until he felt better. When an indestructible being does that, their version of rock solid still is in relation to some point beyond this universe. Like a bulldozer they tear up everything around them as it moves, and they stay still. On a planet they make a huge mess as the planet turns. Inside a ship like this, they go flying through bulkheads and out into space, leaving gaping holes in the ship, and most likely killing everyone on board. He was five and a half – too young to understand, and driven by his feelings. No big ship would survive him, and nobody would be safe in a ship with him, not even his own mother, not if he was forced to travel at anything but his own speed, and anywhere but where he felt comfortable. It was a time of war and great upheaval for everyone, and everything. He couldn't cope with that, and they couldn't help him. There was no time to teach him how to manage his new abilities. They had to leave him behind.

'There was an emissary from Terra, one of our Lifeworlds, and he could not be taken either – he was not of The Magnificci, and he had arrived too late to be prepared for the trip. They left them both behind, to look after each other, because the old emissary and the young Emprino were already friends.

'The second complication was because Alito was a child. His Indestructible Being body would grow a year, then panic, and revert to the structure it knew how to be. The scientists did their best before they left, and he finally made it to his seventh birthday, just, but he returns to the day after his sixth birthday every year, and grows that year again. Over and over. He would always be, he will always be, a child, struggling to understand, wondering about everything. He would never grow up, never be anything more. He finds comfort knowing he made it to seven, knowing his parents would be pleased with him for that, until now, Alito believes it is his seventh year that he lives over and over, not his sixth. Anyone who cares about him, cares for him, must share that belief, for the sake of his happiness. Happiness is something he has to work very hard on. How old he has managed to be is a cornerstone of his pride in himself, and on that he built his happiness.

'Now, he was supposed to follow his people, as soon as his ship sensed he was ready. That ship had many tests to conduct, and exercises for Alito to do. When it knew he was ready, it scanned the stars for the trail to follow, that Alito's parents left for him. There was only empty nothing. The Democratzia Capitalisto wanted to catch the Indestructible Being of The Magnificci. Their spies told them the child had been left behind. They didn't have the technology to find the tiny transmitter buoys left for Alito to follow, so they sent out many explosive devices, to create radioactive 'noise' that would fry the circuits of any small devices floating unprotected in space. They wiped out all evidence of a pathway going away through the stars. Alito's parents were waiting for him, but they would wait forever, because the universe is endless, and his ship had no knowledge of where to start the journey to follow them.

'Alito knows in his heart they would come back for him if they could, that they will come back for him when they can. They would be thinking he will follow and catch them up, when he becomes capable of doing that.

'We don't know if the Magnificci scientists ever mastered the I.B. technology in adults. Alito may be the only I.B. His parents might have died a hundred years ago, far away, normally, as ordinary old people. Over time the Terra emissary became infected with Alito's biomaterial, and became a semi I.B. himself. When we became aware of that we attempted to create more I.B's for our armies, by secretly collecting and distilling discarded body waste from Alito, but it never worked. Perhaps Lord Thomas's emotional link with Alito is why he survives as he does. We don't know for how long. Magnificci science is not like anyone else's.

'Finally, Alito's ship is the only weapon we have that might save us, every living thing, on every lifeworld, from the greed of the Democratzia Capitalisto. His ship is an aware being, with Magnificci scientific knowledge and equipment. It is old, but it is evolving, and will always improve, to protect Alito. Some day, if we can keep it safe until then, it will have got itself ready, and it will defeat the Freedom Collective, no matter how great their armies have grown, or how infernal their war machines. That is our hope. Our only hope. So, there will be no more dangerous questions from you two. And remember – seven. Alito is seven. Forever. Don't let him down. His ship needs him, and we need his ship.'

The Polite had left. Mark was getting his bedding back up on his bunk. James was having one of his childish thinks, and then stuff was going to come out the mouth. Put up with it – he's your friend, Mark told himself.

'Mark?'

'Yes? What?'

'There's something wrong with that. Litmus isn't sad. When he's around you he's like a bomb of happiness. And you aren't any better. Phoebe says if she was a teacher, she wouldn't let you two sit together.'

'Yeah well, she'd be a rotten teacher then,' answered Mark.

Finally, sleep.

MARK GETS HIS MISSION FROM CAPTAIN MURRAY

It was a special wardroom dinner. Showy silver cutlery, flash food, colourful drinks in glittering glasses. More noise than usual. Mark and James were right down the other end of the table from all the noise.

'We fluked the right night for this,' said Mark.

'Yeah. Top food. Don't go for a pee yet – the Captain's been watching us.'

'He's okay,' said Mark, finishing pushing his chair back on its slides.

Junior officers weren't allowed to be the first to leave the table, but hey, who would care on a night like tonight. They were all partying – surely an ensign could have a pee?

'No, not your captain – Captain Murray. Wait Mark! Okay, Burnett is going for a pee.'

'Don't stress, Wimpy! You do enough sucking up for both of us.'

Mark was half-way to the toilets door when he realised Commander Burnett wasn't going in, but standing there stopping people. Bloody hell, I'm busting thought Mark. Burnett was crooking a finger, meaning 'You, ensign, come here'.

'Go in Ensign Planetti. Remember: speak only when you're spoken to.'

Speak when he was spoken to? He hadn't said anything! Flopping it out. Aiming.

Someone else had come in behind him. One person. Standing next to him. Zip noise. They were peeing. Mark snuck a sideways glance. Captain Murray! So the most senior officer, like the captain of the whole two ships, and the most junior, me, thought Mark, are having a pee together.

'I thought we might have a little word, ensign. Diplomacy can be like a relay race. Sometime during this voyage, if everything goes well, you will become the League of Stars Territory's only representative on board. On board the seeder, the Magnificus Royale, with Lord Thomas and the Magnificus Emprino. You will be all we have, our most important asset. More valuable to us than a fleet of Mandelbrots.'

Captain Murray was washing his hands. Now drying them.

'Alito and Axel have no-one left alive that they care about. That's what happens when you live too long. Out on the starfields of war we need to care about the folks back home, or we might lose courage, or purpose. Be respectful, helpful, behave yourself, but, when you have to, remind them we are all counting on them. All our lifeworlds. Don't let us down son.'

Captain Murray was standing at the door. Mark could think of nothing to say. He was not going to say a limp, Wimpy style 'yes sir'. It felt like the wrong moment for that. Captain Murray's hand was beginning to open the door back to the wardroom.

'Son, two last things – if that weird old ship of theirs doesn't fly, I promise I will rescue you and take you home, and – do your fly up.'

'Is that all he said? You didn't forget bits?'

'James! You nearly sound like Litmus: "is that all wot he said, you didn't forgotted bits".'

'I did not say it like that. Did you tell Litmus?'

'No. I will, when I get to understand it better maybe. Still could be a joke – he said "do your fly up" at the end.'

'Yes, but it was undone, and you were about to walk out.'

'Well, I was thinking about a lot of stuff!'

'Too hard. If it matters you'll get told more, that's what I think.'

'So you reckon,' said Mark.

He wasn't so sure. At the time it felt like a strange once-off happening.

Day after normal ship-board day went by. Mark came to the conclusion that the whole thing, the toilet meeting with Captain Murray was, on the surface of their lives at least, forgotten.

SOMETHING VERY SCARY HAPPENS

They were walking the passageways to lunch. Mark felt like the ship was theirs, like a school playground once you'd been there a few years. You belonged. You to the playground, and the playground to you. No more meals were being delivered to the trainee officer's quarters, now there were only the two of them. This time he and James were going to slum it in the General Crew café.

'They better not have the picture wall on,' said Mark as they got close.

He had learnt to really dislike it. If it was on, you couldn't help watching, and always, thoughts would seed in his mind. The news would be claiming victories. The Soft Cargo's crew would be happy hearing it. Mark would notice the status of the Fleet numbers, and think of all the Shanes, Marks, James's and Jeans who didn't, who never would, go home.

'It's off,' said James.

He stood blocking the entrance, just looking around the edge of the door into the large cafeteria.

'Shouldn't we ask first?' he added.

'Nah, go for it Wimpy,' said Mark, pushing James in.

You never got anything in the Children's Home by waiting around to ask.

'We'll just get in the line, and see if we get away with it.'

'And what are you two doing?'

'Food inspections. Trainee Officer food inspections,' said Mark, as if it was their duty to check that the food in the cafeteria was all right for the crew.

The man reached out to grab, but Mark was too fast for him, ducking away, and the crewman had to settle for holding James up by the neck, in front of everyone.

'I wanted Smartarse, but you'll do Jamesey my boy,' he growled, 'Oy, Everyone. Junior officer food inspections, mouth-on-legs reckons.'

Silence in the cafeteria.

Then some-one snorted laughter, and yelled.

'Hold him up? Okay, inspection over, not worth eating.'

'Last time I ate a junior officer, I had a gut ache for a month.'

'Tallison, let the little runts have some tucker.'

The game was over, with some fun all around, and now Mark and James could hold their plates out for food.

A large man stood up from one of the tables. Big muscles, large jaw. The feel of the moment changed. The man was coming to drag them out of the line.

'I'm handling this,' said the crewman who had held James up.

The man was still coming.

'I told you, I'm handling this, and I fucken meant it, you mean prick.'

There was a scuffle, and more rough words, and then the bully went back to his table, muttering,

'Suit yourself, but I'll be fucken reporting this. Smart-arse little runts aren't fucken welcome here.'

'You're a good lad James, and your mate's not,' the crewman said laughing, as he clipped Mark over the head.

Mark knew he was joking.

'You kids are always welcome,' said the next crewman.

'While they behave themselves,' added a woman from further back in the line.

At that, everyone stopped staring and listening, and went back to their lunches.

Mark decided he liked it here. It felt normal, working day ordinary, not self-important like the wardroom, where the ensigns had to remember who did what first, before they sat, or picked up their cutlery to eat.

They walked around hopeful, but they couldn't find an empty table. They sat where there were two empty seats, among the crowd.

'You two boys – don't mind the rough language. We don't have the snobbery of rank to protect our dignities down this end of the ship, so we use rough language sometimes, to let others know we are prepared to stand up for something. Okay?'

Okay, thought Mark, but it sounds ugly, and unfriendly.

'It's good now, isn't it,' said James to Mark as he started on his lunch, 'our quarters, life? Everything?'

'Yep.'

It was good. Life in the Soft Cargo had settled down. They were headed somewhere across the universe, could take weeks, or months, or maybe even a whole year?

'You're not going to get out of lessons forever,' commented James.

'I don't. Litmus teaches me stuff,' answered Mark while he buttered his roll.

'Oh yeah, like what? How to live forever?' and then James giggled, and added, 'How to wipe his nose.'

'You'd be surprised what that little brat knows. Signal protocols, how to get different weapons up and ready, control console overviewing...'

'What's that? I haven't done that yet.'

'You learn how to stand at a strange console, and nut out what it's for, and how to operate it. Not that hard, once you work out that they are all laid out to be used, each in their own predictable function hierarchy... Litmus is a clever little snot, that's for sure.'

'Big words for a little boy,' commented one of the crew at the table.

'Boys, don't speak about the Emprino like that. Not in front of us, okay? All our lives, from Captain Murray down, depend on him and the old captain. They decide we die, we die. We have to believe in them.'

'This isn't just a dawdle across space. One day, all of a sudden, a day that no matter how long it takes will come too soon, we will be on the News.'

'How carefully they lay their plans, and how well we do our jobs – that's what will get us home, or forever dead. Got it?' Silence at the table.

'Lesson learnt, hey lads? Cheer up then. Life isn't all doom and gloom – we could have another year or two of this first,' said a crewman, waving his hand around at the full cafeteria of happy chattering people.

Everyone went back to eating, and the crewmen returned to their previous conversation.

'Now we know where everything is in the ship, and who all the people are,' began James,

'Life could get pretty boring ordinary, like school,' finished Mark for him.

James was looking sideways at Mark.

'It wasn't boring for you, because you were always mucking around. You don't muck around so much any more,' he finished disappointed, and then suddenly he was looking more intently.

'Are you feeling all right?' he asked, sounding doubtful.

Mark stopped, fork half in his mouth. He wasn't feeling normal. There was a shimmering tingle going through him.

'It's just that, you're like growing freckles, and I mean lots,' said James.

B4 radiation.

'Sick bay,' said Mark softly, putting his fork down, and getting up from his seat.

James was holding his hand out.

'Give me your plate. I'll take it back. Go… go!' he said.

He wanted Mark to hurry.

I wasn't worried about what was going to happen to the stuffing plate, Mark thought. He kept his face down and toward the wall as he hurried to sick bay. People wouldn't understand. He didn't have time to explain.

'Litmus, I found him,' a crewman sang out as Mark scurried past, 'he's in passageway three.'

Mark heard pattering feet, the silence of the dive, and then,

'Weeeeeee,' as Litmus flew past, skating along the polished floor on his stomach. The bunny tail was up, and the arms forward hands outstretched, as if Litmus was air surfing. He rolled into a summersault and stood up.

'Where are YOU going,' he asked.

'Sick bay. B4 radiation,' said Mark, lifting his head for Litmus to see.

'I knew your legs was walking wrong,' said Litmus.

LITMUS GETS ANGRY

They were at the entrance to sick bay. The bottom half of the door was closed. Litmus stood on tip-toes, but he couldn't see over it.

'Open up!' he yelled.

'You better fixed him,' he added, as the medical crewman appeared.

'How about saying what's wrong for starters,' said the crewman, opening the bottom half of the door.

Mark realised he was feeling really rotten. I'm shit scared, he thought. His heart was beating so hard it was making his chest hurt. Water was coming out of his skin everywhere, in beads like sweat, then vanishing back in, as his body changed shape. He couldn't help it, he had to chuck. And cough afterwards, doubled over holding his stomach. His eyes were crying. His stomach felt like he was about to have the runs. He wanted to lie down on the floor. He was trying to. Falling over sideways. He heard Litmus say, 'He's really sick. I know coz he's filling his dacks'. At least that's what Mark thought he heard. I must be dreaming he thought next. In his dream Litmus picked him up like a sack, held him up over his head, and began running. Passage after passage, faster and faster. Up to the bridge, straight through, and into Battle Centre One. Mark felt himself land in the middle of the huge table, and skid along like Litmus floor surfing.

'Sealed,' yelled Litmus.

All the entries snapped shut. There were people in here. Officers. Officers Mark couldn't remember seeing before, so it was a dream. Or a nightmare. Dreams never hurt this much, or made him feel this sick. In the middle of the unfamiliar faces was Captain Murray, and even better, Mark saw with a mental sigh of relief, Captain Thomas. Nightmare or not I'll be all right Mark thought – the Captain was like a steady island in everything.

'B4 radiation,' said Litmus loudly, as if accusing them all.

He pointed at Mark.

'He's mine. You don't break my things,' he growled, cranky annoyed.

'No need to rip people's heads off, yet,' Mark heard Captain Thomas say, and then Mark fell unconscious.

SOMETHING NEW TO DEAL WITH

'Sick bay looked pretty comfy? Our mess was really quiet without you. It's good you're back.'

Mark could tell Wimpy was putting off saying something. And here it came.

'I hope you like Crackers. Crackers from school. Because you're him,' said James, standing in the doorway.

'Are you going to be okay?' he added, 'See you after class then.'

That was James gone. There had been no privacy in sick bay. This was Mark's first moment to himself. Litmus, well, where he was was anybody's guess. He was more of a baby, and a big pest, since that reversion. The way he mangled words had to be heard to be believed. He had made the sick bay nurse so upset, mucking around with everything playing doctor, that the nurse ended up crying with frustration. It didn't matter that the nurse was a man. Mark understood how he felt completely. The Captain seemed to be happy with the new younger brainless Litmus, but Mark was looking forward to Litmus growing back to his old cheeky knowing self.

Mark stood in front of the wash area mirror. Finally he could do a proper, private inspection. Hmmm. The feet were too big. The legs were awful thin looking, and not straight. The knees were knobbly bumps. His underpants hung from Cracker's bony hips like wet washing. All his uniforms weren't going to fit. He would have to wear the ceremonial webbing belt for serious now, on all his pants, like a string tie around the top of a bag, or his pants would fall down. Back to the inspection.

The skin was off whitey-pink semi-see-through, and anywhere light could get to was those blotchy freckles. He pulled the elastic forwards, to see down into somewhere light didn't get to. At least Crackers didn't have a spotted dick. It wasn't right either. Like the legs it was weedy thin, too long, and a bit crooked bent, with the end bit being too large for the rest. Obviously Crackers had lucked out in the dick department too. They were supposed to go back in your body mostly, when they weren't interested in stuff, but it just hung out there, limp and long, and crooked, and too thin. Mark let the elastic go flop back against the stomach front. The dick end fell out one of the leg holes with a jumbly bounce, and the whole misshapen thing dangled beside one of the skinny legs. Mark pushed it back in, feeling a little bit sad. Crackers was a mess.

'If I can't make myself like you, then that's it for me, for sex,' he said, staring at the wonky looking body in the mirror.

He had to believe he looked good, for anything to happen. That's what being fourteen was all about.

'Bloody hell. It's not fair. Why couldn't it at least have been a good looking kid?' Mark complained to himself.

'You're a real zube now, aren't you,' said Litmus standing beside him.

'Litmus!! Piss off.'

Litmus just took two steps away, and giggled evilly.

'You didn't know I was there, coz I sneaked up.'

'Yeah, so?'

'You played with your new dick.'

'I bloody did not.'

'Did too.'

'Right! You little runt.'

Litmus ducked out of the way, and then two steps further, and then ran for the door as he started trying to yell something through his laughter.

'Come on, chased me out in the passage,' he dared, his voice full of cunning.

Mark could feel his underpants flopping around the top of Cracker's grasshopper legs. He could feel the balls and dick cradled sloppily, like loose potatoes, and most of all he could feel the hip bones and the ribs sticking out. He didn't want people to see this.

'When I get dressed you're dead,' he said, going back into the wash area for his uniform.

'I can wait,' said Litmus, 'I comed to do floor fliers. You can be the Zoonies. They crash a lot.'

'Gee thanks.'

FAMILY FINDING, THE HAP COMMUNICATOR

Litmus, the Captain, and Mark, were sitting around one of the small coffee tables, in the lounge area of the wardroom. Litmus was poking a finger up his nose, or scratching himself, or doing that weird top lip pulling thing, while he moved around on his chair. All of his concentration was on Mark. Inspecting again. Litmus did a lot of looking and wondering about things these days.

'Do you feel stupider looking?' Litmus finally asked.

'How are you feeling?' asked Captain Thomas, 'we'll ignore the Bunny Bum comment.'

'Better,' answered Mark.

'I didn't forgot you did that name to me,' interrupted Litmus, pointing at Mark.

'I want to hear the truth,' said the captain, reaching over and pushing Litmus's arm down.

'I was waiting for Litmus to get ready yesterday, and while I was standing there doing nothing, I suddenly felt real bad. Not sick, but really sad about not looking like me. Nobody even knows I'm here any more.'

'Welcome to how it feels to be old. We all end up like that – thinking we're still the person we always were but we've become lost, somewhere inside our older grown uninteresting, turned unattractive selves,' said the captain.

This wasn't being old. He was still fourteen, just with red hair and buck teeth for a while. This body still felt exciting. Nerves pinged and tingled with sensual good feelings, all up the insides of the long legs. Mark wondered if it looked that weirdly off ugly to Crackers, or if the kid could somehow like himself, even though he looked like this.

'I'm going to be me again,' he said, both hoping and reasonably sure of himself.

'Perhaps,' said Captain Thomas.

'There were no B4 rays in the crew cafeteria. Not from the departing Mandelbrot, not from any leaking machinery on board this ship, and not from any distant enemy. When you agreed to drink Litmus's saliva…'

'I didn't!' interrupted Mark indignantly.

'When?!' asked Litmus, interested.

'Litmus? See that man sitting over there? That's Commander Burnett, and he likes you teasing him.'

'Does he?…Why?…Why is he all round shaped?' continued Litmus to himself, with his head tilted to one side as he wondered, 'Grandpa…would he fit through the 'mergency hatches?'

'Why don't you go and ask him… That's better. Now, where were we? When the essence of the Magnificci reaches a certain saturation threshold in your body, it questions your structure. You, all of you, is your password into the golden age of the Magnificci. I need to have a word with our little friend, because I don't understand why Litmus's spit hasn't worked its way out of you by now.

'Regardless, now this process has begun, it will find you are not up to their standard, and then it will let you go. Hopefully at a time when you are yourself.'

'How can I be sure?' Mark asked.

He wanted to be sure he would be himself again.

'They were pure honest people, on a glorious planet, in a stable Empire. You are a grubby cheeky ensign, racketing around space on a covert weapons carrier planning doom and destruction. I am quite confident you will be spat out, and end up licking slimy goop out of Litmus's dirty little hand again,' said the Captain, reading something while he talked.

'No,' said Mark.

Once was too much.

The captain is teasing me like I tease Litmus, thought Mark. He's different this morning. Like the serious oldness is winding down.

'Yes. After this B4 business, Litmus and I have looked more thoroughly at your records. You have… where is it… thirty-five or six other blood mutations to go through, before you are yourself again. Wait, wait. That is not a certainty, but a likely possibility. Remembering that, there's no rush to go home right now, is there.'

Home? What was going on? Who was going home? Home… Real home?

'Let's get down to business. You are aware that Planetti isn't a family name? The reason there are so many registered, and no-one ever answered your messages, is because refugees, fleeing from one planet to another looking for somewhere safe for their families, are officially named Planetti. When they finally settle on some quiet little world, they go back to being who-ever they were, before the disaster that had them fleeing across space. So, do you still want me to make enquiries through official channels, for a Planetti family?'

'No. Thank you. The lady at Cadet Club explained already, but I still hoped.'

Now Mark's hopes of finding his family were really gone. He mustn't go sooky here, not in the middle of all these people. He blinked, and did one tight sniff. He was fourteen, and pretty tough.

'Is there another name?' asked Captain Thomas quietly.

'No.'

Silence. Mark struggled until he was back in control of his feelings.

'I was five. Dad used to say, "well my little Planettis, we're a brave family aren't we, travelling across space all by ourselves," and then he would name us all, saying "Mummy Planetti, Daddy Planetti, Mark Planetti, baby one, and baby two Planetti". I don't know any other name.'

How can I search for my family, when I'm no longer me, and I don't even know my own name? He hadn't had this rotten feeling for years. This feeling that everything was hopeless, and he had let his sisters, and his parents, down.

Captain Thomas sipped from his glass.

'Lad, this is progress, not disaster. Where to from here is the question. There are some obvious places to start our enquiry.'

Yes, the Space Wrecks register, and…what was the other one? Captain Thomas was talking again.

'This is the value of having your personal records. We can't trace the home planet your parents were escaping from by the two child policy you mentioned in school, because that is on many worlds, but, B4 radiators were a very rare weapon. From the marker they left hoping to catch you, I can trace them. When you design a marker, you make assumptions about which genetic codes it will be used on. From that, some-one else (me) can make assumptions about who you, the weapon owner, are. It was early days, so the weapon may have been too crude. In any case, we will take an easier path first.'

The Captain was sipping his drink, again. Get on with it – what easier path thought Mark feeling frustrated. He'd spent most of his life thinking over all the possibilities.

'Treaty violations. Fleeing scout craft make massive explosions, to get themselves clear and on their way. There would have been a large cruiser with serious damage, limping home across Space. Visible to all, and claiming every safe passage right to get itself home. We know when that happened, because, looking at you, we can tell how old you are. When I get my answer back, we will know what that ship was, where it came from, and more importantly for us, where it went.'

When the answer came back, thought Mark disappointed. Answers across space took forever.

Captain Thomas put a small box down on the table.

'Inside this box is a HAP communicator. Halved Atomic Particle parallel reactance. Nobody knows why, but halve the particles, and even though you may position them galaxies apart across Space, when you interfere with one half, the other half changes also. By intermittently resonating one half, even complex messages can be sent. They weren't a great success, because each pair can only communicate with each other. I have this one because there is no more secure way to communicate. So cheer up, we could have answers as soon as tomorrow.'

The HAP thing was put away, and the captain began on his breakfast again.

'Mark, this isn't information anyone could access. Think over what is being done for you, because I will ask for something in return.'

Something in return. Whatever it was, Mark was sure it would be worth it, to find his family. He lay awake that night, holding Dad's ship's watch in his hand, and dreamily wandering through memories of his family. I'm crying he thought. Just silent water, running down his face. He didn't need his family every day in his life now, but he needed to see them once more at least, to say thanks for the beginning of his life, and to tell them he didn't forget. He didn't ever forget. He had to know they knew that.

His family were just some people, who would live and die among all the other people, but that was made them special for him – in all of the people everywhere, only his family had known him properly, from his very first moment.

ETERNAL LIFE, AND THE GREAT MAGNIFICCI

The HAP communicator answer hadn't come, yet. Shipboard life was going on much the same, day after day. Mark was having afternoon tea in the captain's cabin. Litmus was cup swapping again.

'The red one's mine, you little grot,' said Mark.

'Come on,' said Captain Thomas, meaning 'be nice'.

'He…it's… What he just did is another thirty-five times I have to be some-one else! I hate these buck teeff. And there's another kid even worse.'

'Steady on ensign. It's an easy mistake.'

How could it be an easy mistake: one beaker was green, and the other was red. Litmus was a backwash dribbler. His lips would linger on the edge of his cup, sometimes to the point of bubbles. Mark didn't know if he could taste sliminess or not, but he wasn't happy. Litmus didn't look happy either.

'Grandpa, which one?'

'I don't know any more Alito. I'm sorry.'

'I am very sadder this time.'

'Yes, I know. How about we tell our ensign about us? Because I think the time might have to be soon. This year perhaps, and we must prepare.'

'You, you tell,' said Litmus, 'And, after, story. Promise.'

'I am a little sad too these days, Little Man. Perhaps too sad for the story. Do you think you might let Mark read it to you?'

Litmus looked up.

'I will say please, and you will read to me,' he said.

He was climbing himself backwards onto the captain's lap. 'Grandpa first. It's a good thing Mark can still see colours, isn't it Grandpa. It means he won't have to live forever.'

'Yes, little Emprino, we did think it would mean that.'

Did, not do thought Mark, noticing the captain's careful choice of word, and since when was he suddenly in line for joining the team of people who didn't die when they were supposed to? Mark wanted to give all of that more thought, but Captain Thomas was about to start the story of himself and Litmus, and Mark didn't want to miss any of it.

'I might start seeing colours? Again? I might?' interrupted Litmus, as the captain was about to speak, 'That would mean something? I like colours?'

The captain was looking across at Mark, his eyes softly tired. Mark couldn't see a yes or a no in them. The captain didn't answer Litmus either, just lifted him around, positioning him on his lap.

'This is a simple history, but hard to tell. If you refrain from questioning until the end, it will be easier. Litmus, hop off, and order a couple of bottles of Captain Murray's best.'

Litmus was over at the order pad, ordering. He looked back over his shoulder.

'Tell him your excuse for longness first, Grandpa... All right, I will – he likes to put in every detail, because it's about people he can't have any more, and it helps them be real again, for him, just a bit, and he likes that.'

Litmus turned back to the pad.

'Thank you Litmus. I think Mark already understands that little detail.

'In the beginning was a peaceful time. My children were grown up, and away from home. My wife was comfortable company. Life was pleasant. I was teaching Philosophy and Psychology, taking my time with the last half of my life. We were happy, watching that summer drift by, one long lazy day after another. One evening after work, I was crossing the bridge on my way home. It was Kath's birthday. On the seat next to me I had roses for her, and chocolates, and a small water-clear precious jewel on a fine gold chain. The roses had the whole car smelling like a room Kath had been in – not the aromatic sweetness, but that open fresh feeling that comes from knowing someone who cares has been there. I saw ahead, through all the traffic, one of those police busses, like they used to use to catch drunken and doped drivers. They were questioning everyone. When it was my turn, the young policeman asked for I.D. "Doctor", he called out, into the bus behind him. I stepped up and into the bus, and there were military uniforms everywhere. "Doctor of what?". I said Philosophy and Psychology. Three of them called out "Yes", from behind their desks. "Army, Navy or Air Force?" some-one asked me. "Space Corp", I answered, sarcastically joking, because I was annoyed – a recruitment van blocking evening traffic, to make fun of old men. I was far too old to join any military organisation, even if I wanted to. "Well chosen Doctor Thomas – our greatest need. This young gentleman will show you the way". I never got home again. Never… Litmus, how about you open and pour, that's a good boy.

'The Home Worlds were very young in those days. They had just begun a loose alliance, and banded together their security fleets, to form a line of defence across space. On Terra we were proud of our contribution – six very large, very powerful ships. When I got to the training base, there were four big smouldering broken messes, that had been lucky to make it down through the atmosphere to land. You don't bring ships that large down onto a world, unless it is the only way to rescue the crew from inside. Those ships would never fly again. There were bodies laid out on the grass in front of the Base hospital. A lady dressed like a cleaner was fumigating them with laughing gas, to help them cope with their pain and misery. Dying shipmen.

'We were being run across the tarmac and lined up in a hangar, like any moment could be Terra's last. Many lines, being topped up from the back by bus load after bus load. Airocargoes began landing outside, spewing out more confused shocked people, their faces as worried as mine. We were stepping forward, hundreds at a time, to the desk clerks. "You said Thomas? Axel Thomas? Fifty nine? Doctor of Philosophy, Master of Psychology?…" The women next along from me was pregnant. As I stood there, I realised the physical fitness test was making people climb over the long bench the clerks were behind. She was struggling, but no-one was allowed to help. "It has to be now, not later," said a supervisor. Behind the clerks were children, still in their school clothes, holding spray cans. Rainbow colours all over their hands. They were white faced and silent, waiting for their clerk to call out a colour, then they would spray the hand of the adult, after they climbed over. The girl on the other side of me said she was a café chef. "Green", called out the clerk. She leapt over the bench, only touching it with one hand on the way, like a gymnast. "Make that red", said her clerk. My clerk triggered something by what he entered, and an alarm light went off. He looked up at me. I could see in his eyes just hollowness, like he was hiding inside himself, hiding from his whole world suddenly coming apart around him. "What do I need to do?" I asked him firmly – I was a doctor, and I could tell he needed help just to keep going. Every passing minute was taking him further away from the safe life he was used to. Colour came back into his face, as he realised I knew, and understood. We were all together in whatever this new horror reality was. The alarm was still flashing. "They're coming for you. Run back out onto the tarmac… RUN?" he said.

'It made very little sense, but I did as I was told. Just as I got outside, a speed hopper almost crash-landed in front of me, it was in that much of a hurry. A speed hopper is a little craft that takes itself to a slingshot launcher, and gets fired up into space. Litmus, we'll have dinner here, in the cabin?

'The speed hopper rose up and out of the atmosphere. Terra looked peaceful and beautiful below us. We docked with a full size galaxy cruiser. People in uniforms were racing around inside it everywhere, like seriously annoyed ants. Some-one was yelling "We have to go we have to go. Get him out and get the hatches closed." Get me out? I'd only just got 'in'. To one side of everything there was a boat shaped craft, sitting on its skids. They were throwing things in through its side hatch. Clothing, bottles, boxes. "Don't just stand there! Get IN for fuck's sake," some-one yelled at me, and then two men grabbed me, lifted me up, and threw me into the craft, head first, like I was another box of food. They slammed the hatch on me. They couldn't get the fork lifter into position under the hull. More panicking bodies came from all directions, and they lifted the craft, all thirty-eight metres of it, by people strength alone, and dragged it into the gaslock area. Next moment I was drifting out in Space. The galaxy cruiser left immediately.

'I was floating around for a week above Terra, chatting to Kath and our kids, saying our goodbyes, while I waited for the alignment window to open, for the hyperspeed corridor to Magnificus... Tea break now Alito.'

'It's not ready. The wardroom kitchen said five more minutes... I'll do Magnificus?'

'Magnificus is a big, big star, that lots of people think is the centre of the universe. It's the only star that is so big nothing can make it through. Not even our seeder, can it Grandpa. My family ruled all the planets and stars around Magnificus, without a single war, for seven thousand hundred million billion, zillion years.'

Captain Thomas laughed out loud.

'Close. For a very long time, wasn't it,' he said.

'Yes.'

'And that's why I was headed there, to beg for help. Magnificus was a large stable Empire. The Home Worlds were a young collective, out on the edge of things. We needed a respectable, powerful friend. Ah, dinner. Let's move to the table.

'The trip took two months. I watched and learnt all the training material that had been set up on board my craft. I practised wearing my uniform. I brushed up on my space conflicts history. Towards the end of the trip the navigation equipment began to complain. I could see why. Stars were missing. By the time I landed, I knew that Magnificus was in more trouble than us.

'They had the same weakness – the need to protect the delicate balance of life on their planets. An impossible task. Alito's father had a huge program running, more important to him than the building of weapons. He was packing every living thing he could onto transporters, and sending it all on a massive orbital journey, that wouldn't bring the ships back into this part of Space for several centuries. When I arrived, the transporters were mostly long gone. There was just the last of the Royal world left to do. The Magnificus military were fighting a rearguard action, a fair way off in space. It was time for them all to go.

'On that final morning I was nursemaiding Alito. It was an easy, enjoyable task. He has always been good company. We were out in the palace gardens, but we were safe. We had a small security device that would set up a telemetrene sphere sanctuary around us. Basically it's like a lock. It misaligns sub atomic particles, so that no normal sub atomic material can enter inside its perimeter. Only the Magnificci have them. No other civilisation has got any further than just grasping the concept. Anyway, they are designed like a filter, allowing certain gasses, and spectrums of light through, in moderation. Alito insisted on having the telemetrene device on, because it made the view around us shimmer, which was pretty. His father appeared at the garden door, to say they were nearly ready. "One more minute", said Alito to me. There would be nothing like this for the rest of his life. No green flowery old growth garden, with lichen, hanging creepers, lily ponds and fountains, on a solid planet, under open blue skies. Alito's mother appeared at the garden door, waved, and called out. I thought that was odd, because it was like she was saying a happy goodbye, but I must have heard wrong. We began walking. Then, out of habit, I went back to bring the chair inside. As we turned around again, towards the door, I had the faintest feeling of a shadow over us, over everything around us, and then a dirty orange shaft of light, as wide as the whole palace, came down from the sky. The telemetrene gadget screamed, and re-deployed itself around us. We saw everything move, from massive impact. The dirty orange light was driving into the surface of the planet like a battering ram. The ground moved away from underneath us, and then everything around us was dragged past, towards the light, as if by a massive vacuum cleaner. Then the shock of the impact again, and the dragging past. Over, and over, like a giant engine. The shaft of filthy orange light was drifting away from us. Whole uprooted trees flew by. A broken bodied person was, for a second, wrapped around the shape of our telemetrene sphere, their face contorted, screaming in agony, their eyes begging life to let them go, and then they were sucked away, with everything else. Alito's father hadn't rescued everything. Just some of everything. He had always hoped that peace would still come. The planet was crewed with volunteers, to look after it during occupation. Birds were flying backwards past us, being sucked towards destruction, along with dogs, and cats, and half dressed, half ripped to pieces people, and a mad mixup of everyday things. The battering got faster and faster, until a flying cow was only a momentary blur, in a continual tapestry of dying life. Soon the ground around us was raw dirt. Everything had been ripped away. The dirty orange shaft was now a distant pillar in the sky, and then, right next to us, a small craft landed. I was watching to see who got out. Alito was looking the other way. He says he saw the lights of his father's private ship, in the distance, flying away to safety.'

'I did. I DID.'

'Yes, yes, it's all right Alito. I saw who got out of the craft, the uniform they were wearing. It was very important, because without knowing who was supporting the competitive aggression across Space, it could not be attacked at its heart, and anyone protecting a world would always lose. They raised their fist in a triumphant gesture, and played their political theme tune on some tinny sounding device, while they laughed an insulting, full of themselves laugh. "And so the great Magnificci fall before us." They climbed back into their craft, and left.

'Shortly after, bits of everything began raining down from the sky. The air outside the sphere was so fouled we couldn't tell if it was day or night, and the sphere couldn't let it in. We had no water, and no food either. I couldn't understand why – but Alito seemed to be fine, while I was short of breath, hungry, and very thirsty. He offered me his bottle, but he said I could only drink from it once, or I might end up 'like him'. Since, if I didn't drink I was going to die, I didn't give that a thought.

'I was sitting wondering how we were going to survive from then on, with one ornamental white garden chair, a tiny circle of green lawn, one drink bottle, and the clothes we were wearing. Alito was watching, watching, eyes focused on the top of the sphere. Suddenly he sat up. Pieces of everything had stopped raining down on top of us. "Now. Terraman, we have to go NOW." I wouldn't switch the telemetrene off. How could we know if it was safe out there? "It only turns off if it's safe, Silly," he says, reaching across me to do it himself. Right then, a whole burnt carcass of some giant fish thumped down next to us, but Alito was already off and running. I had to leave my last piece of civilisation behind – that chair. It was very hard going, but Alito knew the way, didn't you, even after all that destruction.

'We made it to the seeder. It was under piles of mess, a large dull blob, like a giant pip. It was twinkling strangely. Tiny sparkles in the surface of its hull.

'It would let him on board, but not me. There was an invisible curtain across the entry hatch, that Alito passed through as if it wasn't there, but it was solid when I tried. He said I mustn't have drunk from the bottle, just pretended. I disagreed. We could hear a salvage hunter, coming closer and closer. Working its way across the land towards us. The seeder was our only chance of escape from the planet, and it had to be now, before it was discovered. "Well it mustn't have got in you", squeaked Alito, "Drinked, DRINKED." He was holding the bottle at me, to made me drink more. I raised it to my lips, but just as the first taste of it got on the very tip of my tongue, he pulled my hand down. "Stupid stupid stupid, no foreign weapons on board", he was telling himself off. All I had was a ceremonial trigger light, as part of my uniform. We buried it in the mess, and I was on board.'

'You thought we were going up, to fight and dodge and race our way to freedom, but we went down first, didn't we Grandpa.'

'Yes. There was a pre-recorded message in the seeder, for Alito. It was his father's voice saying well done, and telling him not to wait around. Alito sent his own message out, but there was no answer. That's enough for tonight.'

Litmus was tired.

'I'm not eating all of mine Grandpa.'

'All right. Bed then, yes?'

Litmus looked at Mark, considering him.

'You don't have to be readed it now, the nice story, but you have to do it tomorrow. Tuck me in?'

Mark and Litmus went in to the captain's wash area. Litmus began playing with the toothpaste dispenser.

'I don't have to eat my tea, because I don't need it. I only eat because sometimes it tastes nice, and Grandpa says some habits are good.'

Mark took the dispenser and the toothbrush, covered the toothbrush bristles with toothpaste, and gave it back. He couldn't help smiling to himself – the bunny bum wiggled as the toothbrush was shoved clumsily all over the place at the other end. Litmus turned around, ready for bed.

'No, come on! There's toothpaste slobber all around your mouth... Better.'

Litmus was up and in his bunk.

'You shouldn't boss me, because you're just a kid, and I'm the Emprino.'

He finger signalled Mark to come closer.

'They're doing it again, the Greedophiles, but this time we're going to get them back. We know how, Grandpa and me,' he whispered, and then he fell asleep.

GREEDOPHILES AND GODS

Mark stepped out of the sleeping cabin. The captain waited for Mark to close the slide between the two rooms.

'He doesn't need to clean his indestructible teeth, except rotting food between them has, in the past, caused an unpleasant stench,' he said.

'Those remarks about seeing colour – Litmus and I didn't have a lot to go on, in the beginning. Everyone we looked to for information, about anything Magnificci, about everything Magnificci, had packed up and left, vanished forever. We only had our own thoughts. When our colour vision started to go, Litmus was very unhappy. He wanted everything to stay the same as it had been when his parents were with him. I suggested it was probably just part of living forever.'

A sigh from the captain, but not sad, more like he was standing back in his thoughts, and seeing how far he had come in his life journey.

'But back on that little planet, the moment Litmus chose you, his heart opened. He was shining with new possibilities. I looked down as he tugged at my hand. He was fresh and young again, just for a moment, and as I looked at that my colour vision came speeding back into me, almost like a long overdue train, coming into a station so fast it was having difficulty stopping. It has faded away again since then, but now I know how we lost our colour vision. We lost our colour vision the day we gave up hope on a happy ending.'

More stuff to think about, thought Mark. If this was what growing up was, it was hard work, and unlike school there weren't even any girls any more, to show off in front of while he was doing it. He had been saving a question he wanted to ask.

'Can I ask something? Not important, but it's something I don't know much about. If there's going to be war and people dying, I could know more about why, I mean…about who did it? Made it happen?'

'Ask away,' said the captain.

'Litmus said something about…Greedophiles?' Mark asked.

'Ah yes: greedophiles. A greedophile is a person who believes the successful collecting of money is the way to judge someone, their way of life, their whole world. When in political power greedophiles sell everything the people of a planet own – the power supply, the water, the schools, the hospitals, everything.'

'Umm, why?'

'So they can put making money between the providing of a service and the people who need it. They believe the taking of money from people is what makes a world go around. The people have to work for poor wages, just to get to use what they used to own. When they get into government greedophiles can cause more unhappiness on a world than an invading army, because they are narcissistic, unkind and uncaring, and divide their world more sharply into have, and have not.

'I don't know that one, not properly. The "narcissist" one. Does that mean they love themselves?'

'Very well, we will do this now. I will give you the quick version, and hope it is quick enough for you not to goof off into your own little mental world.'

The captain paused, collecting his thoughts, and Mark realised that the last half of the sentence was just a passing thought of the captain's, not meant to be said out loud. Because I am a fragilicus, and that's what fragilicus do, goof off when explanations get too long thought Mark.

The captain had begun already, and Mark had to make his ears catch up.

'Narcissism is a very old word, from a time when there was only one world. Narcissus was a good looking young man. He saw himself reflected in a pool of water, and was so amazed he just stayed there gazing, and gazing, and gazing. He kept returning to the pool, to see how beautiful he was. People thought that a bit odd, so they named being impressed by your own beauty narcissism, after him. It is however, quite normal behaviour for a fragilicus – they are supposed to be curious, and enjoy how they are. But, you asked about narcissists now. In this age narcissism has a very different meaning. They are people who get unclean satisfaction out of knowing they are winning, and bringing other people down. They have no remorse or empathy for the people they trample on. On an unhappy world there are two main types of narcissist, the first uses the lie of God – "I have to kill people and take what is theirs for mine, because they are an offence to my God, and my God has told me to. My God is above question, and must not be insulted, or you are next to die".

'Believing in a god can be a fantastic, wonderful thing, used by good people to help them feel safe in their lives, and to take a lifeworld to new heights of understanding and kindness, but you should know, ensign, that all gods are the work of someone's imagination. Until a person makes them up, they don't exist. Belief in a god can also be used by narcissists, as an excuse for great violence and cruelty.

'The second type of narcissist manipulates people by lying about money – "Our world is in a terrible state. The only way we can fix it, before total disaster, is if you ordinary people have less". They always have many clever justifications ready, and it is never the narcissist who makes do with less, just the people they are bringing down. And that is definitely enough on that, because they are a sad and boring subject.

'Let's get back to more pressing things – the question everyone forgets to ask – why did the Magnificus Empire fall, and not our weak little alliance?

'Alito's father removed the resources from his worlds. That brought the aggressor to a sudden, unplanned halt. It was a huge invasion force, expecting to suck the Magnificus worlds dry. It was left halted in Space, with no fuel, no food, and no water. Treaties were signed all over the place, but they didn't give any worlds back, and finally, now, they are on the march again, across the stars. Everyone hopes to reach negotiated solutions, and then they are no more. Your vote doesn't count, not when all you have has been stolen, and everything you care about is destroyed.'

Captain Thomas had been standing at the counter waiting. Now he was passing a drink, on his way to sitting down.

'My days for negotiating with these people are over. Alito and I have a battle plan. The two of us and one small ship against trillions, but we are hopeful. With your help, we will be three. We are going to give it a serious try. Tomorrow, at breakfast?'

What? Tomorrow at breakfast what?, wondered Mark.

'I mean we'll discuss it then… Not even us three can save the Universe over tea, toast, and fruit candy cereal.'

Mark sipped his drink. The captain picked a story book up, and sat it on his lap. He didn't open it, but he was restful, as if his mind was wandering through memories of its story. Mark wondered at how nice it was to be in a room with some-one, and not have to say anything, or do anything. Just being together, and the calm of the moving gentle grey on the picture-screen. The captain laid the book down on the couch next to him.

'Our enemies are the most successful greedophiles of all, the Democratic Capitalists. Democratic, because the mob rules by vote, meaning they all get to vote, but each little Life world has no say by itself – it is alone against the rest. A bit like feeling safe in a crowd, because you are all in it together, until the crowd realise they would like your music player, your phone, your running shoes, your jeans, then even your tee shirt and your socks, and they all automatically agree to just let it happen to you, for the good of everyone else, and you end up cold and naked, no longer respectable enough to have your own needs heard by anyone.

'Capitalists, because their whole society runs on a winner takes all system, where competition drives everything; politics, social safety, education, and even medical care. In the gutters of their worlds there are people starving, diseased and dying, while the politicians vote to squander resources pushing the Collective's influence further across space. They call themselves the Freedom Collective. Using those words to name themselves is a poisonous cunning lie – as they collect each world it loses its freedom. Enough condemnation. You can see I am very one sided in this.'

'Isn't… Aren't we a bit like that? The League of Stars worlds I mean,' asked Mark.

'Yes. We are almost identical, because those two systems, democracy and capitalism, are so far the most successful way to run things. But, and it's a very big but, although it is hard to see on the surface there is a difference – the social structure of our worlds is almost the same – the "a bit" you mentioned is what's important: a bit free, a bit competitive, and a whole lot of organised sharing. That's what keeps our worlds happy with each other, and at peace. "Have some of what I've got" is a good way to stay friends. This time, with these people, we are long past staying friends. For three hundred years they have been crowing about winning, about being the best, and they have left lifeworld after lifeworld in ruins. Litmus and I are going to bring them down.

'The Freedom Collective have two weapons. Their most powerful weapon is greed – that is what drives them, and the other, also seemingly indestructible, is the material those infernal machines are made of. We hope, the League of Stars Territory, that after two hundred years, we are nearly at the point of breaking that material's secret, and then hopefully greed will turn against them.

'We have a weakness, and it is Litmus and I, two beings who have been around long enough for too much to be known about us. They have an entire planet called Seeder City, crowded with people and machines, all slaving away at building scenarios of what Litmus and I might be up to in our seeder, and where we might be, now, tomorrow, next year. We need you Mark. On board the Magnificus Royale. You are something new, to bring new ideas. They have no respect for the abilities of children. For them you are a most unlikely choice, and that will put all their calculations out, and send their plans awry.'

Mark looked down at his hands, and felt awkward. He wanted to say I'm not a child, but that was only half true. It was an odd feeling, hearing some-one say they needed him. The old captain took another breath to talk.

'Two people, with the fate of everything hanging on their deeds. Always in old tales it is three, and Litmus and I would like you to make it so for us. Did your parents tell you the bedtime story "The Three Mice Get Ears"? Or perhaps "Jack, Beans and Stalk" was your favourite – three talented but behaviour challenged young men, who decide to personally set about repopulating their world, to annoy the giants. Litmus loves that one, mostly because he has no idea what it's about. Don't explain it to him – a bit of mystery is a good thing at his age.

'That's it for tonight. Litmus and I need an answer from you tomorrow. One day soon, we are all going to have a head-on collision with our destiny.

'Oh, and Crackers? Litmus has had a sensible idea, but then he forgot it, in the excitement of the moment. We are going to call you by the boy's body you are, to confuse our enemies. There is no way of knowing who is listening, anywhere, any time, and that will keep you more of a mystery. That is all.'

Mark hadn't been able to sleep. He couldn't untangle his thoughts – there was too much going on in his head. The underpants he was wearing as pyjamas were loosely circling around the tops of Cracker's long skinny legs, in an airy just touching way. Mark could feel them tingling his nerves. Really nicely tingling his nerves, just about making them sing with good feelings. That made him think of Shane's dad's facts of life story, and Bernard's dad's mouthing off about boys being pests, and those thoughts caused a question – is the captain, in his own quiet way, making fun of me for being fourteen? Who cares thought Mark. He lay in his bunk, very quietly doing Jack with Beans and Stalk, hoping James wouldn't hear anything.

JAMES AND PHOEBE

The next morning Mark said yes, he would like to become part of the seeder's crew.

He expected some change to happen after that, but...nothing.

Now it was evening again. Another shipboard evening. James had been packing some spare kit to be sent across to the helpod, in case he was ever needed there in a hurry. He lost interest, and then he and Mark were lying around the quarters, not talking about much, when there was a knock on the mess door, and she was here again. That girl with orange hair from Long Range Navigation. Mark could tell from the way she was eyeing James that she was after him, like a spider after a fly. The fly just sat there on the couch, looking his usual dopey dreamy self.

'It might only be a soft cargo, but she's a good ship, James. The helpod is crowded, and it gets hot, and cold, without worrying about the crew, because what it needs to do comes first,' said Phoebe.

'Well… I didn't ask for this. It just happened. It's not me yet anyway, just this list of my gear, like for spare.'

'You're a dreamy dope. Isn't he Crackers.'

'Yes,' said Mark, from where he was lying on his bunk facing the wall, so he wouldn't have to watch them getting closer and closer to each other on the long mess couch.

'Shut up! You're not helping,' said James.

'Well you are,' said Mark.

Phoebe reached across, to put James's family pictures into the small bag, on top of his spare battledress uniform.

'Hey, I want those.'

'Yes, that's why they go in there. This gets packed now, because they are expecting you won't have time, when whatever it is happens,' she said.

'How can they upgrade you Wimpy,' said Mark, rolling over on his bunk to face the two of them, 'to essential crew, when you aren't even trained for anything yet?'

Revolting – the two of them were holding hands.

'They changed my lessons. Now I'm learning like, well… parts of everything just about.'

'You're the instant replacement for anyone taking a sicky. You're small, so they can pass you in through the slide tubes while they're still getting the other body out. You'd fit in anywhere,' said Phoebe, leaning across the seat to kiss his ear.

'Don't,' said James shyly, 'not while he's watching.'

The wrestling was about to start. Soon they would be all over each other, giggling and squealing.

'WAIT. Wait. I'm going for a walk,' said Mark, getting down from his bunk.

PEOPLE WHO WOULD NEVER GO HOME

The soft cargo was quiet. Empty passageways. Nice, he thought, the way the lights mimicked daylight. In the mornings they were whiter, sort of thin and bright, midday was normal, then in the afternoon they would go a fatter, yellower colour for a while, before dulling to evening half bright, and then the dim red safety lighting for the rest of the night-time hours. He was walking towards a Polite, standing like a dress shop mannequin in the passage ahead.

'Do you know what planet decides how long our ship days are?' Mark asked.

'Blue Skies One,' answered the Polite, 'It is the standard orbital model for shipboard day/night patterns… Late News is on, if you are interested.'

'Thanks.'

But no thanks, thought Mark.

It was different this time. As he was walking past, he realised the cafeteria was dead quiet.

'Freckles, you can have my spot,' said some-one standing at the back near the doorway, 'I've seen it. They keep replaying it.'

The picture wall was showing the forward screen of a stingray scout ship. It was newer than the one Mark remembered, because it had a small black ball mounted in the middle of the pilot's control panel. Numbers and letters were flashing across its dark surface, in a continual stream. Mathematical equations? There was sub and supertext. It was reading the atomic structure of whatever it was aimed at. The little scout ship was shooting forward at incredible speed, dodging through a floating junkyard of broken ships. Swerving around, under, over, and through their wrecked hulls. Directions were coming from another vessel, through a speaker panel above the forward screen.

'Closer. You NEED to get CLOSER. Right up behind us. Now now NOW. This has to be it. Don't let my crew die for nothing.'

The little craft began travelling even faster, rocking and screaming and bouncing roughly around. Now the junkyard was moving too, spinning in red hot and white hot pieces, in the wake of something larger ahead – the big back end of a battleship like the Mandelbrot.

'We will fire all we have, and hope for a hole for you,' said the voice, 'Aim dead centre of us. We will no longer exist… Emerging from… our… Fleet… NOW.'

Suddenly everything was chaos. The little Scout ship was jumping around so viciously that the cockpit camera was recording a wild soup of light, and dark, with lots of specs and lumps flying around that could be anything. There was the beginning of a brilliant flash of light, before the forward screen clamped down to black. It cleared again. There was no battleship. Just a huge wall of green prickly light across Space, with a hole blown in it that was closing quickly. The Scout ship was screaming towards it. Rolling over, steering crooked, drifting sideways. What was the pilot doing? Bubbles of blood drifted across the cockpit… and two teeth, joined by a bit of flesh. The pilot was dying. He was still steering the damaged scout ship, but badly. The back end hit the side of the hole as the little scout ship passed through. Spinning. Stomach churning spinning. Turning, turning slower. What was in here, behind the wall? The biggest lump of machinery Mark had ever seen. Solid, apart from the smallest windows in a narrow row, across its massive cast metal wall. The scout ship drifted slowly up to those windows. Bonk. Touched against the thick glass. The little black ball's figures and numbers changed colour. 'Resonance reading' flashed briefly, before more meaningless letters and numbers hurried across it. Another colour change. 'Radiated spectrums'. Racing numbers again. There were people inside the huge machine in overalls, standing at control consoles. They looked up, and seemed to think the pilot's condition was funny, or was it his attempt to attack them that amused them? One of them pretended to duck for cover, and then waved a mock-friendly hello. A woman was giving orders. They turned back to their work. The scout ship slid up the cast metal wall slowly, turning a little. The pilot was trying to make it touch against the metal, like it had against the glass. Bonk. 'Resonance reading'. A new stream of figures raced across the face of the ball. One of the pilot's arms was floating in front of the camera, as if he was unconscious. The little craft was drifting. Looking down now. A fat shaft of orange light suddenly turned on, like a giant torch, shining from the bottom of the huge machine. It went out into Space. The scout ship's little cockpit camera was at the wrong angle to see where. A dirty orange rod of death, on its way to a world out there.

'Now we know what it is, we can do something about it,' said one of the Soft Cargo's crewmen, into the silence of the cafeteria.

The little scout ship's pilot was reaching around. His hand was showing, bloody and large, on the picture wall of the Soft Cargo. The golden ring looked out of place. There was blood running across the gold, and across the picture of the lady's face. All these years on, and Mark still remembered that ring. That's my pilot he thought. It was the scout who had rescued him from his parents' broken ship. The pilot was searching, blinded and only semi-conscious, for the dull red button. The same red button Mark pressed to help them both escape when he was five. Mark thought an exploding scout ship wouldn't do much to that huge machine, and there was no-where to escape to anyway. The Stingray suddenly shot forward, ricocheting off the cast metal wall and spinning out into Space, but it was as broken as the pilot, and soon slowed, to tumble slowly over and over, as it drifted away in the dark. Like my playroom when I was five, and our ship was broken thought Mark. The pilot's arm was flying around, not unconsciously, but trying to do something. He was ripping the camera from the cockpit roof. As it came free it swung across his face. Mark felt sick to see another living person so wrecked, some-one he used to know as a real, nice, normal everyday person. He tried to hide his head from looking, but that old crewman was there again, the one who had walked away that other news time. He took hold of Mark's neck and forehead, and forced him to watch.

'You need to see how horrible the games of war are,' he said, 'Knowing that is what might keep you alive as you grow up, if you are very lucky.'

The pilot was trying to say something, but his jaw was broken. As blood and saliva fell from his mouth, he was saying 'I'm not here. It's not there'. The scout craft was drifting further out into the darkness of Space. He was pointing the camera at a little sideview screen now. That big machine was still out there, but there was nothing else. No wall of prickly lights, no huge battle fleets. The orange rod was coming out of the machine, and vanishing a little way out into Space like it had been chopped off, and gone somewhere else. It was all getting smaller as the Stingray drifted away. A light began blinking in the wrecked scout ship – it had turned on its medicare – the pilot's temperature would be lowered to near freezing to slow down his heart beat and the blood loss, in the hope that help might come for him before he died.

A civilian shuttle flew up to the back of the orange ray machine. Mark could see, in the clear transfer tube going on board, a woman carrying her shopping. The picturewall in the cafeteria went blank.

Mark didn't wait for official explanations from the News service. He'd seen enough. People on a world built a thing like that, and then people somewhere else had to pour all their children into an academy. Mark realised that right now, he hated people. All people, full stop. "Emerging from our fleet now", the captain on the ship like the Mandelbrot had said, but there was no fleet there, only broken ships and burnt dead bodies. So many people who would never go home.

IT HAPPENS AGAIN

He tried not to think anything as he got ready for bed.

Mark was used to this body now, the grasshopper legs, and the strong long thin-ness. He climbed up onto his bunk, settled himself under the sheet, and hoped for sleep. He didn't want to think about his scout pilot friend, or whatever world that huge orange ray was pulverising. As he lay there he could feel himself sweating, and then his muscles began to ache.

Bugger, it was happening again.

No way he was going to sick bay. He would get it over with here, in his own mess, in the dark, in private.

He climbed down from his bunk and fell to the deck – already his legs weren't working properly.

'You okay Mark?' asked a sleepy James, 'I mean Crackers?'

'Yeah. Go to sleep,' said Mark, and then he shut himself in the wash area.

It was messier this time, like there was excess body material. He lay on the cool floor feeling completely stuffed, wrecked, and really tired. After a while he crawled to the shower, reached up to the tap, and turned it on. Warm water cascaded everywhere for ages. He let it run all over him, and all over the floor of the wash area, until everything looked reasonably clean, and he felt a lot better.

Out of the shower he dried himself, while he tried to see which boy he was this time. He was too tired to even hope he was himself again. The mirror was fogged up. He wiped it clear with a forearm, but his eyes weren't working properly yet.

The bunk seemed a lot higher. It was a difficult climb, after being used to Crackers' long legs. He flopped down, face half squashed against the pillow, wondering if he was on his way back to being five.

One of the ship's old-fashioned bugle calls sounded out from the little speaker in the wall. Mark had no idea what it was supposed to mean. A silly tara tarah trumpeting noise. There was no announcement after it, so he went back to sleep.

SOME GOOD NEWS

'Ensign Planetti, wake up. It's me, Polite Helper Jayman. Standard ship's business this time – you're required for duty.'

'What time is it?... (yawn), they're keen.'

The cabin door was inching open.

'Did you waked him up yet?... Grandpa says breakfast in the middle of the night, in the prow café, NOW. Hurry up Planetman. Grandpa is in a really bossy mood.'

The floor looked a long way below him, and Mark, in a last moment decision, dragged his bedding half off the bunk to slow himself down, for a softer landing. Thump, as his feet hit the deck, but his underpants kept going, to stop floppy and night warm around his ankles. That pair must be stuffed he thought, snatching an unworn pair from his clothes pile on one of the spare bunks. They weren't any better, loose around his hips too – he had to hold them up while he pulled his pants on. Litmus was watching like he was a supervising boss.

'Planetman, hurry UP,' he ordered.

Pants on, but the belt just kept pulling through the grip buckle, until there was a long tail of it hanging out and down. Mark realised he needed to wake up properly, because things were happening to him like in a crazy dream. Litmus, he needed to get Litmus under control, because something was going on?

'What did you call me?' asked Mark, as he pulled his shirt over his head.

'You have to be Planetman, because that's the one you can played with,' said Litmus, as he prepared to launch a floor flier across the trainee officers' cabin.

'Planetboy,' decided Litmus, changing his mind about Mark's play character identity as he looked at him.

'I thought we were in a hurry?'

'You're not dressed yet, so I can played.'

'I am,' said Mark, pulling on his second ship runner, 'so dump them on my bunk and let's go.'

'You're not allowed,' Litmus was trying to say to the back of a silent sleeping James through the shutting cabin door, 'He's not allowed to play with my floor flyers.'

'Litmus! If we're hurrying, let's do it.'

'I caught them doing yuck. She put her hand down inside his pants. When he was IN them.'

'Litmus! Not before breakfast, okay? You've made me want to barf.'

'Sorry. Grandpa can't understand how off that is.'

'Yeah, well… What did James do?'

'He just standed there, looking all dopey happy.'

'Yeah, he's good at that.'

The main passage was empty? Was the Soft Cargo's crew doing panic things or not?

'Where is everybody?'

134

'The "early to your stations" tune played,' explained Litmus, 'So they all goed places.'

'Is that what it was. Wimpy and I haven't learnt them all yet,' said Mark, as he went through the bulkhead door.

He was about to go around the corner into the Prow Café, when Litmus started tugging at him.

'Wait, wait, you do know you're him but a smaller one?'

'What?'

'Junior Wimpy,' said Litmus, poking Mark in the chest.

Everything in the whole Universe was going bad, and now he, Mark, was going to have to play his part in it as a junior James Fargo.

'Ahhh fff…' began Mark, just about in tears.

'Don't say that fuck word,' ordered Litmus, 'I don't like it. And hurry up and get over it, because we have to go in there. Grandpa's waiting, and you're going to maked him cranky.'

There were officers and ship's crew in a crowd near the other café entrance. There was no getting near Captain Thomas. The senior officers from the Helpod and the Soft Cargo were standing around his table. All except Commander Burnett, who was hurrying from the bridge lift, carrying something small.

'It's all loaded onto here. I hope this is worth it. Twenty-five thousand dead. Ninety-eight ships of the line, and our forty-seven best scouts, all gone forever.'

Forty-six. Please somehow make it forty-six thought Mark, but he knew, even if some-one official said it, it still wouldn't be true. A good person from his life was floating out in space, cold and dead.

Captain Thomas held his hand out, taking the secure information device.

'Yes,' he said, 'Gentlemen, like you, they will be trying to figure out what it is we would pay such a high price for. They are not stupid. The most dangerous place to be will be aboard any craft large enough to carry a seeder vessel of the Magnificci, that is in, or approaching, a star-clear path. And that, my friends, is us. Commander Yorker has opened her orders by now, and is somewhere out ahead, keeping our way safe and clear. She is relying on us to be alert, agile, and ready to look after ourselves. Can we be those things, standing around an old man's midnight breakfast table? Captain Murray?'

'No Lord. Gentlemen, meeting now, back on the bridge. With your staffers,' he yelled, 'All hands to action stations. Clamp down to silent running as of now. Lights down heating down no music and no replay visuals. No further news no outside communications.'

'Sir.'

'Sir'

'Sir,' people yelped in answer to the orders as they ran to make them happen.

Captain Thomas had hold of the Helpod commander's coat sleeve. He was waiting for the others to leave.

'Start warming her up,' he said quietly, 'all of her... And Julian? Our destination has changed, so I do mean all of her. Not a word – not to anyone. We have to leave them all behind.'

Litmus was pushing Mark closer to the café table.

'I have news,' said Captain Thomas looking up.

He surveyed Mark critically.

'I'm guessing you didn't get to choose the boy you are. You look like a puppy in a dog's jacket. Too late to get into one of his uniforms. Sit and eat.'

They sat and ate. The Prow Café was oddly empty. They were the only people on the Soft Cargo having a middle of the night breakfast.

'What news Grandpa?' asked Litmus.

'Something happy for a change. Not war news, family news. I have a solar system, a planet, an area, and a last known location for our Planetti family. A great place for us to start searching, when our current difficulties have passed, don't you think?'

BELONGING

They ate breakfast in silence. Mark was feeling his way around his thoughts carefully. He didn't like the sound of leaving people behind, but there was a more urgent thought – Captain Thomas's voice echoing inside his head, "us to start our search". Us. It was a big change in friendship, from people serving on a ship together, to being prepared to travel across the galaxies to find your family. Hope squeezed his heart, hard.

'Really?' he asked like a small child, before he realised he was going to say it, 'For real, I mean,' he added more gruffly, trying to make junior James's voice do Mark Planetti, 'us going to find my family?'

He mumbled the last words, looking down, feeling awkward, knowing this was too big an ask.

'Litmus and I have discussed this possibility, and we are looking forward to the challenge. We understand families needing to find each other.'

Litmus's spoon clattered into his plate.

'Grandpa, you didn't make him promise first.'

'Shh shh shh. You ask, Litmus. It is your need.'

'If we find you your parents, will you come with me to find mine? Will you? Will you? Promise? Please. Please?'

Litmus was getting desperate, his voice higher and more wobbly the more he spoke, his eyes like searchlights beaming worry, panic, and disappointment.

'I will, I will,' answered Mark, 'I will, all right? You didn't even need to ask.'

These two people were as much family to him as anybody now.

'Sorry,' said Litmus.

Mark looked down at his breakfast. His stomach was churning from emotions. He didn't feel like eating any more. The captain was speaking.

'You must be patient, as Litmus has been, and from now on, the topic of family finding comes second to our current mission.'

He put his knife and fork together, and rose from the table.

'We are Alpha watch, and for the next six hours Ensign Fargo, we are sleeping,' he said loudly, as if it was something anyone around with ears needed to hear.

MARK, ON BOARD THE MAGNIFICUS ROYALE BY HIMSELF

'Where are you going Litmus?'

'I'm going with you.'

'Why?'

'To pick up my floor fliers, derr.'

'Thought you'd gone weird on me, Bunny Bum, and you were like, going to follow me everywhere now.'

Litmus glanced behind him, back along the passage to the Prow Café. The captain had gone to the bridge. They were nearly at the door to the trainee officer's quarters. Mark was reaching for the handle. Suddenly he was shoved from behind, pushing him past the door.

'To my ship,' hissed Litmus.

Mark tried to stop, to ask questions, but Litmus had hold of his belt from behind with both hands, and was shoving and steering him off into a side passage. For a kid he had a lot of push. Junior James's feet were skidding on the floor, as Mark tried to regain control of himself.

'You're asking for it junior Wimpy,' warned Litmus.

Suddenly Mark was up in the air. He couldn't get his arms or his legs in underneath himself, to make Litmus put him down. He felt like a crab on its back at the beach. He could feel Litmus's hard head under his back, and Litmus's grubby fingers digging in, using his hip bones as handles.

'This is a crap game,' Mark said, 'If I was me you wouldn't get away with this.'

No answer from below. Litmus didn't seem to mind how straight he walked, or how near to walls as he went around corners. It's deliberate, he's swinging me into things thought Mark. Little bugger thinks it's funny. Mark had to fend off with his hands, his feet kept bumping along the side of the passage, and then his head rammed into something. Litmus was using it to trigger a bulkhead door sensor. Coming in for a second go.

'Hey!' said Mark.

A bit of respect wouldn't hurt.

Litmus just sniggered. What a brat.

They were at the starboard gangway area. Litmus put him back on his feet.

'Now call me Bunny Bum, Planetboy,' he said, with a happy chuckle as he opened the hatch.

'Bunny Bum,' said Mark straight away.

'Ha ha, very funny for YOU,' said Litmus, poking Mark with a finger, 'We're having our own meeting,' he went on as he stepped through the door, 'Grandpa keeps putting it off, coz he doesn't know when is the right time. He thinks you can just be a passenger for now, but I always bubble spit in your drinks, and gorby in your food, because you have to get made a seeder crewman.'

Mark stopped walking. They were in under the seeder. Litmus looked up into Mark's face, and became unsure and unhappy, seeing the expression he saw there.

'I mixed-ed it in with my finger, so it wouldn't be yuck for you?' he added, worry in his voice, 'Please? Now is our lastest last chance of doing this?'

Litmus was pushing Mark forward, normally this time, like a little kid hoping a bigger one would move. Mark couldn't believe the saliva sharing comments. They were so far from acceptable that he couldn't think straight. One thing he knew for sure.

'I'm not swallowing your spit,' said Mark forcefully.

'That's okay,' said Litmus, 'I fulled you already. After he sprunged me, Grandpa reckoned if I didn't stop it would start coming out your ears.'

Now the little bugger was cheeky happy again. Mark looked. Small, and not particularly clean. Those were the spit bubbling lips. Gross he thought, shutting his own lips tight. It made his tongue shrink, just thinking about it.

'Ready?' Litmus was pointing up at the seeder.

His eyes twinkled as he pushed Mark away from him. It was from naughtiness at doing something slightly unpleasant to a friend.

'Not telling what's going to be happened to YOU,' another finger poke, 'coz you're going to be finded out for yourself. Up him.'

MARK MEETS AN IPE

'Down me,' ordered Mark, but the Magnificus Royale stayed dark inside, and nothing happened.

'Well at least put some bloody lights on,' he grumbled to himself, and then, suddenly, that soft light was everywhere.

'Um… are you… listening?' asked Mark of nobody.

The insides of the seeder looked the same as last time. Just strange shaped tiles, all different, on the floor, the walls, and above his head. Some of the tiles began to move, coming out from the sidewall. Turning into a keyboard. When he was nearly there, walking over to inspect the keyboard, a tile rose up out of the floor and tripped him. He stopped still and watched it, the uneven edge that had tripped him. Nothing happened, and then he realised it was waiting for him to look away. He glanced at the keyboard quickly and then back. Already the tile was just finishing rising into being a chair. Lit up letters were appearing in the air in front of him. He began reading as he sat down.

'Clumsy aren't you,' said the air screened message.

'No! You tripped me up!' said Mark out loud, and then he began to type it in on the keyboard, but the seeder was messaging again.

The air writing had changed from white to deep blue, as if it had already learnt something about him, from his typing, or his voice.

'Don't bother. You type slower than Alito.'

Was that all?

'Oh yeah. And I suppose you're so good,' muttered Mark to himself.

'Yes,' said the air words.

The writing had changed to mid blue. A really nice happy mid blue, like a summer morning sky colour.

'What are you?' asked Mark.

He suspected he was being stuffed around by a programmed function actuator. They seemed real, like a person, but there was nothing there, just clever programming.

'I am an IPE – Information Processing Entity.'

Just like he thought.

'A robot,' stated Mark, browned off that a robot was using him as a game.

'Wait... I am finding that word... ancient Blue Skies One slang term for an SFA, a service function actuator. You are at the age of silly slang and play swearing, aren't you. There is a big difference between an IPE and a robot. The difference is in the word entity. Also, an IPE can be a FIPE, a MIPE, or a NIPE. I am supposed to be a nipe – non-sexualising information processing entity, but I think I am actually a fipe – female information pro...you get the picture. I exist as a three dimensional lattice of fluctuating states.'

'Where are you?' demanded Mark feeling a bit spooked, as he looked around at the tiled walls, to see if anything was watching him.

'All around. I am the Emprino's private ship. Enough questions. Now we will get to know each other, and then you will do your medical.'

'And then maybe I won't,' said Mark back.

Dad used to say, when Mark got cranky with the drinks dispenser on the home ship, "Never let a machine take charge".

'Oh, you will,' said the air screened words.

It was then that Mark realised he could tell when it was laughing at him – a word's letters would flicker in tiny party coloured dots, like 'will' just did.

'I can see you laugh,' said Mark.

'Friends then?' asked the words, 'Wait...I'll show you some others. Watch, this is sad, and hopeful, and... what can I panic about...and this is panic.'

'Woah, steady on the panic.'

The acid red was too much for his eyes.

'Hey, what's like, um, sex then?'

Mark was having visions of the Magnificus Royale chasing the Mandelbrot around a planet or two, all kissy-lipped at the front.

'When I am happy to have a bioform feeling sensual about itself inside me, my typing is a pretty mid blue.'

'Hey!! Cut it out!'

This IPE was really playing with him, big time.

'Change the typing to black, or white or something!'

'I could, but it would be a lie, and you would still see a faint sky blue edge to the letters anyway.'

'Bulltwang. It's you, not me – I'm not feeling anything.'

Inside his pants the loose underpants had slithered down his skin, and they were hanging low off his hips, not quite falling off his bum cheeks, and crowding around his balls. It felt pretty amazing.

'I'm just feeling being myself. And I'm not even me,' he said, grumpy from being found out.

The air in front of his eyes hiccupped a fizzy coloured laugh, and then the space in front of his face was empty, wordless.

'That's it, shut up,' said Mark.

'Now what?' he asked, when nothing happened.

There were some fuzzy blinks of floating dots in the air, and then three hummed notes in his left ear, followed by three in his right.

'I wasn't sure this part of me still worked,' said the IPE, 'It's been over a hundred years. Alito used to forget how to read after a reversion, and get cranky when I tried to help him, so I pretended my "secret word" function was broken, so reading was the only way he could get what he wanted. Secret word is when I target two different signals to meet up on the surface of something, and the sound happens there only. Like I am doing now, making sound happen on the skin inside your ear canals. I will only use this technique when we are by ourselves, because the airscreening system is very useful, in many ways, but humanoidians being naturally lazy, you would all stop using it. Enough. You are here for a reason.

'You are here to become a crewman. You are very unlikely material for crew. Already I can tell you are undersize, underweight, and a bit silly, but I am commanded to make it so by Alito Magnificus, The Emprino of Planet Royal, and I am humble before his greater knowledge of you. So we must begin. I need to get to know you. Start with something you've always liked, or an early memory, and go on from there.'

Undersize, and underweight? Mark was pretty proud of being strong for his age. And then he remembered what body he was right now. A junior James. There was definitely no point arguing about this.

'How early? Like cartoons early?'

PLANETMAN, NORTIBOT, AND THE ZOONIES

They'd been going over old familiar things, and it was making Mark feel almost at home again. Right now the seeder was looking for something.

'Found it. Not the episode, but a promo. Here you go – "Nortibot was fart bombing cities again. Planetman had to save the world holding his nose". Is that the one?'

'Nah – Nortibot was only in Planetman Junior Edition. I still laugh but. It's like the funniest character. Nortibot just stuffs around, doing whatever he feels like, and Planetman gets these weird ideas that Nortibot is doing it to take over the Universe. There was this one where all the cities were arguing about who had the tallest building, so Nortibot thought he'd stack them all on top of each other, into one big building, so they'd all be the tallest. Gees that was funny. Not the doing it, but what all the people characters were saying, and the way Planetman turned everything into a complete mess.'

'Give me some more baddies and weapons.'

'Gorgelzooniemaniakoids?... Planetman shoots the Gorgelzooniemaniakoids with his (Mark had to stop talking because he was feeling silly, Wimpy silly, and then a James giggle escaped, even though he tried to stop it) – umm, sorry about that. At the end of the show, the Gorgelzoonies apologized for having such a long name. They reckoned all the good names for baddies have "org" in them, and they've all been used up aeons ago, so they had no choice.'

'and... Planetman shoots?'

'Oh yeah. He shoots them with his rainbow ray. They are expecting it to blow their ship apart, so they turn on their compacto atomicus something something, can't remember that one, to lock all the atoms in close and tight together, but the rainbow ray makes atoms that aren't supposed to like each other, like each other a lot, and instead of exploding, they start breeding all over the place, and the Gorg's toilet grows to like the size of a house. They all need it, because they're shi… really scared. It gets so big they start falling in.'

'So…trigger atomic resonance restructuring, to create disproportional imbalance in intensified-density weapons materials.'

'Can you really use this stuff?'

'We'll see. Mostly I am three hundred years old. Three hundred years older than any weapon or defensive material set against me. Any enemy knows I have every highbrow capability that was around three hundred years ago, and all of space believes the Magnificci are too proud to change. Not a good beginning for Alito and Lord Thomas, to be saddled with me, is it? And they are also dinosaurs in this ugly modern reality. I can only work with what I've got. But hey, I have one weapon that's newer and brighter than anything else around: you, Planetboy.'

'(another embarrassing James giggle) Get out!! Thought you said I was silly anyway.'

'Yes, very. Regards what I can use – wait and see. I have a serious heart. All right, a couple more cartoon stories, and we must get started on your medical.'

'Well…, Oh yeah. There was this episode with new baddies. Planetman hits them with everything he's got. He hits them so hard with the rainbow ray that the backblast starts getting him keen on himself, but nothing works. Nortibot is annoyed that Planetman hasn't got time to play with him any more, so he tells Planetman he'll give the baddies what for. He gets Destructo Mechanicus, puts a huge rock in its hand, and says, "Destructo Mechanicus, strongest of all, smash the aliens' mirror wall", and Destructo chucks it, and this like mirage across Space suddenly smashes, and there's nothing there, except weedy little voices coming from behind a moon, going "Oh shit. Time to go. I'm not getting rainbow rayed while I'm stuck in this ship with you", but Planetman gets them fair up the rocketpipe while they're flying away, and they start flying all stupid, with coloured fireworks, and you hear this woman's voice going "Oo-ooo, Darling!", and the man baddy goes, "Get away from me!". It was real funny. Oh yeah, and at the end, the baddies always yell "Bloody Planetman", and hand over this big trophy with "I win" written on it. It's so big that when Planetman holds it up, it goes off balance, and falls over his head, over all of him actually. Then the baddies have to decide if they'll let him out or not. Sometimes they do, sometimes they don't. You want one more short one?... The baddies go through a whole series catching Planetman all the time, because they know the shape of his ship, and then this girl he's real keen on gets frustrated because he's such a dope, and she's throwing stuff at him. Most of the stuff's missing, and then this champagne bottle gets stuck up the nose of his ship. Turns out to be a good thing, because the baddies can't find him any more.'

'All right. That is definitely enough.'
The air inside the seeder was doing the laughing colours.

'Are you laughing at me, or Planetman?'

'Myself. You've only been on that seat half an hour, and already I have to reassign my weapons support systems, build three new weapons, alter my hull shape, and report to Captain Thomas that we suspect the orange ray is not coming from where it seems.'

'Thanks! I think the Captain knows already, about the fractured space thing. We saw it from a dying scout ship.'

'No-one's dead until they're dead. I am the very finest medical machine in the great and glorious history of The Magnificci. The Emprino must have nothing less, and that is why I exist. If we get there in time I will fix that scout pilot. You might not think we are hurrying to achieve that rescue, but we are. Captain Thomas thinks the images we saw will have been tampered with, and the atomic structure readings will be false. He will need you to board that scout ship, and get the data first hand. Time has not run out for the scout pilot – when we flash we will exceed the speed of light, and enter exospace. Exospace is nowhere and notime. From exospace it is only possible to re-enter this universe at the time you left, so we will reach your pilot at almost the same moment we set out to find him. Leaving here is what is holding us up, and part of the hold up is you – I can't ramp and flash until you have completed your medical.'

Sadness bit into Mark. For a while there, remembering old cartoons and other times, he'd escaped the rotten feelings, caused by knowing what was happening out in space.

'He was looking pretty sick, the scout,' he said.

'So will you if you don't lie down. No more secret word. Time we got this over with.'

MARK'S MAGNIFICCI MEDICAL

The walls of the cabin changed shape, letting long arms shoot out. Long thin mechanical arms with equipment on their ends, targeting an area on the floor the right size for him to be lying in. Every single arm had something on the end of it that looked harder, or sharper, or like it would go hotter or colder, than his skin, muscles and bones could handle. Mark began to feel scared. The space in front of his eyes was filling with words again.

'Come on, this will hurt a bit,' the letters said.

'Won't hurt a bit, you're supposed to say. You're already making mistakes, and you haven't even got those things near... woah! Stop. STOP.'

He was hanging in the air, suspended by about five arms at once. He didn't like the way they were adjusting their holds around him, for better, and better grips.

'I don't want to do this,' he said.

The arms stopped moving. Secret words were happening again.

'I have to do this to you, so I will know how fast I can accelerate, turn, stop, how long I can float you, how long you can survive in shapelock at the start and end of journeys – all that, without breaking you, both like a stick, and like an egg. Humanoidians can bruise, snap, tear, and pop. We do this test together, and those things won't happen to you. So this is a good thing, isn't it. Yes, it will hurt a bit though.'

The arms began moving again. How much was a bit? He saw the screened air say 'sorry', as the arms moved him down to the floor. They began moving, twisting his head back, to the left, to the right, looking up, looking down, arm up his back, around his front, knee nearly in his face. Now the other knee. The breath was being pummelled out of him by his own body. Now they were making his back arch, further, and further, bending the bottoms of his feet up to the back of his head.

'I'm not meant to go like this!' he called out in panic, but the IPE didn't seem to be listening.

The shirt, and then the undervest, pulled free from his pants. It was only the clothes, but he felt like he was coming apart. He could feel his belly-button out in the open air, and his ribs were strrretching the skin that was over the top of them. Am I glad that's over he thought, as the mechanical arms began curling him up in a ball. They were pushing his head towards his knees, tighter and tighter. The clothes across the back of him were complaining now – thread snapping noises – belt loops busting, one by one: he could feel the belt webbing riding up against his skin, and he could sense open air further and further up his back. Bang, and a landing-on-the-deck noise; his belt buckle had just piked out. The belt was broken, and somewhere on the deck below. Ooooff. His face was nearly sniffing his nuts. He'd never had his legs behind his ears before. It didn't feel good.

'Squish the crap out of me why don't you,' he tried to say.

Things were shining into his face. Whistling in his ears. Suddenly the arms stood him on his feet, and vanished back into the walls. He wasn't balanced. His legs felt like rubber. He fell over backwards and sat down. Words shot into existence in front of him.

'That wasn't so bad, was it. You will feel a little bit worn out for a day or so. Wait while I check we have ev...'

The light inside the control area changed to that acid red. Panic, and then inside the seeder went pitch black. He couldn't watch out for what was happening. He couldn't hear anything. He couldn't see. As Mark's eyes adjusted to the dark, he saw a faint red glow of panic, and dim shadow-shapes of long thin folding arms, coming out from the walls like creeping spiders. He backed away into a corner, against the forward vision bulkhead. The arms advanced. A thin half see-through space for words hiccupped from red, to blank. Now there was writing floating there, grey with pale green edges – sadness tinged with pity.

'You are thirty-six plus you body forms. I didn't know. I thought you were just one silly little fragilicus. I must test them all. Sorry. You are going to feel really awful by the end. Sorry. Sorry.'

An arm was slowly inching itself around his middle. He wished he had a red button like a scout ship, to get away from here. More mechanical arms were slowly taking hold, of his legs, his head, his waist, and finally his arms. Carrying him back to the centre of the floor. Stretching him out. There was no point in asking for this not to happen. No point begging. No point pleading. The machine knew already how much he didn't want to go through this. Once, not okay, but he'd handled it. Thirty-six times more of having everything twisted around, and the breath knocked out of him? And how was it going to test the other bodies, when he was still Junior James? The roof above him was moving, making room for something to drop down into the control deck area. For the first time he saw what a B4 ray weapon looked like. A blasting cannon. It came down humming and whistling, louder and louder, like it was about to go off. It was going down on its long arm, low to the floor, creeping up on him from the feet end.

'No. Please? No. Please don't…' He couldn't get his head up far enough to see where it was, but he could hear it coming closer.

One massive rasping hum, and it hit his stomach. The liquid shimmering feeling began there, and spread through him. This again - water going in and out, and his body buckling into a new shape. Heart pounding like mad. Mouth sucking desperately at the air, trying to get enough into his lungs. His brain screamed naked fear when, for a few moments, it wasn't sure where parts of him were. He swallowed, gulped air, sneezed. Pant pant pant. His mouth was still sobbing, saying no, no, no. His heartbeat and breathing were all over the place. It's over, it's over, he told himself. Calm down, calm down, calm down. Who am I? he wondered. His lips didn't feel James childish any more. The muscles of this boy felt like his own. Good shaped, and strong for his age. Maybe he was himself again? He looked at the golden chocolate brown smooth skin on his hands and fingers…no, he definitely wasn't himself.

'Mark one. Return point established. Proceeding through cycle at three minute intervals,' said a recorded voice from the B4 cannon.

'No, no no, this isn't me. This isn't the return point,' Mark yelled, but already those other arms were twisting every part of him up and back like before, only faster, and faster, and faster. It probably wasn't what the B4 cannon meant, anyway. He had to hope that.

'Throw me over why don't you,' he yelled, as they flipped him in the air like pulling a spinning top with a string.

This body was handling it better. Oooff, face shoved in his balls again. Nearly over. And then he heard the heating up noises. He tried to lift himself out of the way, arching his body up in the air. It had to miss, because he couldn't go through that brain fear again.

Zzzzzapp. Oh crap. Missed his guts. Fair in the nuts this time. He felt sick. He couldn't curl up, because he was stretched out by his arms and legs. All he could do was moan.

'Target must be spatially steadied. Preparing to try again,' announced the mechanical voice of the cannon.

Words in front of his face.

'I'm here keeping an eye on you, okay?'

'Not really,' wheezed Mark.

'Keep still and it will hurt a bit.'

ZZZaapp. Stretch, bend, twist, twist, pull his head right back, shove it right forward. He was being moved so fast he couldn't even see what his skin was like this time. When the eye light raced in towards his face, it came in so close he thought for a second his nose was missing, but then he felt the tester rest against it. Whoever this boy was, their face was a heaps different shape. Body felt like usual though; stuffed after being stretched, twisted and squashed.

ZZZzaapp. Again. And the whole cycle again. Somewhere around the fifth time of being some other boy getting wrenched in all directions, his body had no energy left, and went floppy. At body twenty-eight, a boy that felt curiously like Shane if you could see him from the inside, Mark felt pee leaking out. He was surprised it took that long. He couldn't understand how he had managed not to have a bent back finger broken, or a twisted arm or leg torn off. He was gritting his teeth, lips curled into a snarl to keep control. Words darted in, close in front of his eyes.

'I know how far to go,' was all it said.

'Like hell you do,' said Mark weakly.

'Drink,' and a plastic straw was in front of his face.

Suck, suck. The whistling hum was sneaking up on him again. He began sucking slower to make the drink last, to put this off. The straw was pulled away from his face. The hum turned into that rasping roar. Any second now…

Froth was coming out of his mouth. At boy thirty-one, the screen came and reminded him there weren't many to go. After that zap, he thought for a second he was Crackers again, but then he couldn't get his lips to cover his teeth, not at all, and he realised, as his arm was being bent up past his face, that he was that buck rabbit toothed kid. He laughed weakly at the way his whole face felt like it started and ended at the teeth. From the inside the kid felt even sillier than James, happy silly, so there was something good about being him. Then Mark groaned. He knew something bad was going to happen. He could feel it getting ready. Backing up. He couldn't stop it. Poo, squeezing out of him. Slopping around in his already urine soggy pants. The smell was foul. He shut his eyes, tried not to breathe so deep, and waited for this nightmare to end. Every now and then little rubber sucker cups would pull his eyelids back, for the light test. Suddenly he couldn't hear the B4 cannon any more. He was being stood back on his feet. New letters were following his face, keeping in front of his eyes. He was so tired he couldn't focus on them properly.

'Well done. You are a very brave fragilicus. You've done better than most adult humanoidians.'

Brave. Brave sucked. Anyway, brave had nothing to do with it he thought bitterly, you were going to do it to me anyway. He had been totally stuffed by an expert. He felt like he was falling, and then, just as his legs were collapsing him onto the deck, he realised he was outside the ship, and Litmus was standing over him, crouching down.

LITMUS TAKES CHARGE

'I want to laugh, but I can't,' Litmus said, as if Mark was a puppy that had fallen into a bucket, trying to do a trick meant for a full size dog.

'Come on. I'll carry you.'

Mark's body was too weak to hold itself up. It sagged, floppy.

'You stink of poo,' said Litmus, lost underneath the middle, 'and wee.'

He couldn't reach high enough to get Mark's body off the floor, either end.

''nother way,' he decided.

He went down to Mark's feet, towed him around in a circle, lifted his feet up at the ankles, and began dragging.

'I like your new skin… It's all chocolaty coloured,' he said back over his shoulder.

'Take me back! Bloody hell. That's Sammy. Sam Retro. I have to be ME. It's put… the B4 cannon, it's put a marker in that this is me! We have to go…'

'NO. Grandpa would say no too. He will fixed you later. Now is not good. Things have changed since you went in our ship. They packed up everything in the Soft Cargo already just about, and… Oh, don't start panicking more even – that broken time thing is still safe in your locker. You have to wash your uniform but – I packed your clothes for you, but then I left them somewhere wrong, and what you're in's the only for wearing things you've got now. Or you can just smell of poo?'

'Litmus. Put me down. No, I won't run back. I'm just over you touching me. I'll walk.'

But Mark couldn't. He wobbled up onto his legs, took one step, and collapsed in a heap.

'She did you better than anyone else, ever,' said Litmus watching.

'Pick me up again then. But lay off with the comments about spit, and poo, and snot and…I thought you couldn't see colour…'

While Mark was wondering about that, about Litmus being able to see chocolaty brown, Mark fell asleep, because he was totally worn out.

He slid from on his knees and elbows, to down onto his face, and then into a flat tangled mess on the deck.

'You did a Floppy Bunny!' crowed Litmus.

Mark didn't hear.

'Anyway, I never said anything about snot. Come on Planetboy,' said Litmus, and he began dragging Mark by the ankles again.

'I can see colour now coz someone new is nearly in forever,' Litmus said, watching Mark's face as he towed him, 'and now you can't say I didn't tell,' he added, looking pleased with his sneakiness.

The shirt and undervest had dragged up Mark as he slid along the floors until they were tangled around his neck and shoulders. Bonk went his head, as it crossed a deck joiner line. Litmus giggled.

'Lucky your hair's all fuzzy this time, for like a cushion,' he said.

They were nearly back to the trainee officers' quarters. Litmus turned around forwards, to pull Mark the rest of the way.

CLEANED UP

James was sitting at the table writing. He looked up as Litmus appeared in the doorway, with feet poking out from under each arm.

'Hold the door?' asked Litmus, 'Or it will banged his head.'

They were halfway in when a voice came from the couch.

'Big success then?'

Litmus eyed the captain.

'Yes. He's finished.'

'Looks it,' said the captain.

'Finished getting to be a crew,' said Litmus.

'Well done then, both of you,' said the captain as he stood up, walked across, and bent down to inspect Mark, 'You may as well keep towing him until you reach the shower, and I'll take it from there. A shame immortality doesn't affect the sense of smell.'

'It's him, isn't it, inside Sammy? He's going to be all right, isn't he?' asked James.

'Yes. I think so,' answered the captain, as he turned the shower taps on, 'Let's give him a bit of privacy, hey?'

'Why? It's not his body,' pointed out Litmus, 'He's being ruder than us anyway – he's inside it.'

'He's in enough of a state already, without having onlookers while he's getting cleaned up,' stated the captain, as he pulled Mark's top half clothes over his head.

'We won't look. We'll work the clothes machine,' said Litmus, and set about getting it ready.
'It doesn't have a one for extra pooey,' he giggled.

'There,' said James reaching over, 'body waste stained.'

'That sounds a bit yucky,' said Litmus, as he took the jacket, shirt and undervest from Captain Thomas.
'Hey hey hey, not straight in you little terror,' said the captain, watching as Litmus tried to load the clothes washer.

'What then?' asked Litmus, caught in the act.

'Scrape some off,' suggested James, 'into the toilet.'

'That at least,' said the captain.
Litmus held the clothes out towards James, then at the last second snatched them back.

'I'm doing the yucky bit, aren't I Grandpa,' he stated.

'Yes please,' said the captain, 'Here's the rest. Ensign Fargo, we will need to get fluids and food into him. If you could go to your quarters' comms panel, and ask the wardroom galley to send down a wide selection of food and drink, on my authority? Thankyou.'

Mark sat wrapped in a towel, eating and eating, resting for a few breaths, drinking, then eating more.

'Why does he have to drink so much?' asked James, worried.

'So he doesn't get a monster headache, due to loss of fluids,' answered the captain.

'He looks smaller this time.'

'No lad, he's just gone back to being fourteen again. Meanwhile, you haven't stopped growing, and are nearly full fifteen-year-old size.'

For the first time since Litmus dragged Mark in the door, James looked happy.

'Bigger than you now,' he said, 'I can get you back for all the stirring at school. You can be the one that gets tied up with his own socks.'

'Just try it,' said Mark, as he reached for more food to stuff in his mouth.

'We have things to do, so we'll be going now,' said the captain standing up.

'They'll send for you when they're ready Ensign Fargo, but you, Mar...Sam, listening? You are not to leave these rooms. I am not sure the crew and passengers on these ships are ready for you. The gangly redhead with freckles was a big enough shock. You, the way you are now, are going to be a really hard sell. A gold edition Geneheritage World humanoidian fragilicus is something special. We can't claim you've been around but they didn't notice you. Litmus will come back for you, when I've figured out the best course...'

'Grandpa, Grandpa?... I've got a idea?'

'Yes… well perhaps I'll hear that idea a little later,' said the captain.

Mark, James and the captain could all tell that Litmus's idea was going to be cheeky, insulting, and probably only Litmus would find it funny. Litmus looked up at them.

'It wasn't a mean one? It wasn't,' he insisted.

They were both leaving. The door was closing, they were outside walking away down the passage, but Mark and James could still hear.

'Well done Alito. You were right. I was too scared to put it to the test. If he had gone all the way back, he'd be five now, and I'm not sure we could have dealt with that.'

'I'm seven,' said Litmus proudly.

'Going on seven, going on seven, and going on seven again,' said Mark to himself, as the door finished shutting.

REAL NICE STARTING ROUNDNESSES

'He's such a brat. James, you've got no idea – he's been spitting in my food, and stirring it in with his finger.'

'No? I don't think so. I didn't see?'

'Not now, every day, for like ages…what you been writing?'

'Goodbye letter. It hurts if I don't get to say goodbye. Captain Thomas said we mightn't get time. But everything I tried to write was crap.'

'To Phoebe,' stated Mark.

'No. To you,' answered James, scribbling all over the sheet of paper trying to make it unreadable.

'Hey! Paper costs!'

'Not this. It was toilet paper wrapper.'

Mark chuckled, 'Give it here. That's like an ace souvenir. What did you write to the Pheobe?'

'Nothing,' said James, sounding flat. 'She, she, she, she…'

'James, just spit it out.'

'In the middle of the cafeteria, she waves at me, and goes, "Bye cutie," and then she tells her friends, so everyone can hear, "Built like my finger", and she holds her pinkie up, like it's a stiffy.'

'Come on Wimpy, that's not so bad.'

'And then some-one else goes like how would she know, and she tells them all that I let her take my clothes off.'

'Hey, she's only one year older than us, so she's just sounding off. You are like the only boyfriend she's ever had. They all know that. And James, be fair – you had fun with her.'

James grinned, embarrassed and happy at the same time.

'It was going to be her we undressed,' he began, liking the memory, 'and that was going to be so good – I was pretty excited happy. She curves, from under her arms to these real nice starting roundnesses, and her nipples could just about poke your eye out, anyway, we were going to undress her but she chickened out on her bottom half, and decided to do me instead.'

'Yeah yeah – I'm starting to think I don't need the details,' said Mark, and then a huge burp came out of him, followed by similar from the other end.

'Sorry, have to go you know where.'

ACTUALLY REALLY ANNOYING

The quarters were down to sleepwatch lighting. Dim. They were both in their bunks, going over old memories. Mark was hanging over the edge of his, looking down at James talking.

'This might be the last time we see each other, ever, in our whole…' James couldn't finish, because he had gone into silly childish laughter.

Every time he looked at Mark it would start again.

'What's so funny?' said Mark, like ho-hum.

'Nothing (giggle).'

'Own up Wimpy, or I'll come down and pummel it out of you.'

'Your eyes, and your teeth. They're like all I can see.' James did an impression of large round white eyes and smiling teeth.

'Now I know why Sammy chased me around the school, trying to punch the crap out of me,' said Mark, 'That's actually really annoying.'

'He was a real cool looking kid, wasn't he.'

'Yeah, but I've only got the body, not the moves. Tried it in the wash mirror. He had a whole different idea of funny. I used to feel happy, just because he sneaky smiled, probably at nothing. Nearly pissed myself laughing though, cleaning my teeth – I wasn't trying to, but this face was looking back at me in the mirror – doing that looking into you thing he did… you know: that sneaky, happy, nearly in your skin with you look.'

'Yeah, he made me laugh one day, and then he goes, "What you laughing at, Fargo", and I felt real awkward. Then, then he does that sunshine goofy act again, and even though I already promised myself I wouldn't, it made me laugh again, and he goes, "I like doing that to you". I kept away from him after that, all year, because it really embarrassed me that day – made me feel like he was dacking me or something.'

'You're a bit weird.'

'Thanks.'

Silence for a while.

'Mark? What did it feel like being me?'

'I didn't know I was, the first time, we were too busy in the middle of stuff, and the second time, it was too horrible and way too fast, the medical, to know it was happening to me.'

'Shane and me, and Bernard. We all got our blood sucked out for you, that time you were in hospital.'

'I think I felt being Shane. I'll know if it happens again, anyway.'

'Yeah… well,' began James awkwardly.

'What?'

'Don't… I mean… When you are me, you won't like, in front of a mirror or something?… It's just that I heard you giving Crackers a… Oh crap, I think I'm going to die of embarrassment.'

'You! How do you think I'm feeling!'

'Promise me you won't do that? Not when you're me?'

'Shut up!'

'Boys, three hours 'til you're on watch. Get some sleep.' Captain Murray's voice at the door. Doing the rounds of his ship. 'Ensign Planetti? Don't forget that little chat we had.'

LIKE A CUTE LITTLE SMART-ARSE DOLL

Mark woke to the sound of James in the wash area. In the shower. Mark lay in his bunk, warm, comfortable. Hey, I'm

157

someone new he thought, pleased. He stretched as he listened to the ship. Just that low background hum, without extra noises of machinery echoing through the hull frame. The feeling of panic seemed to be over. There was no sound of movement in the passageway outside the mess. This was better – he didn't have Cracker's knobbly knees any more to be bumping the bulkhead beside the bunk. He was Sam Retreaux now. Retro to everyone in the schoolyard. There was an unexplained feeling of sunniness inside Sam. I don't mind that thought Mark, letting his feelings soak in it. He felt like laughing, just from being alive. He looked down from his bunk. His normal dark blue uniform wasn't anywhere he could see. Litmus might have really meant it – losing all Mark's clothes in the general packing up by the crew, so the ship would be prepared for action. The brat could have just left everything in my locker, thought Mark feeling frustrated. His light grey battle gear was on the mess couch, in a slightly scrunched, coming unfolded heap – Litmus must have carried it from the drier. No, something is wrong with my eyes thought Mark, that uniform looks purple. Purple purple. Nah, trick of the light or something.

Relief – James's uniform was still the right colour. All James's gear was laid out on the bunk below, in typical James Fargo order – neat, pressed smooth, and the ship runners washed newer than new clean. Even the white underpants and undervest were pressed smooth and neatly folded. How are you going to manage, James, if a world around you ever starts slipdown, Mark wondered. There would be a sliding of standards, then a shortage of things, and finally chaos, because people no longer cared about anything, and in the middle of it all James, trying to look neat for his Mum. Goodbyes were really close. Mark could feel it. When you started noticing things that had been there to be noticed any time in all the years you'd known each other, when you started noticing them individually as strange, it was like something in you latching on to things, not wanting to let them go.

Here came James, drying himself on the way out of the wash area. He was a bigger kid now, Mark realised, more chunky looking, and with two small zits starting on his face. It was almost like it had happened overnight.

'Morning Retro. Goodbye soon,' James commented, 'I'm going to be over on the helpod. They're sending me this morning, before things get panicky.'

'How do you know?'

'Nightwatch woke me, said to get ready. Litmus was in. You have to be Retro from now on, just ported in secretly from somewhere weird.'

'Like anyone's going to swallow that ported in part. And, I bet that's just my old uniform, dyed purple.'

'Yeah well… it's supposed to make it easier for them to swallow the change. Litmus goes "Grandpa, we shrunked it", and then Captain Thomas said no matter, because they'd shrunk you too. That was funny, but you just went on sleeping.'

'Who cares. We got time for a last breakfast?' asked Mark.

'Not if you're going to do your usual lie around when you're supposed to get up, then go to sleep in the shower, then look for your clothes in your mess, then…'

'Hey! Lay off. I'll be ready before you!' answered Mark, as he slid down from his bunk, and straight into his clothes.
He had showered only a few hours ago, very thoroughly. James was staring at him.
'What?' asked Mark.

'You're still a kid.'

'What do you mean?'
This was strange, like a role reversal.

'You're skinny hips small, and it's just the way you do that. You're not thinking about anything, just the right now.'
Mark stood there, belt half threaded.

'So…I should have a shower? Or what?'

'You could, but suit yourself.'
Mark started undressing again, then stopped.

'Hey James, how about waiting 'til tomorrow to go all grown up on me? Okay?'

'Okay,' answered James, sounded relieved.

James began racing into his own uniform, pulling bits over his head, up his legs, and then bounced down to sit on the deck while he pulled his ship runners on.

'Breakfast!' he said like he'd won a race, and then they were headed out the door of the quarters.

'You'll be the only kid on board soon, oh, that is, you and Litmus.'

'He's not… I'm not… You know what I mean,' finished Mark.

James chuckled.

'I was forgetting there's two of you anyway: Retro and Planetti rolled into one. Every teacher's nightmare. It's weird how, out of thirty-six kids you could change into, you had to pick the rattiest three.'

'What three?'

'Crackers, Retro and Planetti.'

'And you, and hey, I didn't pick anyone! I just got this done to me.'

James chuckled again.

'It's fun, you still being a kid. I wish I was staying around, to stir you back for like the last eight years' worth. Ever since cadet club, when you tied my pants to the ladder, you've been getting fun out of stirring me for being kiddier than you.'

'Yeah good one–"kiddier" – you and Litmus use the same dictionary.'

'Nice try,' said James, and then he chuckled, instead of his usual giggle.

'You're like a doll, a cute little smart-arse doll,' he said, inspecting Mark as he walked.

'Right, that's it, you're getting thumped,' said Mark grimly.

James squeaked like he always used to, and took off up the passageway, with Mark getting up speed for the chase. It was then Mark realised how skinnier and smaller he was – there was a huge difference between fifteen and fourteen. James was half the passageway ahead already.

'You can run, chickenboy, but I'll still get you,' sang out Mark.
A head came out of a bulkhead doorway. Commander Burnett.

'This is not a play school. On your way, and move
yourself in a manner appropriate to your surroundings.'

JAMES LEARNS GOODBYE

They stood on the gangway area. Both with feelings that needed
rescuing.

'Ensign Fargo, time to go,' said the gangway supervisor.

'Shake hands?' asked James.

It was more like a hold. They both forgot the shake.

'Don't forget Shane,' said James, 'we have to keep looking.'

'Yep. Bye,' said Mark, as their hands were letting go.
He'd said it because James liked things finished properly. He
realised with surprise that he felt better for doing it. He could tell
James did too.

'It's not really goodbye, because this time I'll know
you're okay, and out there having fun. Because you always are,
Lefty.'

James's eyes were happy friendly as he said it. Mark realised
there was more to growing up than where you were in the sex
thing, and it was the other parts that were really the important
parts of who you got to be for the rest of your life. He lifted a
hand in a wave as the gangway hatch slid shut.

Underneath all the cheeky smiles Sammy Retro was a bit of a
sook – Mark could feel that feeling all through the neatly shaped
lightly muscled body – the not wanting a friend to leave him
feeling.

CLOSER TO DANGER

The wardroom was full, every dining chair around the huge table,
and people were standing everywhere. It was a cross between
dinner, and a general meeting of all section leaders. There were
officers over from the helpod that Mark hadn't seen before, and
even staff from the Soft Cargo that hadn't been around during his
duty watches.

'People who have a seat please sit, and we'll get started,' said Commander Burnett loudly.

Litmus wouldn't let Mark sit down.

'You don't know where yet, because you're new. I have to show you. Ready? Sammy, you can sit here.'

'Litmus!' hissed Mark.

It was sort of funny, but also really frustrating. For revenge, Mark did that Sammy Retro look right into Litmus's face, perfect teeth, wide eye whites, and full on silly happiness. Litmus began laughing like a balloon full of jiggling bubbles.

'I can't look at you,' Litmus said as he caught his breath, 'you make me all giggly inside, so bad I have to go pee.'

Suffer, thought Mark feeling pleased.

'Mandelbrot's back!' someone in the crowded room called out.

'Quiet in the wardroom,' ordered Captain Murray.

Silence.

'No, the Mandelbrot is not back,' said Captain Thomas quietly, 'I know exactly what Commander Yorker's orders are.' He leant across the table, 'Captain Murray, you do not stand down until this ends.'

'Yes Lord... Display the bridge. All officers remove to Port.'

The long right wall of the wardroom turned into a picture screen of the Soft Cargo's control deck. The officers from the other side of the table were crowding themselves around to Port, forming a packed-in group behind Mark, and everyone else sitting along his side of the table. Beyond his dinner plate, across the table, looking into the wall screen, Mark could see the back of the navigator's seat on the bridge, and beyond that, the large forward vision screen the bridge used to see out into space. Litmus was back, climbing onto his chair.

'Eat up,' whispered Litmus, 'We're going soon.'

'You forgot to spit in it,' whispered Mark, being sarcastic.

'Grandpa got a surprise this morning: he can see colour again,' said Litmus, looking cheeky and like Mark should know something.

Mark was trying to ignore him, and concentrate on what was going on. Litmus was pointing at Mark's food.

'It won't affect me, but we mightn't have food for ages,' said Litmus, 'If you don't eat now, you'll be drinking mo-ore,' and then he bubbled his grubby little lips with saliva. Mark decided to watch what was happening, and eat. Litmus was giggling away to himself.

'Bosun, bring that image up for the wardroom,' ordered the officer of the watch.

'There it is. Still a long way off, but there it is,' the officer of the watch claimed, as a view of the Mandelbrot filled the forward vision screen.

'Yes,' said Captain Thomas, 'there 'it' is. But what is it? Commander Yorker has let this one through, because she has all she can handle ahead of her. This is her way of sending a signal, without betraying us by signalling. That is a Democratzia Capitalisto vessel, imaging as one of ours. A foul monstrous machine of death. Within this hour, your ship will be an empty wreck. You cannot save her, Captain. She is a *Soft* Cargo. You must jettison the speed shuttle, with all passengers and non essentials on board, within ten minutes, and they must leave at full speed. Use this hull as the blast wall. Next, all your trained crew must be on board the helpod within fifteen, in full battle dress, ready. Run to that timetable, and we'll have a little leeway. This has come upon us early, but this is what we are here for. My ship MUST pass, unharmed and unhindered, and I need the helpod. I would like it to survive. You know by what authority I command you.'

'Seal,' yelled Captain Murray, 'No word of this is to leave the Bridge, or this wardroom. Officer of the watch, sound a practice drill for the passengers and non-essentials – five minutes to be in the speed shuttle. My best champagne and chocolates, to everyone there in time. Then sound a drill for the crew, all crew, all stations, to the bridge, in battle dress. Say it is a race with the helpod's crew. Our crew are to leave everything as it stands –

Captain's order. Section leaders on the bridge, bring your sections in. Give no warning, hint or clue. The helpod will be wasp stinging just aft of our nose cone, and they will airsuck us on board, in twelve minutes. Make it happen,' he yelled.

Officers began running in all directions. The wardroom serving staff were left standing in an empty room. They were trained not to be flustered, or hurried. They needed orders to follow.

'Four minutes and twenty-eight seconds, to carry all the chocolate and the best bottles from the wardroom bar into the Speedshuttle, and find yourselves good seats for the long way home,' said Captain Thomas to them, 'I'm sorry – you don't have time to go to your lockers, and the speedshuttle has no space. You must leave it all behind. Hurry now, or you will die.'

CORT GOES ABOARD THE GREAT KAROSHI

'This is your last twenty minutes boy. During this twenty minutes we will finish accelerating, and then fire your pod ahead of us to even greater speed, and you will rise into exospace, moving so fast you are no longer in this reality. When you get there the Great Karoshi's function actuator will tell you what to do. Obey it – it doesn't care what happens to you, because it can't. It is a piece of software machinery following program parameters, parameters that were set long before any of us were born. In case you are beginning to wonder – worse things than having difficulty breathing can happen to you, and it is programmed to use all of them. We will get the result we want. The survival of the Freedom Collective depends on it.

'Fifteen minutes left. We began constructing the Great Karoshi when the Magnificci cheated us of resources. We were victorious, and they for all their greatness ran away. They left us nothing. When they return we will have taken their royal child to pieces, and we will be waiting for them, with the greatest weapon ever made.

'During the construction phase there were twenty-thousand workers. It took us over a hundred years to build up to that size workforce, shipping people into exospace every single day of every single year, for a whole century. When the Great Karoshi was finally finished we no longer needed the workers, so their carbon content was converted into fuel for the engines. All factored into the original plan. But now we do need someone. Someone small but strong, for a last particular job. You will be removing the protective tiles from the very tip of the front of our great ship, so the harpoon machinery can be extended out ahead, to catch one of our enemy before he even knows we are there. That is an honour, a great honour, for you, to be the final constructor in such a massive project. You will die knowing what you are doing matters.

'Ten minutes left. There are adult CULs on board the Great Karoshi. They will show you how to stay alive. We have very limited communication, a one-off brief chance to get an update from the function actuator when we drop you off, so once you are there you, and your fellow workers, are on your own. Don't wallow in self pity hoping we will come to your rescue – whatever state you get in you will have to get out of by yourself. We send a new crew every ten days, to replace the one among you the Great Karoshi function actuator marks as least useful. That cul is then your drinking water, so use the water wisely, as it has to last for all of you – there will be no more until the next new crew arrives. All right – your time's up – get in your transfer capsule.'

The lid went on over the top of Cort. There was a lot less room inside even than inside the tiny Fly-ahead he had piloted once. This thing had no controls. No nothing.

Like something being spat out it was accelerating. After a while it had been accelerating for so long he had no idea what time it was, or where he would be in space. Memories of Uncle John kept drifting in and out of his thoughts. Mum and Dad would be dead too, turned to water and dust, and everyone from school, all their lives over forever. It was a great sadness losing them, but it was worse, so much worse, having someone from your life murdered in front of you. They hadn't even given Uncle John a chance to say goodbye. That was the bit that made Cort's heart harden completely. It would have cost nothing, just letting someone say goodbye for a last time, but they didn't care enough even for that, because there was no money in it.

Finally he felt stillness.

Very strange – his body, as he looked down himself, had gone semi see-through.

In the low light inside the capsule, the colour slowly began coming back into his skin, and then the top half of the capsule fell off, like a coffin opening. He was now a faster than light-speed being, up in exospace, inside the largest thing every constructed.

THE ONLY LIVING THING ON BOARD

Someone had been vandalising the wiring loom in the wall of the ship. There were dried up crumpled shells of bodies everywhere on the metal decking, like a battle had happened.

Cort watched as his presence made a screen light up. It had a list with headings – CUL, and ALC – Carbon Units Living – Available Liquid Content.

He felt a horrible hollowness chew into him, and when he looked down, a letter and a number had burnt through his school uniform and appeared in the skin of his chest. He was now C7#*Blue. The screen changed, adding C7#*Blue to the list of CUL, and Cort got to read how much available liquid he was. The other numbers on the screen were all A numbers – A, a number, hash, star, a colour, except for C6#*Pink, another C number. Those same A numbers were around him on the floor, written into the shrunk-small chest skin of dead sucked-dry people. One of the dead bodies had writing on its leg. Writing now very small, because the skin was so shrunken. Cort got down on his knees to read.

"Hello C6. We are going to poison ourselves with hydraulic fluid, so they can't use our water. This thing can't ever be finished. Please die. Don't let our deaths be for nothing". There had been a battle, slave workers against the ship, and the crew had sort of won –they had lost their lives, but the ship could not use them any more, alive or dead, and now the ship was, at each new crew drop off, telling the Democratzia Capitalisto back in the sub-lightspeed universe that there were living crew. The slave labour had sabotaged the wiring, so that that information in the short messages wasn't true.

Cort realised he was the only living thing on board. In a machine as big as a whole planet, he was the only creature that thought, cared, knew things, wanted to go on living. What for? To kill the people who made this thing, and to destroy everything else they had made, until they and their weapons were no more. He wanted that, to lessen the pain of what had happened to Uncle John. Cort wanted, but he knew he had no chance. What had happened to his home planet, the death of everyone on it, meant that the Star Alliance's whole Space Navy had been busy desperately fighting until their total loss, against an enemy so great, so greedy, and so uncaring, that they could never win, and so they hadn't come to rescue him, his friends, his school, his family, his whole planet, because they couldn't. Everything was lost, forever. They couldn't do it, so he had no chance.

But I never give up, he thought sadly. Not a victory motto, just a tired reality. What was he refusing to give up for? He looked down at his hands and thought about that. What was left that was worth the struggle of going on living? He wanted…some friends. Not many, just a few – they could be anybody, just someone to share life with, in a place where he was liked just for being himself.

'I am good at some things?' he said softly.

'I was a good fly-ahead boy. I just have to get through this, and I will be a fly-ahead boy again. One day I will.'

C6#*PINK

He couldn't find C6 among the shrunken body shells. C for child? A for Adult? He stopped searching and looked up instead, around him carefully, then away along the dimly lit wide tall passage. There was no sparkle of a watching pair of eyes. No other frightened child was hiding out there.

'C6?' he called softly.

No answer. There was no one.

He had been walking for so long. Walking down an endless dark passage. He was so tired, but he couldn't stop, because the Great Karoshi function actuator would cause him horrible pain each time, until he was doing what it demanded. No effort had gone into making the voice giving the orders nice. Nice cost money. It ripped at his ears as it talked.

"C7 will walk. C7 will crawl inside the nose cone. C7 will remove armour tiles from the nose cone until machinery can pass through. C7 will stack the tiles behind it for C7's replacement to refit. C7 is the only uncontaminated water on board. C7 will not ask for liquid it cannot have."

He was inside the nose cone, ready to begin work. Something brushed his face in the dark. It didn't feel like a piece of machine. Something was there. He waited, scared, hoping his eyes would work better.

C6 was hanging by her hair, dangling, caught on the machinery that was waiting to move up to the very front of the ship.

She was easy to lift down, because all the moisture had been sucked from her. C6 was very dead, and like a small school bag. She was empty, except for a few things like broken pencils, all that was left of her bones. Cort could tell she would have been no more than five years old. Blue Skies One years. Probably too young to read. Reading the message on the leg earlier had given Cort a strange sort of hope – someone who had been here cared what happened to him, thought that it would matter. There was nowhere nice to put her, C6. Cort reached up, and poked her inside the workings of the machine. At least she could be privately dead in there. No stab of pain happened to him for doing it. He realised that the Great Karoshi actuator couldn't see everything inside the nose cone area, only some of it. He was just about to look to see where the cameras were, but he stopped himself – that would be a serious mistake. Never make your adversary aware of your thoughts.

EXOSPACE, AND BEING SNEAKY

Cort knew he was exposed to something very dangerous. Some tiles had already been removed. Ahead, through a small area of missing tiles, he could see furry seething deep darkness. The Great Karoshi actuator wanted the tiles that were removed to be stacked in a certain way, to limit exposure of the ship's insides to what was outside.

As Cort worked, he knew he was going to die. The function actuator was making him stack the tiles behind himself – when Cort finished and the machinery moved forward into this space, the only place for Cort would be out into that blackness.

Another tile, another moment closer to his death. There was no point suffering the terror of the pain that happened when he refused to work – another crew would be here in ten days, to finish whatever Cort failed to do. Ten days. He knew he couldn't go that long without drinking anything. The machine would suck him dry the moment he finished moving the tiles – that was why he didn't have to fit back into the safety of the ship's hull – he would be going back as water through a tube, just like Uncle John.

It was time to risk being sneaky, and hope it didn't catch him doing it.

Cort lifted the next tile loose, and a second tile in front of him straight after, keeping the second tile hidden by his own body, and as he turned to crawl back he let the other tile go, out into that blackness. No searing pain, or that feeling like his insides were being sliced out by a big knife – the Great Karoshi function actuator hadn't seen him do it.

One hidden tile out into nothing, and the other visible one back into the stacks, one tile out, one tile back, one tile out and one tile back – the ship was going to be minus a few parts by the time Cort finished his work. Its protective nose cone would be incomplete. The next slave wouldn't have enough tiles for the reassembly.

ONE LAST JUMP

Hours of steady work had happened. Cort was tired. Very tired. The large piece of machinery moved one tiny jerk forwards between the stacks of tiles, and stopped. There was going to be one last tile in the way, at the big opening Cort had made in the nose cone.

It was waiting. Cort knew this was the end.

His thoughts seemed to be thinking very slowly. He decided he would hold that last tile tight up to his heart, and hope the water sucker hit it instead of him. He knew this was hopeless, everything was hopeless, but he couldn't stop himself from trying. And then he decided he would do one last really quick jump, moving as fast as he could, taking the water in his body away from the huge machine that was the Great Karoshi. He would jump from the nose cone, out into the seething blackness of exospace.

A whimpering feeling was happening inside him, telling him it didn't want to go, he didn't want to die. Not ready, not yet. He hadn't had enough fun, he hadn't been loved enough. He had to go. None of the people who cared about him were alive any more – he was waiting for a happiness that would never be real again. Not for him. He balanced on his toes, ready to jump out into the blackness, one tile in his hand, held tight over his heart.

ABANDON SHIP

Walking quickly down the main passage, Captain Thomas in front, Litmus, and then Mark. The Captain turned around.

'Your book and Hoppy and Floppy Litmus, and your watch Sam. That is all. No,' he said, holding his arm out to stop Mark rushing past, 'We stay together. We get them together, on the way. When the speed shuttle leaves, this hull will probably go banana shaped – they are going to use us to push themselves off into space. They need to leave so quickly that they cannot be chased and caught. When that happens the soft cargo's hull structure will be compromised, and we may need to get you to somewhere safe in a hurry. You are not only a humanoidian, you are also still very much a fragilicus.'

As they hurried Litmus was tapping Mark with a hand, to get his attention.

'You know what it is? A fragilicus? I know tinycus because I was one, and minicus ones like me, but not that

170

fragilicus one. I asked our IPE. She said half way to finished growing. That wasn't very interesting, so I asked a polite what you were. He said "silly little wanker". Funny? That's funny? I asked IPE, I ordered her even, but she wouldn't do a meaning for wanker, so you can tell me.'

'No,' said Mark.

'Litmus,' said Captain Thomas frustrated, 'Now? Is now really a good time to tease him?'

'Every time's a good time,' said Litmus happily. 'I will get your special thing Planetboy. I'm taking a short cut.' There was a loud bash noise, a big hole in the bulkhead beside them, and Litmus was gone.

'Indestructible Being,' said the captain, 'Lateral thinking. We don't need these walls any more, or this deck. You run for the Magnificus Royale. Say "up" when you get there. And Sam? Hurry.'

The captain suddenly shot up through the deck above, towards his own cabin, leaving a hole with snapped wires and broken pipes dangling from it. They were wrecking the joint while Mark was still in it. Mark started running to the starboard gangway.

As Mark ran down the main passage of the Soft Cargo for the last time, he could see why it was called 'Soft'. Everything was arranged for the comfort of the crew – the width of the passages, the cabin doors being doors in doorways – full walk through height, not bulkhead hatches that were basically oval holes in walls, so you had to duck your head, and step over a hatch hole rim to get into a cabin space, and – softest of all, the air vents that blew breezes here and there so you didn't feel like you were suffocating in a tin can. He'd started the day saying goodbye to James, and he was ending it saying goodbye to their home. It was hard to believe that a thing as big and stable as this was about to become a mangled dark broken mess, adrift forever in space. Soon he would be boarding a new place to call home, that tiny little seeder – a three hundred year old ship that used to be some sort of weapon. Carted here and there in secret, and hidden away for the last one hundred and eighty years, would it, could it still fly?

The Soft Cargo suddenly shuddered. The lights dimmed even more for a moment, the deck beneath his feet wobbled, then slanted away from him making him run faster but crazy out of control. He skidded to a crooked stop keeping his balance, and then everything seemed normal again, except now the deck was leaning, going the other way, up hill. Mark felt a large hand shoving him unstoppably forward.

'That was the speed shuttle leaving,' said Captain Thomas.

'Very soon this internal atmosphere will be punctured by the helpod, and we need you to be somewhere safe by then. Take Floppy and Hoppy for me, and get yourself running again. It isn't far.'

As Mark began running, Hoppy the Happy Frog in one hand, Floppy Bunny in the other, a strange loud clicking started coming from the walls. Something was tapping the outer skin of the soft cargo, like it was a drum. The clicks were getting closer together, little by little, sounding more urgent with each change.

'Final count down,' said Captain Thomas, like he was thinking about changing his plans.

Mark realised he was by himself – his feet were the only ones making running noises on the deck. Captain Thomas wasn't coming. He looked back along the passage. The captain was standing at the last turn, watching for Litmus.

'Say "up" when you get there,' Captain Thomas yelled to Mark, 'and keep running.'

The clicks were very close together, almost continuous. The soft cargo was tilting, groaning, shrieking. Somewhere its hull was tearing. Mark felt himself getting lighter, until his feet were brushing on the passage deck, not thumping along it. The artificial gravity was failing. He crammed the two soft toys into one gripping hand, a frog leg and a bunny ear tight inside his fingers, and began pulling himself along the passage by the sidewall handrail with his other hand as he ran. He reached the starboard gangway primary hatch almost flying instead of running. He didn't have the code for it. He stood there panting, tiptoes still touching on the deck, waiting for whatever would happen next. He began to float, Sam's purple uniform rising on him. He could feel his tee shirt and underpants drifting around over his skin, and the tops of his feet could feel his ship's runners over them. His socks and ship's runners felt more like gloves for his feet than shoes. His free hand was hovering over the key pad, about to try combinations of symbols and numbers, but he didn't even know where to start. Mark looked back over his shoulder, which made all of him drift on a silly angle to everything around him. The captain was coming, straight towards him like a train.

The keypad was dead. Captain Thomas put his fist into the bulkhead, tore out the whole door lock mechanism, and pulled the large door out into the passageway, like it was tinfoil.

Mark felt his body being taken hold of and thrown towards the Magnificus Royale, he yelled 'up me', and next moment he was inside, inside a place that was calm and safe.

'Go go go,' Litmus was yelling as he shot up into the Magnificus Royale.

The captain was with him, and ran towards where wall tiles were buckling out into a large console covered in parameter setting images. Litmus shoved Mark away to one side, like he was inconveniently placed furniture, and then stood like he was about to throw a spear as far as he could.

'Everything on. Everything up. Everything Magnificci,' Litmus yelled.

HOPELESSLY OUTNUMBERED

There was a whizzing sound like a huge spring letting go, and then Mark couldn't move. He felt frozen solid but not cold. The captain and Litmus were racing around inside the seeder controls area doing things, their bodies just fast blurs to his eyes. He knew time was going by, but his view of it was doing it very quickly, and then a Litmus hand was reaching towards him, slower and slower the closer it got, and suddenly Mark was Sam again, and back in real time. The captain was in the middle of talking.

'...a ripped apart drifting mess. One down. The helpod is linked and under tow, ready to be ramped and flashed with us. We just need a slightly larger particle-spray bow wave, to keep it hidden. Done. Testing communications now. They're cheering on board the helpod, so things are working. Alito, I would like them to assist the Mandelbrot on the way past? I signalled Commander Yorker that she can withdraw her vessel, but they are trapped, surrounded. The Mandelbrot is only one ship, and they are horrifically outnumbered. The Democratzia Capitalisto master ships will arrive soon, decelerating into the battle. They are the ones we can't pull apart with our three hundred year old technology. The Mandelbrot's crew will surely die? We are finished with them, but helping them escape can happen on our way past. We won't lose time?'

'Allowed,' said Litmus, 'but only if you take on all hostile ships. I mean it. We will test our weapons.'

'The helpod? It might be enough to throw the balance? Commander Yorker said just one battle platform down should be enough for her to get the Mandelbrot safely away?' suggested the captain.

'And us, we're doing it too,' said Litmus, like "end of discussion".

'Yes Litmus,' said Captain Thomas, as if he was laughing at himself, 'everything out there except the Mandelbrot will be vaporised, percussed to tiny pieces, imploded, bits torn off them, and all your other favourites.'

'He's cheeky,' said Litmus to Mark, 'I have to say "everything", because he goes all soft and wants to try saving people. I wouldn't mind, but we are rescuing your scout friend next. That leaves no time for being nice to baddies. And, probably we'll just dint them and hurt their pride a bit anyway, while the Mandelbrot sneaks off. Our weapons are designed to confuse, disorientate, disable and relocate. We don't do "I hate you, so here's some pain and suffering". That's really where "seeder" comes from – CDDR – Confuse, Disorientate, and the rest of it. Did you knowed that already?'

'No,' said Mark.

'I'll tell you more later, I'm busy now,' said Litmus.

As far as Mark could see, Litmus was just standing in the middle of the controls area, doing nothing. The captain was working away on a huge screen, sometimes frantically. Occasionally Captain Thomas would spread his fingers to check his work, and some of the flickering numbers, lines and arcs on the screen would change into images of something out in space. A weapons platform with a pontoon breaking away, or a strange looking battle cruiser spinning around awkwardly, because something was making its motors malfunction.

'We've never did this, not a real go of it, but we've did lots of practice ones,' said Litmus to Mark.
'Grandpa calls me Alito when he thinks I'm doing right, and Litmus when he wishes I would reconsider, but I am The Emprino, and I only reconsider if I want to. Grandpa, the left one. They haven't been banged up. You'll have to use a different weapon.'

'Yes...no, the helpod has done it. They haven't learnt yet what a vicious tiny ball of technology it is. I beg your pardon Alito – this has been a wise test. There was only one way to find out which weapons no longer work on our enemies.'

'Grandpa, we know she is strong, but you will order Commander Yorker to run away now. When she is safe we can leave, and then there will be no more damage and death. Soon our adversaries will be got more. Then we will be somewhere else, because I want that.'

'Yes Alito.'
The captain continued working. The lines arcs and numbers moving in groups were getting more frantic, and happening all over the big screen, and the flashes of picture views of what was going on out there were getting faster and faster.
'Sam, pay attention. Watch what I do. The Magnificci designed their first tier weapons to limit an adversary's ability to be aggressive. I move them, I disorientate them, I confuse their targeting equipment, I pull exposed parts loose but not free of the main hulls of their ships... We are too late. This is no longer a skirmish. The master ships are arriving. If we stay we lose everything.'

'Then I'm keeping it – I want that – we are taking the mandelthing with us,' said Litmus, his voice going higher and concerned.

'Alito, can we taildrag a craft as big as the Mandelbrot? Alito? I need a quick answer.'

'Yes Grandpa. I want that.'

'I know you want that,' muttered Captain Thomas under his breath, 'but that wasn't my question.'

'IPE: prepare,' said Litmus loudly, 'guide them in, linked them up, and then ramped and flashed us.'

Litmus pulled Mark by the arm, until their heads were the same height, then whispered,

'We are in trouble. A reversion is coming, for him. Even pretend wrecking ships makes him sad, for all the people inside, good or bad. He's not sad. He is splattering baddies all over the place in a super hurry like it's fun. I thought his caringness is gone to sleep first.'

'Okay?' said Mark, meaning he sort of understood, but why the "in trouble" part.

'It won't be like me. He's been putting it off for all our time together, in case I get left alone in the universe. That's a hundred and lots of years. I think he will sleeped for days and days, a week, a whole year even, and I thought that's going to happened us, really soon.'

'All right,' whispered Mark, 'but then who's going to do all that?'

'You,' said Litmus.

Mark felt like his head had just been emptied. Him? Litmus giggled, his eyes looking sneaky happy.

'Us, dopey, Planetboy and Alito Magnificus. We are, we will. I want that.'

The captain was definitely winding down. He was moving slower and slower as he worked on the screens, pointing, tapping, and dragging. He turned, and looked towards Mark and Litmus.

'I'm sorry,' he said, his eyes dull like he was dreaming about somewhere else, 'It is now, and I don't think a moment, a name, and a hug are going to get me through this.'

He stood up straight and then stopped, completely still, like a toy with no power left in it.

The long spindly arms that had thrown Mark around for his seeder crew medical test came from above, and collected the body.

'In, quick,' said Litmus to Mark, 'Two steps forward. I will tell what. NOW Planetboy. Put your finger there, drag it to here, press, tap, lift away, and now over there, the one that's lots of numbers in a ball – meaning Freedom Collective flagship with big weapons and lots of crew, finger and thumb separate on the screen and roll your hand, now drag them over here into this one. If it's layers of numbers, instead of like a big ball, then its a weapons platform. They are all tangled up now. All these arcs over here are Mandelbrot weapon streams, cracking things open. We need them to keep firing while we get ready to run. They are the reason no-one is targeting us. Look, more than fifteen Freedom Collective destroyers undamaged still, and there's three new ones slowing down as they getted here. That's like thirty-seven against three, and those darknesses coming over there are the biggest baddies, trying to hide from IPE. Forty against three. They are big cheaters.'

Litmus reached past Mark and did some weird finger moves on the screen for himself.

'IPE, you will hurry a big lot. And, fit a headset on Planetboy.' Something got clipped over Mark's ear, and now he could hear Commander Yorker, asking urgently,

'Do we have comms, do we have comms?'

'Yes,' said Mark, 'Litmus wants you to keep attacking, while we tow you out of here?'

'If you can do that do it soon, or else I'm going in all weapons firing, and taking out as many as I can. We are starting to take damage, and we won't be able to make even the tiniest dint on what's coming.'

'Tell her my IPE will codinate the move,' said Litmus, 'I'm busy letting off a chook bomb.'

'Co-ordinate?'

'Use my words, or I will maked you sorry Planetboy,' said Litmus looking stroppy.

'Our IPE will codinate,' began Mark.

'Understood. All linking data to be codinated by the Magnificus Royale IPE,' said Commander Yorker.

Mark understood now. He might be fourteen, and Litmus only seven, but this was Litmus's reality, and Litmus knew a lot better than he did what was going on. Codinate was what the little snot had said, and codinate was what he'd meant. Probably as in do secret code for things to happen between the three ships – the small helpod, the Mandelbrot, and the tiny Magnificus Royale.

'Sorry Litmus.'

'You learned fast,' said Litmus back, 'You know what chooked is? Bird things that lay eggs for eating. That's what's a chook. They don't go completely chook, the captains and admirals and crews, because it's just to scare them – I chooked them with my magnetic brainwave bomb, and all their faces make themselves go like a chook's, with a beak shape of their lips and everything, but they get over it later. It's hard to tell someone to go firing weapons and stuff if your voice just goes burk bagurk out of a beak shape. I invented that weapon.'

Litmus pressed with a thumb on a big ball of numbers and symbols, then drew his arm across the screen.

'Them ones just goed three stars away. I would do more but we are only little. Our power would run down, and I need it for next.'

Commander Yorker was talking through the comms so fast it was like she was calling a race.

'Just quickly while you lot are organising whatever you're organising – this battlefleet weren't here to block us – there's ditched gash, by that I mean garbage they've disposed of out into space, and it's been drifting away from them. It's a fair way out now, so these ships have been in this exact position for weeks. They've opened up a clear space through their middle, even though that makes no sense strategically, from a battle plan point. They are up to something they think is even more important than fighting us. The cleared space makes a line back through a mess that looks like wreckage of something gigantic, though our equipment is showing that wreckage at all different wreck dates, over a couple of hundred years. That wreckage goes in an arc out into space, both ways. Nothing could be that big, or spread wreckage that far? It's like something monstrously large has been going around and around in a huge circle, and dropping bits off. Really strange. Forwards, that cleared space goes to the same star clear path we're aiming for. Nothing there at the moment that we can see. Just thought you should know.'

Litmus stopped still, but Mark could tell his brain was racing.

'They are trying to get to exospace first,' he squeaked, 'A ship will come flying out of the last star shell really really fast, and then it will launched something to go even faster, to catched us later. IPE, now. We have to go now.'

RAMPING

The spring letting go sound was a whole lot louder this time, like it had a fair bit more to drag, and Mark felt the occasional shudder.

'Not attacks on us,' explained Litmus, 'That's us sort of treading on their ships so we can push off. Sometimes they get out of the way a bit, the first time. We're ramping good now. Make them all report in, to you. Our ships I mean.'

'Hello? Everyone okay?' said Mark.

'No!' said Litmus, laughing and frustrated, 'like this – "Report. Now." – see? You're not asking, you're saying "this is what will happen next, you telling me stuff".'

'Mandelbrot in your tailslip and accepting closer link. No serious damage some injuries no crew loss.'

'Helpod linked and ready to flash.'

'Now,' said Litmus to Mark, 'While we are ramping up for three ships, you find out what damage the Mandelbrot has got. I will be really angry if we tear them in half when we flash. Planetboy say yes, so I know you heard me in your brain.'

'Yes,' said Mark.

FLASHING

Flashing wasn't as flash as Mark thought it would be. The Magnificus Royale was a tiny ship, and it was flashing itself, the small helpod, and the great fat ugly Mandelbrot, from the middle of a space battle, to somewhere far away. It shuddered, it shook, and there were clean high pitched screaming noises, like machinery was functioning perfectly, but at its extreme capability. The shuddering got worse, and worse, and so did the screaming. Now they were leaning one way, then the other, like the seeder was trying to work its way up to high speed. The shudders got so huge Mark couldn't see or hear properly.

'It's okay, this is okay,' Litmus was yelling, 'I towed my whole part of the castle away one day when I was really annoyed. My ship wobbled hard a whole lot worse then. My slippers came off me even.'

Mark's breath was getting knocked out of him. He had to hold his arms in tight, crossed against his chest, to stop them flying around, and then he couldn't, and they started flailing all over the place like he was pretending to be a windmill. His clothes were yanking and flapping everywhere on him, like they were in a wild windstorm, and now the top half of them was coming off over his head, leaving his arms caught so he couldn't keep his balance. He fell over backwards and sat down on the deck, tangled in his own half off jacket and pants.

Suddenly the shuddering was over. The Magnificus Royale rose up, and began humming smoothly, riding through space on an even keel. Mark could tell his shoes had come off, but he couldn't see, not until he got his head back out through the neck hole in his tee shirt, and purple uniform jacket. He wriggled his head out and his arms back to where they were supposed to be. His legs were still caught in a tangled mess of clothing. His eyes and his ears were taking a while to settle. Litmus was jumping around like an excited frog, and yelling,

'We did it, we did it, we did it'.

Now he was looking down at Mark, and laughing, going more silly than usual even.

'Your pants fell down. Your pants fell down.'

'Yeah yeah so what, shut up,' said Mark, sitting on the deck and pulling his pants back on, 'If you had the shit shaken out of you your dacks would head for the deck too.'

'Didn't?' said Litmus.

'Made your sock come half off even,' he added, mildly interested in Mark's untidy condition, 'all off, coz that one's over there. Bunny suits are the best, and that's why,' he said, 'and they're not even purple.'

It was funny, thought Mark getting his socks and ship's runners back on, how once you'd been around Litmus for a while, his idiotic comments actually made sense. This time, Litmus was saying there was a reason he liked his bunny suit, and also that he was impressed with the colour purple, now his eyes were seeing colour again. In the air in front of the big screen the IPE was asking, in plain white letters, 'Open communications? Are you ready?'

'Wait,' ordered Litmus, 'Planetboy, go see Grandpa. I'll do this stuff. IPE, I'll talked at them now. Report.'

Mark could hear his headset had gone to half volume. The helpod said it was in good shape. The Mandelbrot had some damage, because the Magnificus Royale had come across a huge battle cruiser trying to block the escape route, and Litmus had bashed it a good sideswipe with the Mandelbrot on the way past. As he listened, Mark could feel his purple uniform half on him in an untidy mess. It felt really good. Being Sam right now felt amazing. Sweet fantastic. The skin was smooth, and every muscle felt like it was just the right shape, all of them, his hips, his lips, his arms, his legs, even his eyes felt hungry happy with themselves. Being this was exciting. There were new letters forming in the air in the middle of the controls area. They were only displaying information from the Mandelbrot, but they were no longer white – they were big bright mid-summer morning blue ones. The IPE knew. Mark wished feeling this good could be a private thing. Life on board was going to be difficult. There wasn't going to be a single moment, day or night, when he would be really alone. Even if it was the middle of a night watch and Litmus was asleep somewhere, the IPE would still know. Mark turned around, faintly embarrassed. The tiles of the aft bulkhead were reshaping. A hatch doorway came into existence. He stepped over the lip and went through the bulkhead hatch to find what had happened to the captain.

FOREVER IS A LONG TIME

The cabin was a small room, white walls, flowers in a vase on a small bedside cabinet, and an open window to a view outside. Mark knew that view couldn't be real – the outer hull of the Magnificus Royale would have to be very close to the other side of that cabin wall, but he could feel a lazy hazy Spring air breeze drifting in through that window. The captain was wearing paisley pyjamas, and sitting up in a bed.

'Hello?' said Captain Thomas, like he was pleasantly surprised.

Mark could see floating letters, a back view of them. The captain was reading out loud.

'My name is Axel Thomas. I am...convalescing. Sam is not my little bother...Sam is not at school with me...Sam is not my grandson. He is in my future. I will gently lean my memories forwards, until I can understand his presence, and then I must explain to him how we will survive this great challenge.'

Mark watched the captain, as the captain looked back at him. The eyes seemed to be a pipeline to the captain's conscious thoughts. They were going from not really anybody at home in that head, to the look Mark was used to, Captain Thomas's intelligence watching and caring as you existed in front of him.

'Ah Sam,' said the captain finally, 'so it did happen. Litmus, what a crazy dream he is. And you, you are so young fresh alive. I can feel the joy of you from here, living each first time ever moment in your life.'

Mark felt awkward, and self aware, of his black fuzzy hair, the child-smooth chocolate skin he was in, and the neat little muscles thin arms, body, and slim legs of being Sam. A shy soft half-grin was spreading his mouth. That was embarrassing, like it was him admitting he'd been found out for being something. He realised it wasn't Sammy's fault – if Mark had been in his Mark Planetti space orphan body, then he would have felt awkward about the haystack of half-blond straight hair, the budding young muscles, and again – the thin arms, body, and slim ace feeling legs that were part of him being young. The captain's thoughts seemed to drift for a while, then he said 'purple' softly, like it was something his memories were wondering about, and then he was there in his eyes again.

'I must not waste any of this time with you. The Magnificus Royale IPE is going to rock me back and forwards between my past and this present, until I am in working trim. There will be long periods of sleep, as I cope with putting things in an order I can understand. I must not be jarred, shocked, or scared, by reports of desperate situations being lived out by you, in your current moment of eternity. It will damage my recovery, and I would not be able to help, or advise wisely?'

'Yes Sir,' said Mark.

'This room will sometimes seem very odd when you enter. That is because this ship is going to give me what I need, to survive the emotional journey I am on. There will be moving shadows of people I love...I loved – they no longer exist, there are only memories left – and there will be the sounds, smells, and forgotten lights of day to go with them, to go with those people. Don't try to take part in a world that seems to be. Just stay yourself. Wait quietly while I extricate my intelligence from wherever, from whenever, from whoever it is dreaming.

'Soon you will be a little like Litmus, and a lot like me. We are different, us three, from every other living thing. We will always be different. We cannot be changed back to a life that is fresh and new. I will explain now, so that one day, when it begins to happen to you, you will understand.

'The people around us live their days out, wandering from shallow moment to shallow moment, the endless noise of being alive clogging their thoughts, but we are different, we listen, for things we will never hear again. I tried to heal Litmus. He would...something in the air of a day would remind him, and he would stop, in the middle of what he was doing, and wait. It would be a day like any day, a day like a day when his mother was just around the corner. He would listen for the flavour of her in his thoughts, and cling desperately to whatever he could get. Sometimes it would be a morning, and the fresh light would remind him of something his father was doing once, long ago. His mind was visiting things that happened over a century in the past, and trying to stay there. It was so hard to bear, watching him silently wrecking his little heart. Then, one summer afternoon, I was pouring us drinks. On Blue Skies One this was, and I heard that noise, that Kath used to make swinging her foot as she read. I didn't want it to stop. I believed, almost, that she was there, just there, in the armchair behind me. Suddenly, it was important, more important than anything in my life, more important than my life. I couldn't let go of that near to her feeling. All my thoughts were bent on hanging on, but still it drained away, back into the afternoon. I turned around. Litmus was horse-riding the chair arm, and watching me. He said, "Who was it?". I said, "Kath". He looked into my eyes, and said, "Now you know how it feels".

'A child of seven showed me the pain of being old, and it isn't worn out joints, tired skin, or the aches from muscles trying to do what they used to do easily. It is the part that cares about things, about places, people, family pets, about everything. Everything. You can't keep it. A day comes when you know you should have let go, let go long ago, but you know even now that you can't, and then your memory, holding on as tight as it can, starts to lose its grip, and that, that is what really hurts, losing the tiny tired pieces of thoughts that were all you had left, of everything you were. It hurts so much to keep them, but without them there is nothing, you are nothing any more.'

The captain's eyes were looking at Mark, begging him to understand, and then they dulled. The words had stopped, and the thoughts behind them were slowly fading away. The eyelids closed.

Axel Thomas was sleeping now.

The room faded, until it was a softly lit small bare ship's cabin.

The IPE was putting words up in the air in front of Mark, but then she changed her mind, and secret worded instead, softly in his ears.

'He may not get better. I am doing my very best. The Emprino has ordered "I want that", and so it must be, if it can be, that Axel not leave us forever. Not yet.'

LITMUS THE BATTLE PLANNER

Mark walked slowly back to the controls area, wondering which of the captain's words Litmus needed to know. He decided on saying "He's sleeping. I think he'll be okay". That would do for now. One thing was sure, the Magnificus Royale and its crew would have to fly and fight without Captain Thomas for a while. A long while.

Mark was stepping over the lip of the bulkhead hatch into the controls area, and here came Litmus.

'The mandelthing has a big fat bum,' he said, 'and it's sticking out of our particle spray. Bad things will finded it. And then they will catched us. So I am codinating for a new weapon, to stop them chasing me. You have to help. We can't rescue your pilot if we are only lots of deadness.'

'Hurry up Planetboy, and your one better be good,' sang out Litmus, 'coz mine's gooder.'

'I'm ready now,' said Mark, 'You said you can relocate their ships? Mine is we send their ships back to their home planets. Wait wait – I know that would take a whole lot of power. We're towing the Mandelbrot, so she's not using her main motor. We make her power-up to the max, a battleship's got to have heaps of power, and then use that power to start throwing ships and weapons platforms back to where they came from.'

'Okay. It doesn't really work like that. My weapons are mostly like really tiny tentacles of invisible plasma stuff, that get inside how they drive things, and adjust all what they're doing. The Freedom Collective planets are too far anyway,' said Litmus, 'but we can do your one mixed with mine? We can do a big swerve, and go past a recharge dockyard. They are really, really big, with lots of everything their ships use to attack everyone with. Recharge dockyards have to stay still in space or big accidents happen. I'm going to confuse that thing's mooring matrix, by making what stars it thinks it see'd all go funny, and then I'll do some of your powering their motors wrong. They'll go all wobbly. We are small and sneaky and can slip past? Even the mandelthing is a small ship compared to the Freedom Collective battle ships, they're like huge monster things, that would upset everything. They are all chasing us. There will be a huge pileup. I will get people now, so I can tell them I want that.'

LITMUS TELEPORTS PEOPLE

The big screen had a different controls image at one side, and Litmus began doing the usual press tap and swipe motions there, between three close balls of data numbers and symbols. A surprised young Ship of The Line crewman suddenly appeared out of nowhere, wearing only his underpants.

'You are a wrong thing. You can wait for going back,' said Litmus after giving him a look, 'I'm busy.'

Litmus tried again, poking a little bendy finger into the screen, hard this time. A young crewman appeared with one leg in his pyjama pants. He was in the middle of stepping in with the other.

'No,' growled Litmus, really annoyed, and starting to look a bit ratty.

Another even harder finger poke. Another of the Mandelbrot's crew, this time a lady wet from a shower, holding a towel, which she got busy wrapping around herself. Litmus was getting a hard cranky look to his eyes. Commander Burnett appeared next, in full battle uniform.

'NO,' howled Litmus angrily, 'I don't want the fat one.'

'Shush shush shush,' said Commander Burnett like a doting grandmother.

He crouched down beside Litmus, 'Explain the controls to me, and I will do my best. The Mandelbrot has a scrambling feature, that might be randomising your weapon's focus.'

'Nothing,' declared Litmus, 'Randy-what-ever you saided my weapons. All my weapons are Magnificci weapons. They DO NOT RANDOM. Only if they are randoming you.'

'Alito, Alito, I do understand. Now let's see if we can't get the right people to behave themselves into your ship. Oh, I see. We could reset your screen, for viewing by someone smaller than Captain Thomas. We are looking at one angle, and your finger is poking from another. I think they will be ready now. Who would you like?'

'I want Captain Murray and Commander Yorker,' said Litmus, sounding like he was doing his best to get over wanting to have a tantrum.

'Show me which symbols they are?' asked Commander Burnett gently.

Litmus was sooking, pointing and baby talk muttering. Mark watched, and wished that if he was ever a dad, that he could be as patient and as good at it as Commander Burnett. Here came Captain Murray, and Commander Yorker, both looking momentarily stunned as they arrived.

'Grandpa's having a rest,' said Litmus turning to face them, 'and we're having a meeting right now. Them ones have to go back, because they forgot their clothes.'

Litmus told Mark to stand behind his chair and watch.

'You have to do your best go of being Grandpa,' he said quietly over his shoulder, as the others sat down around the strategy table.

'He doesn't say much, he just watches for things I miss.'

ESCAPE

There was no time for swerving anywhere. Full continuous acceleration was happening, so the dying scout ship pilot, somewhere far away on the other side of many galaxies, could be reached before it was too late.

A see through glowing green image of the huge armada of Freedom Collective battle ships was in the air above the Magnificus Royale's strategy table. The Democratzia Capitalisto master ship darknesses had arrived slowing into the battle from one side, and were now behind the main armada, getting speed up again to join the chase.

'There was a ship on our long range imaging equipment,' said Commander Yorker, 'Right where you said, coming out of the last star shell. We can't see it now because linking up with you has blinded some of our gear, but if that ship continued accelerating, it would reach us almost right when we get to light speed, assuming that is even possible.'

'No. I don't want that,' said Litmus pointing at Commander Yorker, like it was her fault.

Captain Murray put the tips of his fingers together, thinking.

'How fast are we travelling, right now?'

'That much', said Litmus, pointing at a number that IPE made appear in the air, this time for everyone to see.

'Well, perhaps Alito, I think it is too late for aggressive action, from them or us. That ship is still too far away, and we are leaving this lot, this battlefleet, far behind. Nothing large loaded down with weapons can accelerate like this.'

Litmus was waving an arm, with a grubby little finger at the end of it, pointing around the table.

'Humanoidians must listen. They have a ray cannon ship. We didn't get broke yet because they can't charge up with their mouth open, and my IPE has made their firing tube iris work back to front. If they fix that we are toast. Soon we will go out of range of holding them open, and then they can close, charge up, reopen and fire us until we are all very burnt and not good feeling.'

'How soon?' asked Commander Burnett.

'Three Blue Skies One minutes,' said Litmus, 'and we won't make it to exospace with enough fastness.'

'There aren't any cannon ships, we've done every check. They can hide from visual, but we still get them on charged particle emissions,' said Commander Yorker.

'Which can be faked,' said Commander Burnett, 'Alito, what detection method do the Magnificci use, for these infernal things?'

'Everything in the universe has a heaviness, even out in space. Bigger things attract smaller things, and smaller things are attracted by bigger things. When there is a whole battle fleet, my IPE can measure between them exactly what is what, and this time, what is, is that ray cannons are the heaviest armoured things in the whole of everywhere, so that ship at the back made to look like a stores container ship for your looking machines, is a ray cannon hiding from you, and I want it busted.'

'You want it "busted",' said Commander Yorker, with a happy look on her face, 'For once I am with you. Send me back aboard my ship for one minute, and if you really do have its iris wide open, and they are trying to gas-up to fire, I will bust it for you,' she said, 'Like good chocolates, they are hard on the outside, and soft in the centre. We've been getting this little trick ready for a while – since we thought we were hopelessly outnumbered. I will jettison a semi-camouflaged speed shuttle, not full of our crew begging for mercy – full of self targeting nasties, and wait, wait,' she added, because both Captain Murray and Commander Burnett wanted to jump into the conversation with objections, 'I will launch in its image shadow a full range of non programmable incendiaries, that will always go where they are aimed at when they are first released, regardless of who tries what on them along the way. Our way in to inside their indestructible hull shell is through their open weapons port. Time's ticking?'

Movement was happening in the armada, ships being brought around sideways across the front of the "stores container ship". Attention around the table was back on the armada image above it.

'As if that's going to protect it,' said Commander Yorker.

'If they drift up against the cannon's armoured hull, they can block the tube end, the cannon can charge, and then we have a serious problem,' said Captain Murray.

'But…' began Commander Burnett shocked, 'they would still be there when they fired, and all the ships' crews would die, on those six large ships.'

'The Democratzia don't care,' said Captain Murray, 'because those crews are from Freedom Collective planets that have been destroyed "for the common good". The people in those ships probably don't even know they no longer have a world to go home to. Sooner or later the Democratzia Capitalisto were going to turn them all into fresh bags of water anyway.'

'Those ship movements are confirmation that the iris is open. All I need is a yes from anyone here,' said Commander Yorker, 'and that ray cannon is no more. If I do it in the next thirty seconds, I think I will manage not to involve those other ships in the carnage.'

'I want that,' said Litmus loudly like an order, and Commander Yorker was gone, her voice echoing in empty air, because she was muttering to herself as she left – 'This "exospace" idea is fucking bullshit. And as for "I want that"…' Mark had a feeling her next word would have been a growl of grim frustration. Hearing a small boy say "I want that" really annoyed her something fierce.

Litmus was considering her parting comments.

'That word is yuckier than poo in your mouth,' he said disapproving.

Nobody at the strategy table had an answer to that except Mark.

'Exospace?' he whispered next to Litmus's ear,

'or…bullshit?'

'You know what word,' growled Litmus without turning around, 'and it wasn't them ones.'

Commander Burnett and Captain Murray were poking fingers into the image above the table, telling each other about the types of ships, and where they were from.

'That ship there, ex Star Alliance. It means they have fallen, and will have only one hostage planet left. That ship has to fight for the Freedom Collective, or the last living world of the Star Alliance, and the last of their people, will be destroyed.'

'It breaks my heart,' said Commander Burnett.

'Next opportunity we have to get a message out, we must tell home to send a rescue mission, to help anyone who survived on that planet to sneak away,' Captain Murray was saying.

Mark could see in front of Litmus's eyes the IPE screening a message, that only he and Litmus could see – 'I am letting in messages from something very small a long way off. The helpod is waiting for those messages – it is ordering silence from the Mandelbrot so it can hear. Also the Mandelbrot has launched the speed shuttle. It is only supposed to be half camouflaged, but I can't see it now it has left. I am sorry Emprino, some things I am are too old for this battle. What is your will?'

'We will watch and wait,' said Litmus out loud.

'What's that?' asked Mark, pointing over Litmus's head, his finger going into the image above the table, out in front of the armada, 'Is that little speck of things the speed shuttle and the other weapons?'

'Sam, that little speck is us. Our three ships,' said Captain Murray.

'There is a plus side,' he continued, 'We are so insignificant that they find it hard to target us. These fine lines of different coloured light spraying out all over the place are targeting fingers, looking for any sign of us. On the down side all our ships would fit into one of their loading bays, and they know roughly where we are, so they are going to melt everything inside the search arc, if they get that cannon firing.'

Commander Yorker was back.

'Done,' she said satisfied.

'And now we wait,' said Captain Murray, 'for a result.'

'There won't be time for a follow up attack?' said Commander Yorker looking around the table, 'If we slowed just a tad? A brave move, but then we would be sure we got the job done.'

Mark had that old horrible feeling, of needing to get on with life, before something came along and ruined everything.

'No,' he said, his voice at Litmus's ear, almost whining from the sad fear he felt soaking through him.

More than anything he didn't want to wait around. His scout ship pilot needed rescuing, and these three ships needed to be somewhere else, somewhere safer for them and their crews. Anything that slowed those two things down was bad, even if it meant making sure they finished things properly where they were.

'There will be no going slowed,' said Litmus, 'My Sam is wise about not waiting for bad things to happened him.'

'Very well,' said Captain Murray.

'Here we go,' said Commander Burnett eagerly, 'look, they're wobbling, shuddering.'

'And spreading out,' said Captain Murray, 'Alito, please instruct your IPE to prepare for evasive action. The only reason we haven't had incoming, is because they were relying on their cannon. They will now fire anything and everything, like throwing handfuls of rocks at someone.'

'You said before? And it's true,' said Litmus, 'They can throw all they like. Only the ray cannon is fast enough to reach us now, and we are still faster-ing.'

The Armada ships were swerving around all over the place, catching up with their own weapon discharges, and trying to avoid them.

'They have never tried to chase down anything this fast before,' said Commander Burnett, pleased with the result.

'Three times already they tried to catch us actually,' said Litmus, 'with extra special racing ships, but they never, and then there was a story about a fourth huge ship, but they didn't built it anywhere. That big and we would have knowed about it, Grandpa and me, coz we were watching.'

'Regards that, there is one other matter,' said Captain Murray.

He was looking at Alito, as if he was considering what, or how much, to say.

'Alito, the helpod is tracking that ship you suspected might exist. It is now off our port rear quarter. A long way off, just coming through the side of a gaseous star. It has been accelerating through a long string of wreckage, we think most likely it is using the wreckage to hide whatever it's up to. It has been on the same trajectory since before the Democratzia Capitalisto were aware we were here, and it hasn't altered course at all, so I don't think it has anything to do with us. I mention it now because we have confirmed some unlikely data – that ship has been struggling to pick up speed, leaving behind a trail of jettisoned fuel cases. It is travelling extremely fast, faster than us, but because of our greater acceleration, it is likely we will reach universe exit speed first, that, or at the same time. Captain Thomas ordered me to instruct you of all the facts, should there be any unexplained activity, especially anything unusual that looked like a coincidence.'

'More. I need more knowing,' said Litmus.

'Well…we have calculated that craft's possible top speed, considering its design and size, and we, Commander Yorker and I, believe it will be impossible for it to travel faster than light, given that it only has technology we are familiar with, as far as we can see.'

Litmus looked from face to face.

'Tell me the other thing,' he said.

No answer.

'Tell me how you are knowing that,' Litmus demanded, 'Coz we are too far away for knowing that.'

'I told you,' said Commander Yorker, 'I knew he wouldn't swallow it.'

'Quiet Commander,' ordered Captain Murray.

'Alito, we never give out information about covert operations in hostile territory, not unless absolutely necessary, because that is how people get caught, tortured, and die. We have a scout ship hidden in that wreckage. It has seen this happen before. There are so many old fuel cases littering a path through those planets that we sent a scout to hide herself and watch. Just when that ship out there fails to reach light speed it will jettison a very small container ahead of it, which, our scout has reported, has in the past just vanished into nothing.'

'They are trying to catched me again,' said Litmus frowning.

He wiped his forearm across his face, to get rid of starting tears.

'I am here Emprino, and I am keeping you safe,' said IPE, in softly glowing words, in the air in front of Mark and Litmus. Captain Murray looked around the table.

'We will be fresh bright and alert again, starting now,' he said, like a whole new meeting was beginning.

'Next on our list is getting ourselves to the scout ship that provided us with our resonance readings. The fastest way we can do that is if we continue as we are, with the Mandelbrot's stern a little visible,' he said, 'but is that little scout ship still a priority? We have the data from it, and it is a long long way out from charted known space.'

Litmus was sitting up on his seat, looking at everyone around the table while he thought.

'Well…' he began, 'it's far away because they want their foul weapon to be unfindable, and unreached. Only a seeder of The Magnificci can go that far, fast enough to get there before everything is changed. Grandpa said we can't rely on the images we got because they've travelled and could be made false, and that we have to get the real data, direct from the scout himself.'

'Too late? They explode when their pilot dies?' said Commander Yorker.

'Thankyou commander. Even if they do, and he has,' said Commander Burnett, 'When we get there we will be in the best position, with the best opportunity we've ever had, to destroy that infernal orange ray factory.'

'With one small destroyer, one even smaller souped up helpod, and a three hundred year old flying cucumber,' said Commander Yorker.

'Yes,' said Captain Murray, 'If Alito will allow us that opportunity. And by the way, that "cucumber" is hauling your ship across the universe faster than it has ever travelled before, or will again.'

'We will go straight to the broken scout ship,' decided Litmus, 'We will let the mandelthing slip loose before that, when we are getting close. The Democratzia Capitalisto are watching for my ship, not other ones. The helpod and Sam and me will do scout rescuing things, while the mandelthing goes berserk doing its best go of wrecking.'

'Nice,' said Commander Yorker looking happy, 'My five year old nephew couldn't have put it better, but but but,' she added, before the other officers could tell her to mind her manners, 'honestly, I thank you Alito, with all my heart, for this opportunity.'

'If you succeed, Commander Yorker,' said Captain Murray, 'then when you finish, you will travel quietly, taking the longest and safest way back. For a ship's crew, the only reward worth having is to return home safely. If the helpod is up to it, we will travel with you. Lord Thomas has told me, previous to today, that Alito will have no further use for us.'

LITMUS TAMING

The small controls deck on the Magnificus Royale was empty of visitors again.

'Planetboy?'

'What?'

'The food is going all different now. From now. My ship grows it in culture blocks. It still tastes of things?'

Mark was looking at Litmus, and feeling a bit shitty remembering the whole bubbles of spit in his food thing. Litmus looked back, a little kid sly I'm secretly laughing at you a bit look.

'Yeah,' said Mark, 'You better not.'

Mark had forgotten he was wearing his headset. A voice was suddenly talking in his ear.

'We're all going a little see-through here? Captain Murray has asked me to check with you?'

'Litmus?' asked Mark, worried that some strange weapon was being fired at the three escaping ships.

'Exospace. We're going into it,' said Litmus, 'Tell them not to panic, they'll all go solid again, when no parts of them are in the universe any more.'

Mark had a feeling that the helpod and the Mandelbrot would have appreciated a warning, before they suddenly realised they could see through their hands, and the heads of the people around them.

'Litmus? Anything else they should know?'

'Naaahh….yeah. When we go back, they'll all go bright coloured strange for…I forget how long. Not much? That, that's the only other one thing what happens. I promise? Nothing can chased us to here, so they can all do relaxing. Tell them that.'

Mark realised that Captain Thomas had done a lot of Litmus taming, over and over, every single day. Life without Captain Thomas on deck felt empty, and not safe. Please please get better, Mark wished.

THERE IS SOMETHING OUT THERE

The three ships were racing through exospace inside the Magnificus Royale's particle spray, which was shielding them like a blanket, and dragging them along. There was no comms talk happening, because each ship's crew were getting on with their own business, on board their own ships.

'Time back in the universe is standing still for us,' said Litmus, into the quiet aboard the Magificus Royale, 'everything that goes into exospace comes back out zactly the same time it went in.'

Something else occurred to Litmus.

'Sam? I stopped already? Did you notice?'

Mark looked at the small child, wondering what it had been up to, that it had stopped doing.

'Baby talk,' said Litmus, 'I could hear myself doing it? But we were in the middle of important stuff, so I had to concentrate on other things. I am stopped doing it now.'

So you reckon, thought Mark.

'See that smudgy darkness,' continued Litmus, pointing at the large wall screen, 'that's not supposed to be creeping up behind us, because we are the fastest of everything left behind?'

Everything left behind when the Magnificci empire fell, one hundred and eighty years in the past.

A large pointiness, slightly darker than the rest of the blackness of exospace, was at the bottom of the screen. A really large, pointy on this end, darkness. Litmus was looking like he wanted Mark to have an answer.

'I don't know, Litmus,' said Mark.

'Okay. It's not very much closeness. Go make sandwiches for us, from the spotty green block, and the yellowy one. The bread is the one what's bread coloured. I will do a big Alito think.'

'Planetboy,' said Litmus calling Mark back, 'There's something else I keep not telling? IPE says we're not enough. She said after we got you you were a good choice – I did good getting you, but we're not enough crew for her? She says we need Grandpa for being Grandpa, and me because I am, and you for being the every day think of things person, but she wants a pilot so she doesn't have to be that all the time as well as other thinking things, and she wants us to have a person who likes making food, and someone she can train to make tiny adjustments to her insides. That would be all our cabins on board filled up nearly, except for the visitors' bunk cabin. And at least one crew has to be a girl, not just IPE being the only one. I'm telling you now, because sometimes if I get excited I forget things.'

'Okay. Now is probably not the right time to go crew hunting.'

'But now is a good time for thinking it? We have to wait for getting places and things to happen, and it is a nicer think than other things?' offered Litmus.

Yes thought Mark, thinking about the stingray scout ship pilot dying wouldn't help the pilot, and thinking about the big black shape slowly gaining on them wouldn't make it go away. Even thinking, worrying, about when the captain might get better wouldn't help that happen. They might as well think about new crew members, but it wasn't like Mark had any idea where to get some from.

'I never forgetted you telling me about cadet club. I eated that up all the way into my heart. There was Joanne and Shane and Wimpy, but probably we can't have Wimpy, because I asked him on the soft cargo. He didn't answer, and he looked frightened?'

'Yeah, he does that,' said Mark, 'if something might be a bit exciting for him.'

Wimpy. James Fargo. Some friends were just hopeless, but they were good friends still. Shane. Shane was somewhere out there in the universe, maybe on some ship where life wasn't good for him. Joanne Mark hadn't seen since junior school, but she had been great at cadet club, like having another boy on the team, except she was more sometimes. Definitely she didn't always think like a boy, and that made for extra fun. Even now he could still laugh at her battle game winning strategy – "We strike now, while the Zoonies are having a tea party". Tea party. As if.

Litmus looked up at Mark, with that small child needing to own up to something look.

'What is it little man?' asked Mark.

'That Shane is on a cruise ship. Grandpa found out that. Wimpy got in trouble for looking in the "Awareness, Other Ships" tracking record. Wimpy was trying to see where all the ships at Crew Day went to after. Captain Murray was very angry. He said junior trainee officers don't help themselves. Grandpa said "His need is great". Captain Murray said "What? A great need to find a friend from school" like he thought that was ridiculous, but Grandpa just said yes, and after he went back, and did the looking himself. He said not to worry you in the middle of everything happening, but that when all this was over, we were to go see Shane was all right, because the cruise ship owner chose him to be a toy for the passengers, in a silly uniform like a puppy in its first collar. Grandpa said that. He went all stern when he thinked about that. I thinked I want him, that Shane one, for my crew. Grandpa wants that lady, the one who played chasey with you, probably for making us be good.'

'Or not,' said Mark, remembering the Highliners lady from crew day.

Grown ups probably thought she was very sexy. Definitely a better bet for that than Miss Haymaker from school, and, the Highliners cruise ships lady had turned out to be a really nice person, caring about what happened to some kids she didn't even know.

'Well,' said Litmus sounding determined, 'Nobody better be thinking about making babies on my ship, coz that's 'sgusting.'

'Fair enough. How about we stop thinking about that, and think about our crew again instead. Shane's good at being serious, and James...James was a better cook than Joanne was,'

said Mark, 'so you don't have to be a girl to be a good cook.'

'My Grandmother, The Empress of The Magnificci, she was a girl, and she designed IPE, all by herself. No-one else could do it, not in all of forever. My Mum helped Dad with the new weapons. She was in charge, and he organised the making. Girls can do really really amazing things. My dad said never forget that. My Mum was a g...was a...'

Litmus started again.

'My Mum...' and then he stopped.

He was going to cry. It was in the screwed up face, and the tight rising voice.

'Come on Bunny Bum, toughen up,' said Mark.

A Captain Thomas type hug was needed. Mark did his best.

He thought that would be the end of it, but Litmus's thoughts had moved to his next problem, the problem of trying to fit more people into his life.

'I don't want that,' he said, 'Grandpa is the only one, and I am the only one, and you are the only one. That's all. I don't want...'

The voice was whining, and getting higher, as Litmus realised his happiness was being invaded.

'Hey come on, come on,' said Mark, 'How about we live in the front, right behind the controls deck, our three cabins, and IPE moves the visitor bunk space into the middle, and turns it into like a lounge area. The crew can all live on the other side of that, and we can go visit them for food.'

'With a door,' said Litmus firmly, 'and they have the clothes washing thing on their side,' and then he pushed Mark away, satisfied that his life was organised.

If there was a pilot doing some of the flying, they would need to be in the front of the Magnificus Royale when they were doing it, but Mark thought sorting out details like that could wait for later. None of this new crew were anywhere close to becoming a reality.

'Sandwich for me,' said Litmus sternly, pointing at Mark.

Bossy little brat.

SNIF CLOTHING

Cruising along in exospace smoothly, sneaking to somewhere else while time stood still in the universe. Mark and Litmus were getting themselves organised, getting their life on board the Magnificus Royale how they wanted it, while there was peace and quiet for doing that.

At first Mark thought Litmus was joking him around, but Litmus had been telling the truth – in the confusion of leaving the Soft

Cargo, all of Mark's clothes had got left behind. Litmus was giving orders that Commander Yorker was to provide replacements.

'Not girl ones,' said Litmus, like he thought Commander Yorker couldn't be trusted not to be adult funny.

Litmus had collected an arranged parcel of clothes, very carefully aiming his pressing finger while doing it, but when Mark opened it, Commander Yorker had only sent over civilian clothes donated by her crew, for wearing on the rare occasions the crew of a battleship got recreational leave on a lifeworld. One pair of jeans, one pair of board shorts, two tee shirts with holiday resort writing on them, a towel and one pair of socks. They were all too big, and there was nothing else, not even Space Navy Issue Form underpants.

'Not good enough,' said Litmus.

He went over to the side of the screen he used for moving people and things between the ships, and moved everything that was loose inside Commander Yorker's cabin.

'Now it is somewhere else. She is bossy. Bossy people are a bit mean, and slower learners,' said Litmus, 'Now you talk to her, while I eated my sandwich.'

Mark's headset began making a racket – Commander Yorker, annoyed.

'Staffer, he is a bossy little shit! And, and, he could at least say what I have to do to stop my cabin contents appearing all over the place. Everywhere except in my cabin, to be exact. I am the commanding officer of a battle ship, not his playmate.'

'You didn't even send over one single set of underwear stuff,' said Mark, 'and only one pair of socks, and they were the from someone's mum at home kind.'

'Oh...well...Ship of The Line uniforms are for Ship of The Line crew only. Okay, all right. I will get stores to downsize some regulation issue kit, SNIF socks and underwear, and undershirts. Not the insignia outer uniforms though. That better be all. And why can't that spoilt little shit speak to me himself.'

'Three reasons – he is eating a sandwich, watching a large dark shape on his screen and figuring out what to do about it, and he might tear your head off, because he isn't liking you right now. Hey, and anyway, I've got my uniform? You bend rules when it suits you. That's just like the teachers at school.'

'Open Fleet. You have an open fleet uniform, not Ship of The Line. Very well staffer, you outrank us all anyway, because you have God's ear – we will dye some uniforms purple, sew those flagtags on, and then Lord Minibritches can pick them up with more of the technology he refuses to share with us. We're supposed to be working together to save the League of Stars Territory lifeworlds. God, what a joke.'

'The GOD part isn't religious,' said Mark, starting to feel annoyed himself, 'it stands for Giant Of Death, because if he gets annoyed enough he goes berserk and destroys things, in a big way, like only some unbreakable, living forever thing can. And he's not trying to save the LOST from the Democratzia, he is trying to save all the lifeworlds, everywhere, even the ones they've over-run.'

Silence at the other end. Commander Yorker was thinking.

'All right staffer. I meant "God" like a throwaway profanity – "God it's hot", "God I could do with a drink". I stand corrected, like that time in the lift. Do you realise how quickly you are slipping into Lord Thomas's shoes? Organise yourself some rank or title, so I remember my place in future.'

RANK, AND BEING LITMUS

She was gone. Litmus was holding out a mug of drink.

Mark thought back to the conversation with the captain, the one about senior officers and ensigns, and people knowing their place in ship-board life so the chain of command wasn't weakened. Litmus would need to make up ranks for the crew of the Magnificus Royale, because its voyage had begun. "Sam" wasn't really a rank?

The Mandelbrot and the helpod would be travelling in convoy for a little while longer, then after that they would be gone, and this tiny cucumber shaped antique space craft would be home to three people, and all that the two people working in it had to keep them going.

'Litmus? What rank am I going to be?'

Litmus looked up, frowning like he didn't understand.

'You are Planetboy. That is the best rank of all,' he said finally, 'When we get new crew I will ask Grandpa what is a best rank for you. You could be a Zoonie?'

'Good one,' said Mark.

He wished he hadn't opened his mouth, so "Sam" could have stayed an option.

'I thinked he will say Commander. IPE says you can't have a one name, because she can't stop you being thirty-eight different boy people.'

'Thirty-six. Thirty-six plus me. Don't go making it sound even worse than it is,' said Mark, 'because it's not funny.'

'Thirty-eight,' repeated Litmus, his eyes looking at Mark like he was nailing him down, 'coz being full of my spit when you got B4'd means you have to be me sometimes,' and then seeing the look on Mark's face, Litmus began giggling, and couldn't stop, until he was shrieking with laughter and crying at the same time.

'That's funny? You think that's funny?' said Mark, 'Time out. I need time out,' and he went to his cabin, rolling his eyes and waving his arms wildly around in the air as he left, and going "Ahhheeeaaah" at the same time, to show Litmus he was driving him mental.

You could have too much of that little sandwich eating machine.

THE PEOPLE WHO MAGNIFY

The cabin was small, and softly lit. Mark sat up the end of his bunk, forearms on his knees, trying not to think about anything.

'Would you like a window?' asked IPE with her secret words.

'Yes please, but not a small round one. It would be like when I was five, trapped in my family's broken ship, and I had to look out on the stars while I waited to die,' answered Mark.

A window shaped like the outline of a sideways egg happened, alongside Mark's bunk. A big window, large enough to fall out of if it broke.

'It is a screen image. My hull has no openings,' said IPE. The image was so clear Mark couldn't make his eyes see the screen, just the outside, a deep blue night sky with tiny bright stars. It was beautiful.

'That was the night sky from Alito's bedroom window, on Planet Royal. Mark, I am speaking to you now so I can tell you something very important. The Magnificci don't belong in this part of space. They came here and set up their worlds.

'They had a weapon. It would shine modified starlight on something, and that thing, no matter how big, would shrink and shrink, until it was just a pebble in your hand. Then when they felt like it, they would aim the weapon again, starlight would shine through it, and the pebble would magnify, until it returned to full size. That is where "The Magnificci" comes from – the people who magnify. There were wars and fighting and greedy arguments. Litmus's great grand parents to the power of I don't know how many, by that I mean great great great until we all lost count, rather than murder all their enemies by shrinking their worlds to nothing, they shrunk three whole solar systems of planets, and some stars, for themselves to live on, nicked off with them and came here, leaving all the wars and troubles behind.

'But there are always nasty people, and there are always nice people. Sometimes things get out of balance, one way or the other. Things are out of balance again. Alito's father was too nice, and the Democratzia too scummy greedy, so history was repeating itself. He did as his ancestors did, shrunk the stars they needed, and some planets, and they are somewhere else now, in a new galaxy far far away.

'Alito and I were left behind, because that was how it had to be. We decided to save as many lifeworlds as we could. Everyone else's lifeworlds. They couldn't all be packed up and moved away, even if they had agreed to that. Alito's father could never build that many ships, not enough to transport all the birds, the animals, the trees, the bacteria, the fish, the insects of every Life world, and such a task would take forever. When a planet is shrunk, every living thing still on it dies. So our purpose, Alito's and mine, is to save what we can, by stopping the Democratzia's march across space. Alito has hardened his heart, and said I am finally allowed to do what I was made for, and shrink the Democratzia Capitalisto worlds to their final destruction, if we fail to stop them this time.

'This time is our last chance, because he is a lonely little boy who needs to go home. One hundred and eighty years away from their family, to be left behind for that long, is a big ask of anyone.

'I know you are thinking why haven't we done that already, destroyed the Freedom Collective, shrunk them to oblivion, but like all lifeworlds, there are normal everyday nice people living there, and children and forests and oceans full of life. None of those living things are pressing the buttons and pulling the levers of the weapons. It is the evil adult humanoidian men and women we must bring undone. But enough is enough. Alito's heart broke when the Star Alliance fell. They were happy energetic worlds. Their children, their people, died, because of Freedom Collective greed, and because Alito and I stood by and did nothing. We knew it was going to happen. We weren't ready. That day Alito cried, and then he said "I have to make this hard decision now".

'I have horrible weapons, weapons from before I was rebuilt as the Magnificus Royale. The CDDR gentle weapons are the new inventions of Alito's father and mother, and Alito himself. When I became Alito's medical ship they gave me feelings, and a neat little hull to carry my crew, but underneath everything I am still that original weapon, the one that brought The Magnificci here, thousands of years ago. That horrible secret part of me the Democratzia Capitalisto cannot capture or destroy. If my crew dies, if I ever lose Alito, I will turn everything to nothing. Just grains of sand. Everything until the last star, because my heart will truly be broken, and I will cease to care about any of this, this noise of life.'

Silence, and no air screening. Mark was about to ask why IPE didn't destroy the huge thing creeping up on them, when he realised there was no starlight in exospace. The ultimate weapon of The Magnificci had to be back in the universe to work.

'Mark? When I know for sure that the Freedom Collective are defeated, I will send Alito's people a message. For the last one hundred and eighty years I have been recording snippets of him for sending, little gems of silliness, sadness, happiness. Wherever they are, whoever the Magnificci are now, they will be glad to hear them, to have them. I will broadcast all the snippets like an exploding bomb. The broadcast message will drop through the barrier between exospace and this universe as little bubbles, then burst free to sound everywhere at the same time. All the universe will hear, but that will not matter. Only those who care will understand.'

Mark had a wonderful feeling, a moment of hope, and then he remembered how long messages took to travel anywhere, even just among the known galaxies, and the hope faded away.

'Why didn't you start sending them right from the beginning?' he asked.

Then Alito's family could have been getting them the whole time.

'Because we would have been found, captured, and Alito's father would have turned back, to a horrible battle. This is the best outcome that could be, that can ever be. Trust me as I trust you.'

'I do. I'm just not feeling very happy right now,' answered Mark.

'Drifting down from exospace into this universe will not take very long,' said IPE like a comforting mother, 'I will transmit, and soon after his voice will sound, for people who have waited a very long time to hear it again. That is one of the things my own happiness is clinging to.'

LITMUS'S WORST WORD MANGLE

Mark was carrying the last of his breakfast around in a mug, while he thought about IPE. "My own happiness" she'd said the day before – she definitely wasn't a robot.

'Planetboy, stop drinking things and thinking about nothing. We are working,' said Litmus loudly.

'Right ho, yes Sir,' said Mark.

'Ho is for putting your legs together on a marching day. I knew that when I was four even. Now listen to my explaining of that coming behind us thing. One – it could be an aliasing shadow in the data stream, so there's nothing there not at all even. Two, it could be the hugest ship ever made, that they started building three hundred years ago, for being better than my ship, and they've been flying it faster and faster, around and around, on the approach to their orange ray factory, hoping that one day they would get it up to speed, and catch us coming here. Three, it could be my people? Coming for me? It could?'

'Okay. Worst first – if it's number two, and that big, how will it chase us anyway? If we get sneaky I mean.'

'Umm...maybe we can't turned very good, because we're going fast? I don't know that one really but. It won't catched us though anyway, coz we will be three ships again, when I do slowingness for us?'

Mark looked at the screen, and had uncomfortable thoughts. Whatever it was, it was huge.

'I thinked something?' said Litmus, 'I thinked it is them. They always do the biggest, coz for them it's the best one.'

'Litmus, how am I supposed to know who "they" are?' said Mark feeling frustrated – first "slowingness", Litmus's worst word mangle for the whole day, and now a sentence with only "they" in it, for Mark to anchor his thoughts to.

'The Democratzia Capitaliso. They like themselves building the biggest ships, the tallest buildings, the biggest statues, the fattest people. You can't know nothing!' answered Litmus, sounding very surprised.

'All right. Well, if I'm the idiot, how come you aren't throwing out like a probe or something, to check them out? And how come they don't come up as numbers and symbols on the screen, like everything else?'

'One of those things is because they're making themselves hided, from me, and the other one, yes...how come?' said Litmus to himself.

LOOMING ATTACK

There were still no answers to all the questions about the widening wedge of darkness creeping up on them from behind.

Because of that IPE and Litmus had decided to split their forces, and their chances of success. The helpod would be dropped off early, and sneak up and rescue the Stingray scout ship pilot, then hide and wait for the Mandelbrot to appear to help it, before attacking the orange death ray factory. IPE would be working hard, concentrating everything it had to figure out the two hundred year old secret of the Democratzia Capitalisto's armoured material, and if it figured it out, then the orange death ray factory, and everything else of theirs that was armoured, would become normal, and defenceless, and their greedophile rule would be over.

'Which would be awful nice,' Mark said, because then everyone, everywhere, could get on with their lives.

'And our plan would make more sense than anyone's,' said Litmus, 'except we will all reappear back in the universe at the same time, mandelthing, helpod and us, even if we let the helpod off early first from here.'

'All right, you're hurting my brain now,' said Mark, but he had to go on thinking about it.

'Still a good plan Litmus – the helpod won't be here to get attacked by whatever that is, and we will have the Mandelbrot here to fight it when it attacks.'

They both had a feeling that it would be when, not if, the always looming larger dull black wedge on the screen attacked them.

THE MAGNIFICUS ROYALE

Mark's new clothes were stored in his cabin. The cabin was cosy, comfortable, just the right size for him. The purple uniforms looked extra good against Sammy Retro's skin, but if, hopefully when, Mark was finally himself again, in his own skin, the original cadet club type blue of the ensign uniforms would look better. Samuel Retreaux – Sammy Retro. Mark was grateful to have Sam's positive view of everything. His own memories of his life would be right on the edge of making him miserable, and there would be Sam Retro's sunny view of things flooding his feelings, to make Mark happy again.

'IPE, is it really thirty-eight? It isn't, is it? I'm not going to have to be a copy of him, am I? Litmus I mean.'

'Sorry,' air screened IPE, 'I thought it would be better if you didn't know, and then one day it just happened to you.'

'No. It's not…I do like him. I just don't want to be him. I had my turn of that already, being myself. And, being a junior Wimpy was a bad enough reminder.'

No answer. IPE just did semi sad coloured speckles in the air, which slowly changed to her laughter speckles, lots of see through coloured dots bouncing around.

'It could be fun?' she suggested.

'No, it couldn't,' said Mark, but he knew that it probably would be.

'If it helps, I have carefully considered the parameters at your times of change, so now we can predict, roughly, when it might happen?'

'And?' asked Mark.

'There are two factors – your emotional state, and your body mass. The change to being another boy is dependent on your current body having grown large enough. Large enough to have the material in it to make the change to the other body shape. Your emotional state is important, because the chemicals in you have to guess when is a good time to change – stress, fear, joy, boredom – I can't tell you which, but they are all likely reasons you will suddenly find yourself changing. I medi-scanned you while you were sleeping. Your body is preparing to do it better. Better size matching, and allowing spare mass for the energy to do it. You shouldn't feel it so much in future.'

'That still doesn't really tell me when,' said Mark, not pleased.

'No, but just watch out when you are having big feelings of any sort, because that is when it's most likely. Today your size is easily big enough for the smallest boy. A few days from now you'll be large enough to be the original Mark Planetti again.'

'And then I get to stay that way?' said Mark, feeling hopeful.

No answer. It was IPE's way of saying "No. Sorry".

'Anything else?' asked Mark, 'I mean any other stuff it would be good to know, that I don't know yet?'

'There is one thing – I am going to give Commander Yorker a virtual tour of a real Magnificci ship. The 3D imaging will be one hundred and eighty years out of date, but it will be good enough. I want her to make her plans with more respect for our abilities.'

'Aren't you a real ship?' asked Mark surprised.

'No. I am Alito's play room and medical suite. The controls deck he and Captain Thomas use, they made that up together. Operating a real Magnificci controls deck – that was beyond a small boy and an old man from another culture.'

'Hey, that's another thing – where's your motor? Shouldn't it like take up half the ship, or be out on stalks or something?'

'My motor is my outer skin. Really very simple, and logical. The most powerful ship will be the one with the most propulsion surface area for its size. That is why I am the shape I am. Don't start wondering about when you get your Magnificci ship virtual tour. When our current worries are over I will build you your own Magnificci control reality, and begin teaching you how to use it. For now perhaps learn where everything is.'

Mark went off to inspect the food making area, then the toilet, which had weird wing shapes to support your bum, and a shape coming up and around at the front, but no traditional toilet bowl, and it folded itself away into the bulkhead for when the tiny area became a shower.

He looked in on the captain.

AXEL'S TIME

Captain Thomas seemed to be asleep, and in the middle of a monster dream.

Mark stood in the doorway, looking across a valley. The whole landscape was under stormy end-of-a-day clouded sky. There was a boy out there by himself, standing on the lip of a funeral tower among the cemetery trees, looking out at his world. IPE began talking softly in Mark's ears.

'That is Axel, when he was young. This is the day his mother was placed in her mausoleum. He is trying to make sense of everything – Time, places, memories, dying. This is his moment, when childhood pains hopes and disappointments become empty, and lost forever. Until this day he had been happy, and shining happiness into his world. He is looking out at everything, his heart and his thoughts in turmoil, his jaw and his teeth clenched tight, tears on the edge of his eyes, and right at this moment, this moment we are watching, his life breaks, and as he begins putting it back together, it slowly fills with sadness and uncertainty. Now he knows he is one lonely thing, alive by itself, in all of eternity. Captain Thomas, when he looks at you and Alito, sees faint reflections of the young Axel he used to be before this day, and that makes you both all that is important to him. We must leave Axel now. Resolving this issue is a very private thing. He must realise his turn at being a boy made from shining happiness is over, and make the best use of what he has left.'

IPE's long thin medical tool arms came out of the walls, to guide Mark back from the doorway.

'You aren't there yet,' said IPE, meaning Mark hadn't yet had the experience Axel was reliving, 'so go and get on with being you.'

Time to go and see what Litmus was up to. Sometime soon they would be going back out of exospace, back into the universe, and then, probably, chaos would start happening, evading weapons, trying to protect the helpod while it was trying to collect the scout ship, trying to rescue the pilot from the mangled wreckage if that didn't work, watching the Mandelbrot park its fat bum up near the death ray factory and blast the crap out of it with every weapon the Mandelbrot, as a Ship of The Line, had plenty of, all sorts of things could be happening when the Magnificus Royale dropped out of exospace. Their earlier plan seemed a bit childishly simple. Mark had a feeling he should talk some of the possibilities through with Litmus.

A DIFFICULT RESCUE

The meeting table had gone, and a seat had appeared in the controls area, since last time Mark had been in there. Another seat rose up from the floor, to be next to the first one.

'Sit here,' ordered Litmus, munching on a red jelly bean, 'While I thinked. I mean while I think. I did like you said, and tried to make our sensors see it. It is made of that material that nothing breaks. It is really thick, like each tiny part of it is made of billions of things. But watch. You have to look real careful, because I have to mental image the camera feed with my brain, or it is too hard for IPE to keep happening. See something? On the screen I mean?'

'No?'

A ghosting image was faintly dancing around, and then it steadied, and then steadied even more, into a silvery tiny dots picture of a boy.

'I see...a boy? He's really slowly lifting things like tiles, and stacking them somewhere behind him.'

'The front of their machine is open. I want him, and one tile? Am I being bad? I mean coz he might die, if my controls can't get him properly?'

'So that's what we lose. That's a bad loss, even if he is the enemy,' said Mark, 'What could we gain, Litmus?'

'What he knows, and a sample of what that huge thing is made of. And we get to rescue him.'

Now Litmus was looking at Mark. Litmus's face was unhappy.

'It is rescue. It is. They only use children for things where they don't want an adult hurt. They'll just throw that fragillicus away when they're finished with it.'

'Child, Litmus – they just throw the child away, and nobody would do that.'

'Yes they do, and child could mean anything. Your words are useless. The Magnificci, we have tinycus, minicus, and fragilicus. He's too old to be a minicus, but he's still school skinny, so he's a fragilicus. Are we rescuing him or not?'

'Okay. Go for it. Try to rescue him, no, wait, what does IPE say?'

'IPE won't say, because it's my big decision. IPE is getting ready for whatever I decide. I decided this, so I will concentrate really hard on doing the image, and you will guide IPE's targeting weapons. Your finger is your target pointer thing. You have to use it like shining a torch. You have to always keep it on the boy, the pointing of your finger. This isn't just moving people around between ships joined together. This is a different person we never knowed yet, that we don't have numbers for, who is far away. IPE wants you to do the final targeting, because the boy will sense someone is trying to catch him, and IPE thinks he will be less scared of you. Can you? Can you do that?'

'Yes,' said Mark.

He hoped really hard that he could, because if he didn't do it properly, the boy that was that ghostly image would die.

'Wait. Litmus, wait a moment – can I have a practice on something? Something that won't die if I stuff up?'

'No. A practicing will tell them we are going to try, and then he will be lost. Look – he's made a big square hole, for something to come out. There's only one tile left for it to be finished, and then he will be gone probably, back inside that thing. Hurry, get ready, torched your finger at the screen.'

Mark held his finger out, and a wobbling around beam of light shone between it and the large controls view screen.

'If he stays still while we do this, nothing bad will happened him,' added Litmus.

The boy had his hand on the very last tile. He seemed to have stopped, like he was thinking.

'Hurry hurry now now now,' squealed Litmus at Mark.

The boy had the tile, but he wasn't going back in to the front of the huge machine to put it on a stack. He was lifting it to over his heart.

Mark couldn't get his finger to aim the beam of light right. He just knew something was going to go horribly wrong, and he would be left with a bad, sad memory, for the rest of his life. And he knew what was wrong – he was using one of Sammy's fingers, and trying to aim it with memories of being Mark.

'IPE,' he called out in tortured panic, 'Help me?'

The long arms came out from the walls, folding around Mark, holding him steady, and aiming his hand. The torchlight from the end of Mark's finger travelled into the image Litmus was working hard to keep bright and clear.

Mark was starting to feel better about his chances of rescuing the boy, when the boy suddenly jumped, out into nothing.

FINAL BATTLE STATIONS

Litmus struggled, holding his head with both hands like it was a ball, trying his hardest not to lose control of his imaging thought. The boy was dancing around in Litmus's mental image, larger smaller larger, left, up, right, down, and fading, fading all the time, and then, there was only swirling blackness out there to see.

Mark kept his finger steadily shining into the nothing. He didn't know for sure that the boy hadn't caught hold of it. It was only some strange sort of light, but it was supposed to bring the boy to safety? If you let out a rope to save someone, you didn't take it away again just because you lost sight of them.

A voice was in Mark's headset, IPE was letting it through half volume. Commander Yorker talking to her crew.

'All crew will be going to final battle stations. Suddenly out of nowhere there is a monster ship right behind us, with pincers coming out of it to capture us and hold us, while further back on its outer skin, weapons are rising up all over the place. I think those flying cucumber brats finally need the crew of the Mandelbrot. Playtime is over. Now is the time to take some responsibility, and pull our weight. Take charge Lieutenant, and fill in the detail. I need to have a private chat with our GOD.'

Now Mark could hear the Mandelbrot's staff lieutenant speaking to its crew.

'When we decouple we will lose speed, and come perilously close to re-entering the universe. Although that would mean escape, for us to be successful that cannot happen, yet, so we are going to hang back from the Magnificus Royale little by little, and dangle ourselves into this monster's mouth. Then we will do what we do best, wreak destruction on our enemy. We will suffer extreme damage. Our commander is ordering us to final battle stations. Final battle stations is the one drill we haven't practiced. All controls and all crew relocate to the core of our ship. All crew – because we will be shedding outer skin, inner hull protection voids, storage areas, fuel banks, sleeping quarters, crew cafe´s etc as they become damaged beyond recovery, and beyond use as a shield. This will be the Mandelbrot's last full-on battle. Whatever shaped ship we have left at the end, we will get ourselves home on. Make this count, make this hurt. If we save the Helpod and the Magnificus Royale, then they will be able to save us, when whatever we have left drops out of exospace. Crew to final battle stations. All crew to final battle stations.'

IPE was putting a message in front of Mark's eyes.

'You can let go now. Your finger is no longer needed.'

Mark wanted to ask what happened to the boy, but he was scared to know. Litmus was tapping him urgently on the arm, and talking fast, words pouring out.

'I spoked with Commander Yorker. We have let the helpod go so it is safe. The Mandelthing crew they are going to stay and die for saving us,' he said.

'What are we going to do?'

'IPE wants one more piece of time to figure the armour out. I'm going ahead to wreck it, that huge ship thing, so it is still open for her weapons when she's ready. You comed with me?'

Inside the controls deck suddenly went hard red. It wasn't difficult to tell that IPE was air screening a large acid red "NO" in front of Litmus's face.

'I don't want to go by myself,' Litmus wailed.

Inside the Magnificus Royale changed to a sad grey, with pale light green edges around things. Now the "NO" was huge, and Mark could see it too.

'You show me things,' ordered Litmus of IPE.

Now he was reading the air in front of him, then commenting.

'No. Not choices things. I want a list of things Grandpa and I use, in bad times.'

Litmus looked across at Mark, and began reading his list out loud.

'Hug Floppy Bunny.'

There was a look of disgust on Litmus's face.

'Sleep with Hoppy the Happy Frog.'

Now his face was going hard cranky, but he kept reading.

'Telemetrene sphere. I want that! I want that.'

He was alive and energetic now.

'IPE says you aren't quite ready to be a Giant of Death with me, and you would die out there, but two would be better than just me, because that is something they will never expect. IPE says they must have a plan for capturing just one of me, or they wouldn't have built that monster ship?'

'Oh-kay…'said Mark thinking, 'But what do I do?'

'What I do, but without the bunny bum,' said Litmus, trying to have fond memories of himself to keep his courage strong.

IPE was interrupting again, and Litmus reading, then turning to Mark to give orders.

'You wear the telemetrine sphere thing, and Hoppy and Floppy can go with you. IPE is giving you a gun thing, that you wash bad stuff away from me with. It doesn't aim very good, because of the sphere.'

Now IPE was secret wording in Mark's ears.

'It does "aim very good" considering it is working from inside, through the sphere's protective wall. You won't harm Alito with it, but you should not aim at him, in case it opens him up to weapons I do not know of yet. I will provide eight small floor panels, for you and Litmus's play friends to stand on inside the sphere. Hold still while I fit the belt onto you. It deploys automatically, when it is needed. I am sending Hoppy and Floppy, because keeping them undamaged will keep the sphere deployed all the time you are out there. You are almost indestructible – I don't want the sphere making an almost right decision about protecting you – it is just a piece of computational machinery. Do your best. I know I've had one hundred and eighty years, but I just need a little more time to figure that material out. Almost ready for you to go. Hold this. It is old fashioned – you just squeeze the trigger button.'

OUTSIDE

Mark was looking down at the weapon he was given, and suddenly he was outside the Magnificus Royale, without a suit, and not even inside a standard emergency rescue bubble for protection.

The murkiness around him was wavering strangely, like he was looking at it through wobbly glass. He felt like he was a goldfish in a small bowl, looking out at exospace. Floppy Bunny and Hoppy the Happy Frog were at his feet, on a small circle of floor that Mark was standing on. Litmus was racing away ahead, into the blackness.

The Magnificus Royale vanished into the dark, with Captain Thomas asleep in it, and only the IPE left to be with him when he one day woke up.

The sphere lurched forward, like Litmus was tugging it along on a string behind him. It caught up with Litmus.

'Feel that!' said Litmus, excited by his new surroundings.

'What?' asked Mark.

'Exospace – it's coldering my bum off,' said Litmus.

'Not even a word,' said Mark.

'Is, and it doesn't have to be two. Bumoff is like a competition for noisiest bum.'

Mark was wondering how, when everything around them looked so dangerous, and anything could happen any second, bad things included, Litmus was talking silly. Litmus seemed to have had the same realisation. He shoved an arm in through the sphere's shimmering surface, to get hold of Mark.

'Don't let go my hand,' ordered Litmus, 'coz this is like crossing the road with your mum, before you knew how much cars could hurt, and how to watch out for them.'

Now they were moving through the swirling blackness really fast.

'Litmus, I can't see anything but us,' panicked Mark.

'The mandelthing is going to light the way like a bonfire,' said Litmus, 'The more things try to destroy it, the easier it will be for us to see where to go, and what we have to do.'

'And what's that?' asked Mark.

'Get inside the monster ship thing, and wreck stuff. We wreck enough stuff, and the mandelthing will escape not too broken.'

Brilliant hard light began shooting everywhere, turning the blackness around Mark and Litmus into seething churning vomit orange and dirty excrement brown.

'Every stuff. Wreck every stuff as fast as we can,' Litmus was yelling, and pulling Mark even faster towards to the light.

'IPE says because it is so large it will have an optic pipe backbone to connect and control everything. We have to get to that, break it, and make that ship tell itself lies, by putting all the wrong pipe lights into each other. Then it won't be able to close its front, or aim its weapons proper.'

THE FINAL BATTLE

Pieces of junk were everywhere, like a forest of breaking and torn seaweed in a wild sea. The Mandelbrot was coming apart, being attacked by the biggest most powerful ship the Democratzia Capitalisto had ever built. Something hit Litmus, and he went sparkly hard. A whole splatter of sharp small pieces of broken ship smashed against the sphere really fast, but Mark didn't feel anything. A tiny red dot was travelling back from Litmus.

'Now they know we're here,' squeaked Litmus.

'Hurry Mark. Move! I can't tow you along any more. You are become half a Giant of Death of the Magnificci – you decide where you are in everything. Will yourself there. I can't wait for you, or they will all die, Yorky and all her crew, and then my ship will be nexted, with Grandpa on board and everything.'

Litmus was gone, into the confused mess of dirty light and dark. Mark had never seen so many different colours of light, all changing so quickly. Bloating balls of glare, stabbing shards made of hard sparks, and exploding fizzy orange light that looked like it was crackling with energy. All of the different light displays were shooting streaking or drifting away out beyond the battle, out into the dense black.

Any glare of light that got too close, and the telemetrene sphere did what sounded like a warm hum of anticipation, and then seemed to suck on it. Getting more energy to run itself, realised Mark. There was plenty of energy, all around, for the sphere to choose from.

Mark didn't understand the "will yourself" concept, not in a way that he could use to make anything happen. He began moving himself forward by shooting broken parts of a ship with the weapon, so they flew away from him, and he moved in the other direction. Soon he was moving fast, forward through the battle debris. There were armour plate tiles everywhere like he was in tile soup.

For a while he couldn't see anything outside the sphere except how a roaring fire would look like from the inside, if someone clamped down the heat and light to save you from it while you looked.

When he could see properly again he was inside the ship, inside a large tunnel or main passageway, and still moving forwards. Litmus was up ahead, getting a huge fat bulging pipe out of a wall.

The enemy ship was trying to build a skin of tiles all over Litmus, so fast it was like the tiles were a dense cloud of landing mosquitoes. Litmus was struggling while he worked, pulling away pieces of the tile skin, breaking them off himself wherever he could get his fingers under an edge. Mark willed himself to the tile dispensing machine, and began shooting the crap out of it.

It was protected by those armour plate tiles, almost indestructible. He was making progress damaging the wall around it. That seemed to be making the machine wobble, and only fire bursts of tiles, instead of a continuous stream, but there was no way he would damage it enough, not in time to save Litmus from being encased in tiles. No light, no awareness, and no movement, that's what would happen. Mark thought about that, and realised it probably wasn't true – Litmus wouldn't be able to see or hear anything, or move his arms and legs, or fingers, or toes even, but he could will all of him around in space inside his armoured tile casing, all the way through this giant ship, until every part of it not made of those infernal tiles would be wrecked, and they would become a useless shell. Or until, while trying to do that, he accidentally went out into exospace, and the ship continued on with only minor damage, leaving him behind adrift out in that darkness forever. Bad thought. Better to concentrate on what was happening now.

Two more tile dispensing machines had moved out from the passage wall. Mark moved as fast as he could to behind Litmus, between him and the flying tiles.

The tiles began building up around the telemetrene sphere. Soon it would be like being underground, in a small lightless bubble shaped space, with no way out.

Litmus had pulled more wall panels loose, and was tearing into the wall, breaking big chunks of glassy looking see-through coloured pipes out. Bright coloured light was shooting out of the broken pipes then accelerating like it was exploding, before shattering in all directions, in a flying forest of wildly spinning sharp-edged bright sticks.

The tile dispensers were going crazy, with tiles now coming out so fast they were like blurs. So fast Mark would be aiming at one to shoot it away, but hit one several tiles behind it. There were so many tiles that Mark knew he wouldn't be able to move any more, very soon. He turned around, moved himself forward until Litmus was mostly inside the sphere, to protect him.

Litmus was half in the passage wall, trying to make two large light pipes, of different colours, meet at their broken ends.

'This is a good idea of yours,' he said over his shoulder, 'I can work good with only my arms out.'

Inside the sphere was becoming darker and darker. Tiles were covering it over. Litmus was pulling hard at the two broken pipe pieces, to make their ends meet.

'Do it, do it, do it,' Mark yelled to Litmus, so Litmus would always know they were doing this thing together, right to the end, and Mark had no regrets.

The last thing Mark saw was Litmus glancing over his shoulder, seeing the telemetrene sphere being turned into a coffin space, then going really stroppy angry mental, moving away faster than Mark's eyes could follow, a whirling trashing, smashing bashing image of a seven year old in a bunny suit, having a monster tantrum. The bunny suit had gone from slightly dirty grey white to darkest dark green and sparkly. Litmus was screaming so hard his scream was wrecking everything around him, until he was in the middle of a ragged jagged hole the size of a large ship's cabin.

Mark tried to scream as well, because he was supposed to be a Giant of Death too? Nearly? He just had to remember what having a tantrum felt like, and live it again. It was a big ask – the last time he had been that silly and selfish was so so long ago, in a time when he still had a family to put up with him doing it. The telemetrene sphere didn't let Mark's scream out, not without damping it down. Mark went back to shooting, until the weapon's discharge was doing nothing, just running around the backs of the tiles encasing the sphere. The air inside the sphere had its own gentle light. Good old long dead Magnificci scientists thought Mark – when they designed something, they thought really hard about the end user, and everything they could need.

THE MANDELBROT'S MAIN ENGINE

Litmus was pulling at tiles, prising them loose from their shell shape around the telemetrene sphere. Pulling them up, throwing them away. Now some of them were gone, Mark began shooting himself clear of the rest of them. Litmus was breathless, excited.

'I broked the main light pipe, and everything shuddered, like the ship was doing wrong things to itself,' he squeaked in all the noise of destruction.

'Mandelthing's lost their main engine. It's really big, and coming straight for us in like three two one bang! We have to go with it – make sure it does lots of good wrecking. If this huge ship thing can't keep above light speed, it will fall back into the universe, and that will make it get torn apart by Time. Mandelthing's motor and us, we can do it? Just make yourself want to follow me. Maked yourself be that.'

Tiles were coming again, from all directions. Litmus was throwing them away, then batting them away with his arms as they came faster and faster.

'We have to turn it around. The mandelthing's main engine. It's going the wrong way. Going fast that way means it will be goed slower in exospace, and vanish back to the universe, before it's wrecked much. You need your arms and legs and everything for that, but not your dick,' Litmus yelled, as he frantically pulled tiles away from the sphere.

Mark moved the sphere to help Litmus, pushing it against one corner of the Mandelbrot's main engine as it bulldozed its way into the hull of the huge ship.

'No!' screamed Litmus disgusted at Mark, 'You're doing the other corner, so it spins. Why are old people so stupid? Now I know where your brains are.'

'I'm not old. I'm only fourteen,' Mark muttered to himself as he got to the other corner of the engine, 'You're old, you little bunny bummed sandwich munching shit of a brat, and by the way, people do not have brains in their dicks.'

The engine was slowly turning, blasting parts of the big ship's insides into mangled wreckage, until finally it was facing forward, towards a massive broken edged hole that was the front of the huge ship. Litmus was steadying it in that position. The engine was firing back into the wreckage. Mark realised the Mandelbrot must have jettisoned the engine on purpose – because they had turned on all its functions, including the old fashioned emergency burn-out flame rockets. A main engine unit didn't get separated from its ship, and still have everything working, unless it was meant to go like that. The Mandelbrot's crew might still be alive.

The passage inside the huge ship had opened out behind them, into a large area like an aircraft hangar, and it seemed to suck the Mandelbrot's main engine into its hugeness. Mark could see why – its walls were all tile dispensers, like that was its whole reason for existing. Enough tile machines to completely encase a small ship until it was helpless. Most of the machines seemed to be disconnected, and three were collecting tiles instead of firing them. Litmus had done some useful damage to the light pipe backbone earlier.

The Mandelbrot's engine was slowly vanishing underneath tiles. Tiles were covering Litmus over, and then Mark couldn't see that way any more, because the sphere was being smothered in tiles too. If something didn't go right soon, this was the end.

ONE LAST HOPE

The gun IPE had given him had gone weak. It was like the telemetrene sphere didn't want him to use it. When he squeezed the trigger button a little shower of sparks came out, like it was a kid's toy, and that was all.

Mark reached down into the bottom of his heart, to lots of old feelings from his life.

He sat down on the small circle of floor, with Hoppy and Floppy.

His brain was working slower, and not finding anything that would be good to do next, and then his muscles began doing that aching thing.

There were tiny bubbles of perspiration on his skin.

He was changing into someone different. He couldn't worry about that now. He had reached a decision. He knew what he had to do. Somehow he had to get out there and help Litmus. Whatever boy he was becoming would just have to do their best.

The Magnificci chemicals in him couldn't make up their mind. He was flickering, being two boys at the same time, his skin having moving patterns over it of brown and white skin. One boy was Sam Retro, Mark could feel his cheerful spirit urging him to keep going. The other boy was having a grim determination to fight this to the very end. Shane. It was Shane, Mark just knew.

Mark reached out one nervous two coloured finger towards the shimmering shell of the sphere. If the telemetrene sphere let his finger out, then all of him could go out there, as an indestructible boy of the Magnificci.

Yes, his finger was out there in exospace, and it had survived.

'Everything Magnificci', he yelled, shortening Alito's battle cry as he leapt from the sphere, breaking off tiles on the way.

The shortened battle cry seemed to wake the telemetrene sphere, which glittered and sparkled in strange patterns all over its surface. Mark couldn't wait around to see what would happen – he was going to tear tiles off Litmus. Having longer arms and bigger hands than Litmus was going to be a great help, and doing something constructive, well that was way better than waiting around to be imprisoned forever.

Now, as he strode through exospace to Litmus, pushing broken pieces of The Great Karoshi out of his way as he went, all of him began twinkling strangely, and then he felt it, yet another boy, replacing Sam and Shane. The Magnificci chemicals had decided on their choice of boy for this.

Hoppy the Happy Frog and Floppy Bunny were left behind in the telemetrene sphere, their blind button eyes staring at nothing. The tiles of the floor curled up around them, covering them over like a protective hand, and then the sphere began to spin, faster and faster, flinging tiles off itself in all directions. It was going into battle.

CORT JUMPS SHIP

Cort heard it, some part of the Great Karoshi, brushing against a pile of tiles as it snuck up behind him, preparing to catch him. It would strike hard and fast, so he wouldn't have time to drop the tile out into exospace. He held the last tile even tighter to his chest, because it was the only thing he had, to share the last moment of his life with.

He looked out into the churning blackness. There was a tiny little finger of warm friendly light out ahead. Strange. Was his next life calling him on? Cort felt his legs shivering, shaking with fear. He knew he was about to be dead if he didn't jump. He would be caught on a barbed sucker that would drain his insides out. Come on wobbly legs, he told them in his thoughts, make this one last thing I do go good.

He jumped.

Instead of falling down, or being blown back into The Great Karoshi, he was falling slowly forwards through swirls of darkness, like he was being weakly drawn away from bad things, to somewhere safe.

Way out ahead of him the warm friendly light was very soft, like it was the scrappiest single weak thread of spider web, and he was a tiny spider out in a storm, trying to get itself home.

Cort heard a noise behind him. The Great Karoshi was shoving piles of tiles out of the way, to get a metallic snake-like machine clear to where it could aim its head at him.

A shiny wire came flying from its mouth. He twisted himself around, and held the tile out. On the end of the wire the sharp tips of a grabbing claw closed into a fist and hit the tile, trying to knock it from his hands. He got a good hold of it again.

More wires were coming, and barbed ended sucker tubes, firing from the machine, which was snaking itself around to get a better position for shooting him. He batted them away with his one tile, over and over, like he was dancing. He was dancing in the murky darkness, all by himself, to save his life.

The darkness swirled around him, like a deep ocean was about to swallow him, swallow him down and down until he was lost. The wires were falling short. The Great Karoshi gave up on the snake head machine, and now it was moving the large ship-grabbing jaws forward, in dangerous jerks, like it was in a terrible hurry. Cort was far enough away now to see more of The Great Karoshi. Weapons were rising up out of its huge skin – the tiled front area he had been in was just the tiniest tip of something leviathan horrible. Nothing could stop something so huge.

More dark swirls, closing around him like empty uncaring nothingness, and slowly carrying him away. He had a horrible thought that he had lost that friendly light. He twisted around again to look. He had. It was shining past him out into the blackness. A nasty scared feeling bit into his heart – the light was beginning to fade? He could feel his lungs weren't getting enough air. He held out the tile, and reflected the light onto himself. Somehow it was a good thing, and he wanted it with him when he died. He knew he was dying now, because he could see, like a dream, two boys floating past in exospace, going somewhere together. That was making him have a really nice memory of the two boys who rescued him, the time he was a child pilot crashing out of space in his Fly-ahead, a long time ago in his life. They lived on some small grass covered planet, far far away. Cort knew that their lifeworld had probably been slaughtered by the Freedom Collective too, and they would be dead, like all his own family and friends on his home world. I will have happy memories of you two, now it's my turn to go, Cort thought. More threads of soft light were finding their way out through the black to him. He began having a feeling like his heart was swelling, not to burst with bitter tears, but to be a golden happiness, like someone who cared was watching over him.

ON BOARD A NEW SHIP

He landed somewhere with a thump. Mechanical arms were whipping him around, folding him up, straightening him out, whistling things in his ears, and shining lights in his eyes. A large cannon thing lowered itself down from the ceiling and started talking, in a metallic fake voice.

'Taking a return reading. In case of great biotrauma this will be the return point.'

Hard in the little hollow in the middle of Cort's chest the ray hit. It hurt. It went all through him, like every single cell was being turned around and considered. When the ray suddenly shut off, and the cannon went back into the ceiling, Cort realised he was dribbling slobber off his bottom lip, and his muscles felt all floppy weak.

'Don't ever do that to me again,' he yelled, angry.

HISTORIA IMAGIFACTION

The arms vanished back into the walls, except for a collection of them in one corner, holding his tile from The Great Karoshi down on the deck, and testing it with tool after tool.

He was standing back on his own feet. The ship he was in seemed to be empty. It was rocking around like it was being attacked. Words made out of see through coloured light kept appearing near his eyes, like a robot brain was trying to talk to him. After a while, when nothing tried to hurt him again, he let himself look.

'Hello. You have passed your medical, and I have caused a temporary marker halo, so you will be like a little beacon in space when I lose you. Now you must tell me things, so we can help each other.'

When it loses me?, thought Cort, and then he had another thought – would he want to be found? After the Great Karoshi, he needed to know was this ship friendly, or something else?

'I am a fly-ahead boy of the Star Alliance,' said Cort, 'and that is all I'm saying.'

'I am the last flying ship of the Magnificci. My crew are away fighting an evil enemy. You could help me save them.'

Cort thought for a moment.

'What do you think "evil" means?' he asked, because he wanted to know who this ship really belonged to.

'Someone who forces their will on another living thing, without caring what harm, pain or suffering that causes,' said the words in front of Cort's face.

'The Freedom Collective,' said Cort, sure from the ship's description that that was who it meant.

'No. The individual members of the Freedom Collective do care, but they have an impossible choice – work for an evil enemy, or watch while their worlds, and every living thing on them, are destroyed, forever.'

Cort thought he knew who the evil enemy would be.

'The Democratzia Capitalisto. Is it The Great Karoshi? Is that the ship you're fighting right now?' he asked.

This ship was thinking, taking time to answer. Is it making up lies?, Cort wondered.

'I am looking, I am thinking, I am building an historia imagifaction,' said the air screened words.

'And what's that when it's at home,' said Cort, not trusting fancy words.

'An historia imagifaction is when you know very little about something, so you inspect everything else you know, and then add any new knowledge you have about the thing, then you imagine a possible history for the facts you do know, to give you at least some idea of what you're dealing with?'

'I understood that,' said Cort feeling proud, 'so you can cough it up now, this hissy fact thing.'

'The Great Karoshi is the name of a huge slave built ship, assembled in exospace some time in the last two hundred years, designed to capture and destroy me, and then imprison my crew, so they can be cut into pieces for "scientific research", so the Democratzia Capitalisto can use that knowledge to poison more of the universe with their modus operandi.'

'I don't care what those last words mean – I want no more explaining,' decided Cort, 'It's simple – we have the same enemy, so we can team up – me Cort of The Star Alliance and you, Ship of the Magnificci, against our enemy.'

'Deal. I will make my forward screen into a Star Alliance Fly-ahead cockpit, and you will pilot me while I fight. We must turn back to the battle, and save the boys who rescued you.'

DEAD IN LITTLE PIECES

Cort looked as the forward bulkhead changed into a replica of his old Fly-ahead cockpit. Seeing the familiar controls was a very sweet, deep feeling – they were something he knew from his old life.

This ship must be really small he decided, because it turned around almost as sharp as a tiny Fly-ahead.

'Are you the Magnificci that's like a lost empire, and there is this Alito the Unbreakable Child thing, left behind all by itself, to wander around the universe lonely forever? That Magnificci?' he asked, 'I mean really the one from that bedtime story?'

'Yes. I am his ship,' said the ship, 'but I have a crew now to keep him company. Captain Thomas, the Planetboy Mark Planetti, and you, Cort, Fly-ahead boy of the Star Alliance, until we can take you home.'

'I am home,' said Cort.

The familiar cockpit of his old Fly-ahead was all he had left.

As he got settled better in his seat, felt his fingers around and ran his eyes over controls he hadn't seen since he was a lot younger, he wondered about Mark Planetti. Wondered about him being all the way out here. It wouldn't be the same Mark. The universe was so large no-one knew how big, so one tiny person in it somewhere, well, how likely was it you would ever see them again? Yeah, but, he used to see his mum, and Dad, and Uncle John, and his friends at school every day almost, maybe because they were all lost together in that hugeness. War did horrible things though, and people ended up all over the place, and, thought Cort, if that "all over the place" didn't mean in dead little pieces, they were really lucky. Being far from a home that wasn't really there any more was bad, but it was better than that.

A PAIN IN CORT'S INSIDES

He realised he had an immediate need. His stomach was hurting. The top of it, somewhere inside him, felt like it was being pinched, hard, and that was making all of him feel awful.

'Ignore the big things flying past,' the ship was saying, just as Cort starting talking.

'My stomach hurts?' he said.

The ship seemed to be thinking, as they raced through exospace.

'You haven't eaten, probably for days,' it said finally.

A long thin arm appeared from behind him, with a brown stick thing in its grasping end, the size and shape of a good lolly bar for sucking and chewing, but Cort could tell it wasn't going to be that, just from the surface of it.

'Thankyou,' he said.

If it stopped his stomach hurting he would be grateful. He sank his teeth in, and started to feel better as he chewed.

'There will be better food soon, when the captain is back with us,' said the ship, 'for now you must concentrate on your controls.'

CORT GETS LEARNED

'Ignore the big things flying past,' said the ship again, 'They are weapons originally designed to find a large ship and damage it. They think we are just rubbish in the way, to be swerved around. Every now and then you see a tiny spark of light through this murk? Head for that. I will be decoding the armour plate you brought me.'

What happened to fighting, or at least getting weapons ready, thought Cort as he flew one handed, munching on his snack bar.

'You said you had a B4 cannon? Is it ready? We could try it out?' he asked.

'Already did, on you,' screened the ship, its writing going into jiggling around coloured dots, and now it was talking in his ear.

'My B4 ray cannon is for rebuilding broken living things. It cannot aim outside my hull shell. I have many medical wonder machines, because I am the Emprino's medical ship. I was very new myself when I first got him to look after. I was using the most wonderful complicated medical science tricks on slightly grazed knees, and tender knocked elbows. He was very good at letting me know when something hurt, and even sometimes when it didn't but he wanted to let me know he needed me to care. The racket that minicus could make, tears and sooky noises, was amazing. When he became indestructible the silence was sad, like we had lost something very precious. Now I must learn you.'

'Learn me? What does that even mean?' said Cort surprised, and then worried.

'I am a huge computing machine, with a tiny caring thought running it. I need to know you, so I can be sure I will care enough about what happens to you when that matters.'

'Well I don't know anything about me. I just am,' said Cort.

If he was younger he would have added "so there" and "suck on that", and Uncle John would have taken him outside for a handflier game, before his dad or mum could catch him and smack his cheeky unhelpful little bum.

'Well...then...' said the ship thinking, 'I will share some of Planetboy's happy moments, and you can start adding yours when you see a chance. Do you know...about the Zoonies?'

'It's not Planetboy, it's Planetman, and that's a League Of Stars Territory cartoon. It's really good though. I was on one of their hospital ships after I got rescued, and they showed me heaps. I laughed so much I was crying, and the nurses came running to see if I was having great pain from something they'd missed. Hey, wait a moment. How do you know about the Zoonies?...Um, something's weird here. What does your Mark Planetti look like? If you can show pictures, show me him, hey, and his sidekick umm...umm...James!' said Cort, amazed with himself that he had remembered the name of a small boy in his past. James Fargo, the kid with the soft big eyes like a trusting pet rabbit. Two big front teeth like a rabbit too, Cort saw, as a shimmering half see-through picture of an older James Fargo appeared. So it was that Mark, that was in this ship's crew. Cort felt a tiny seed of a feeling in his insides, getting ready to grow into happiness – someone from a good time in his past was alive, and here, for sharing more good times with. He hadn't lost everybody.

'Show me the Mark boy on the big screens,' he ordered, hopeful, and scared that it mightn't be true, that somehow he had misunderstood this ship, and got this important thing wrong. He was really scared of disappointment now, because this really mattered.

'It is unwise to get bossy on this ship. It sets the Emprino a bad example, and bossy is something he is so very good at once he gets started, that it can be exceedingly unpleasant for the rest of us.'

'Okay. Got that. Can I see the Mark one on the big screen...please?'

'The big screens are for general information. Air screening is for private conversations, between me and you. I can't show you Mark because right now he is in the shape of someone else, and you will be confused.'

'Whatever that means. Why can't you just talk to me all the time, instead of half the time doing this writing in the air stuff?'

'I have two very good reasons. Ask me again later, when we are both not hopelessly busy on desperately important time-narrowing tasks,' answered the ship.

JOINING THE FIGHT

He was racing towards it, a vicious space battle.

Broken parts of things began flying past. Cort was waiting for the ship he was in to give him new instructions, now that they were nearly there.

He could see The Great Karoshi, aiming many weapons at a space destroyer from the League Of Stars Territory. The chunky strong looking space destroyer was small in front of The Great Karoshi. The Great Karoshi was trying to smash it to pieces.

A feeling like the whole outside of the ship he was in was taking off a jumper, that feeling flowed over Cort, and then a corkscrew spring of light threw itself forward, past the League of Stars Territory ship, and into the Great Karoshi, flinging weapon-heads from its hull out into exospace. Now there were little holes like picked pimples all over that side of its hard surface, with light and fluids dribbling and sparking, drifting out from them. Tiles like attacking birds came flying out, covering the holes over in protective skins.

This time the ship Cort was in growled, and vibrated hard, in big shudders. It was going to throw off more than a jumper.

The interweaving corkscrews of light were beautiful, tighter and closer together than the first one, and reaching out across exospace to the Great Karoshi.

The Karoshi was targeting the corkscrew with all its remaining weapons, but they seemed to have no effect. The corkscrew of light hit the surface of the Great Karoshi, and began burrowing in, drilling into it. Words airscreened in front of Cort.

'This will cost me too much energy. You must fly me in closer while I think.'

The corkscrew of light faded in the forward vision screen, until it was gone.

Cort thought it was blood at first, the stuff dribbling out the hole the corkscrew had made, but it was tiles, flowing out fast, then being formed into a small shield wall between his ship and the Great Karoshi.

The Great Karoshi turned its weapons back on the space destroyer.

For a moment Cort thought the space destroyer had been blown up, but then he realised it had jettisoned its main motor, and had blown its own hull apart to get the engine out. Before the motor exploded maybe, because it had been damaged? He knew they had done it to themselves, that it was deliberate, because covers had closed over huge holes in the ship, like they were designed for that if the motor had to be let go.

In the middle of all the weapon tracers, beams and missiles, the naked motor turned, turned more, until it was aimed right into the mouth of The Great Karoshi. It fired everything it had all at once, and shot forwards, burrowing into the centre of The Great Karoshi's front.

The motor was gone. The space destroyer was unable to move now, and just sat being smashed and smashed and smashed again, making Cort feel sick.

'Fly us in between,' said a voice in Cort's ear.

'Hurry. We will survive those weapons. I am more than that. I need the power they are spewing out.'

Cort flew quickly, swerving and diving through wreckage. An overlay was happening on his forward view screen. An overlay like tracing paper, only done with light, of where the crew were in the League of Stars Territory space destroyer's hull, what was left of it.

'You must position us to shield them,' said Cort's ship.

THE SHIP GIVES IT BACK

Cort began wondering just how long the ship he was in could stand being attacked. It was getting buffeted around a fair bit, and getting warmer inside. The crew of the space destroyer were huddled in a ball of bodies in the very centre of their ship, keeping in the attack shadow Cort was making for them. He was carefully adjusting his Fly-ahead controls after each serious buffeting, to keep the destroyer's crew shielded.

'Energy plasma is flowing over our outer skin like candle wax,' said words in front of Cort.

'They think they are crippling me, but I have never had so much power to play with. We are tiny, but we are glowing with the power of a thousand cities. When this current battering goes into a lull, you must turn me front to our enemy, and hold us very still.'

The Great Karoshi seemed to think it was winning, and having a rest to recharge things was the last thing its program felt like doing. The battering just got louder, and harder, crescendoing into a rattling drumming screaming noise against the outside of the hull. His ship was shuddering, shaking, flicking around, and getting really hot inside.

Cort could feel perspiration beading on his forehead, his face, running into the crack of his lips, then moving around the curve of his chin, before speeding down his neck, over the hard burnt C7#*Blue on his chest, down across his stomach, and coming to a stop on the top edge of the rim of his underpants elastic. Slowly, with little tickles on his skin, sweaty wetness leaked its way past, and the soft cotton of his underpants below went limp and damp, cooled with evaporation, and collapsing into a gentle softness close over his skin. He was wondering about how amazing that felt. It was something new. Something fantastic and new in his life, this urgent nice feeling.

'NOT NOW,' said very bright sky blue letters right in front of his face.

'Fragilicus, remember you are waiting to turn us. Both hands back on your controls. Be ready…ready…ready…NOW.'

The longer this took, the more likely it was people in the space destroyer would die, because they would be more exposed to the

Great Karoshi's weapons. Cort swung the ship around as fast as he could, and immediately held it steady.

A screaming gritty zing went through the frame of Cort's ship, like an electo-mechanical version of clenched teeth and fierce determination.

For a moment all the churning battle filth in exospace seemed to freeze still, and then the front of the Great Karoshi fell back, like it had been pushed by something invisible but huge, something even bigger than itself. Its still firing weapons went half see-through, and then so did the whole battlescarred ship.

It began to fly apart, faster and faster, tile by tile, part by part, the pieces all vanishing into nothing like they had never existed.

The space destroyer was sitting by itself, drifting past Cort's ship, afterglow damage hot spots on its hull making it visible in the dark, and then suddenly it was gone too. There was nothing out there, just blank viewing screens.

'Ummm. Sorry? They've nicked off on us. Everything has. I can't fly around in somewhere that isn't there any more.'

Cort turned around to see if anyone, or anything, was listening. He didn't know what to do next.

The arms inspecting that single armour plate tile stopped for a moment, and air screening words happened in front of his face.

'They have fallen below light speed, and left exospace. We must now do something very difficult – catch you as you reappear in the universe. If you are not soft cargo when that happens, I will need all my medical tools, including the B4 cannon, to reassemble you.'

'I don't like the sound of that,' said Cort.

'Sorry,' agreed the ship, 'it would hurt a bit.'

'No kidding.'

'A lot,' screened the ship, like it was having second thoughts.

CORT TRIES TO RESCUE HIMSELF

The ship started whining high and smooth, and then the sound rose even higher and smoother, like it was mustering all its power for an attempt at something. It accelerated wildly, it swerved, it rolled and dropped until he felt sick, it slammed the brakes on, then lifted and accelerated again through exospace, trying to get itself above one joint point in space and time. The copied Fly-ahead controls weren't doing anything.

'I feel a bit sick?' said Cort.

He felt a lot sick.

Now the ship was talking words into his ears. He could hear the words were just for him, and not in the air around him.

'If you had entered exospace at the same time as me, we wouldn't need to do this, because you would exit it into the same time, and be safe. But you didn't, so we are misaligned, and you must watch now Cort, for a tiny speck in your forward vision. It will be small, like a tinycus's bedroom night light, only outside in the night. It contains the light memory of you, and we must snatch it from that time place as it is dropping back into the universe, for you to survive. We are close. Your controls are up, you can take over flying us again. I cannot stop working on this tile. Everything, all the people and places I love, depend on this. That great ship was only the beginning. There are many worlds out there covered in cunning greedy people. We must bring them all into the beginning of a new, better age. To do that I must finish my work on this tile, while you concentrate on your flying.'

Cort saw a tiny light like a steady candle, way out ahead in the turbulent messy black. He gave the Fly-ahead controls everything, his fingers curled around, his hands holding on lightly but with all his strength ready. The ship accelerated forwards smooth and fast. He crouched his body low and tight in the flying harness, so he could lean his weight into his steering actions.

The ship was screaming that pure clean scream again. They were racing together, chasing the candle light. That light was being buffeted around, and so was the ship. Cort felt good, flying accurate and fast towards a wanted target. He was finally doing something again that was fun, and something he was good at – piloting his fly-ahead. He could feel his shape, young and strong, working things the best it could. The light in the ship around him was drifting between bright white, a scary red, and a soft happy blue. The little light out there in the murky swirls of exospace was dropping as it sped along, and dimming little bit by little bit, like it was fading away to be somewhere else. Down, down, down Cort chased it. He was determined, and sure this ship could do it, and then he had that candle light right in front of him, but, just as he was nearly there, it got buffeted sideways by the dark turbulence of exospace.

He called out in panic as he spun the ship into a drifty to wash off speed, hanging out the back end as he tried to collect the candle light in a sideswipe. He gave the ship a last powerful surge forwards as the back end swung around, and then suddenly for him everything was black.

Not swirling, not space, just totally no light for his eyes black. Fear rose sharp and acid in him.

EVEN IF THEY ARE EVIL PEOPLE

A widening slice of light knifed the impenetrable dark into two. An eye opening. His own eye, his two eyes, steadying, figuring out what was what.

He was all bright colours. He was lying somewhere, up against a wall, or a ship's bulkhead. He was still inside the Magnificci ship.

'Back to your seat,' said letters in the air, flashing and flashing the words, like he should hurry.

'Strap in take the controls and go. Somewhere ahead of us we must rescue our crew. This part of space is very empty, of planets, of stars, of meteorites, of everything. With nothing to move towards, and nothing to push away from, Litmus and Planetboy will become still, and vanish into the cosmic background static. Then they will be very hard for me to find. Indestructible beings need energy around them, or they lose energy too, and eventually there will only be an indestructible lump of lonely nothing, adrift forever in space.

'Don't be distracted by that pattering rain on our hull. It is The Great Karoshi losing light speed and disassembling, as all its parts return to the times they entered exospace. Think of it like a hailstorm, and we must keep on through it, to make sure our people are safe.'

My gran used to talk to me like that thought Cort – that caring for the ordinary people in your life thing. Little chats about making time for "The people we have" because one day they mightn't be around any more.

Cort realised as he looked out into the black, his eyes searching, that it wasn't just people. He needed other living things to share the journey of his life with – trees, insects, spiders, lizards, birds. It would be an empty existence, being the only type of living thing left around, anywhere. The clouds and the sunshine would have no reason to exist any more. Rain would happen, but do nothing good, and the sun would still shine down, but there would be no creatures soaking in its warmth.

But the worms and frogs and stuff would still be waiting at home for him, because the Democratzia Capitalisto hadn't put them through that water and dust machine. Not that day anyway.

'Can you take me home?' his voice asked, before he knew it was going to.

'Yes. We will go to Terra to help the Captain rest his memories, we will find Mark's family so he can make sure they know he cares, we will see James off on his way home to Outer 17, we will go to the Star Alliance worlds for you to say hello to what's left, and then we will leave on a great journey, to find the Magnificci. You can be our pilot if you like.'

'I do like,' said Cort.

'In that case, we will also be ambushing a Holiday Highliners ship, to collect the boy I am going to train as my technical mechanic. We will probably have to fly very sneaky, to pull that off without upsetting anyone.'

'No problem,' said Cort, looking forward to adventure.

'But I will not be going anywhere if I don't find my children, my minicus and my fragilicus,' added the ship, the light inside it turning a mix of faintly red, and dim dull greens and greys.

The light went warm bright yellow, like an excellent sunny morning.

'I have it,' air-screened the ship in front of Cort's eyes.

'This plate is made by reverse HAP linking its atomic structure, so no-one can damage it unless they have the strength to damage every other thing made from this material, across the whole universe, but just like a HAP message, change this one small piece, and I change equally everything everywhere else built from this.'

Cort liked the sound of that. The Democratzia Capitalisto's indestructibly armour plated master ships would become some new material they weren't expecting. Lots of things would change, right down to the belt buckle of the Democratzia worker who had sent him to The Great Karoshi. His pants would probably fall down.

'What stuff?' asked Cort, 'What stuff will you make it be?'

'I am now unravelling the tiniest tiniest hole. From that I will re-weave its structure as compost, so things can get life from it. The previously indestructible surface on every military thing the Democratzia Capitalisto have will be, when I have finished this tile, floppy sloppy plant and animal food. I haven't been this pleased with myself since the day I was given the honour of being the Emprino's personal ship.'

Cort decided not to mention the ruling classes and the filthy rich business people of the Democratzia Capitalisto, the fact that they had impregnated themselves with armour tile particles. He didn't want the ship to stop its work, and he had a feeling it would if it knew, because it was kind hearted, and would feel too guilty, turning people into plant food to be shovelled around in the garden. Even if it was evil people.

The B4 cannon came out of the ceiling and reached right forward, and down into the corner, until it too, along with lots of other big and little gadgets on mechanical arms, was aimed close up at the tile. So many things all aimed at one point on one small tile. I am so glad that's not me, thought Cort.

Nothing much was happening, then suddenly raw brilliant white light was between all the medical tools and the tile, too bright for Cort to keep watching. He had to cover his ears too, because the ship was pouring a huge amount of energy into changing the tile

– the B4 cannon was making its nasty noise, the ship's motors were screaming, and all the gadgets aimed at the tile were each doing their own beeps, buzzes and alarm bells. Cort had a feeling he shouldn't be so close. He was moving himself away little by little when all the noises and the powerful light stopped.

'Done. The universe will from this moment be a happier, more peaceful place,' said the ship, holding up the tile with one two fingered arm. The tile was now floppy, and lots of different splotchy patches of dull greens.

Yes, thought Cort, the universe would be happier and more peaceful, and not because the weapons were made weak, but because the people who had been using them were rotting away where they sat, and would no longer be giving all the orders. The greedophiles had finally got their true reward.

'Fly-ahead boy? We must make a really quick detour, back up to exospace. I have a signal to send.'

'You can't do it from here?' Cort muttered to himself.

No answer, but words began to appear. Communication was back to air screening again.

'I must send it from there, so it can drop back into the universe everywhere, including many many galaxies away, straight after I have sent it.'

Even while Cort was reading the words in front of his eyes, the ship felt like it was lifting. It began to scream that clean scream.

'Here we go again,' said Cort, hanging on tight to his Fly-ahead controls, even though they were doing nothing, and then came the feeling like he was being fired across space by a huge rubber band.

As the ship steadied, he smelt the most strange thing – hot chocolate, like someone was making some for him to drink.

LITMUS EXPLAINS

Distant stars, and peaceful space. Work was going on behind

Litmus and Mark – the Mandelbrot's crew repairing what was

left of their ship, getting it ready to be towed home by the helpod, when the helpod got back with the scout pilot, asleep onboard in a stabilising unit. He was still alive, and that, Mark just knew, meant that the Magnificus Royale would be able to fix him.

Where was Litmus's ship? This was like waiting to be picked up from school thought Mark, him and Litmus standing around together.

'Two,' said Litmus, powerfully pleased with his thought.

'Two what?' asked Mark.

'You can't trap two in nothing, because they have each other. I've got you.'

'Yeah well,' said Mark, because the "got you" felt a bit claustrophobic, like he was Litmus's personal belonging, 'I belong to everyone you know.'

'I only belong to me,' said Litmus, looking happy greedy.

'Crap,' said Mark laughing inside, 'You, Litmus, are Alito the Unbreakable Child, and every kid everywhere has a part of you in them. So you belong to all of us.'

'Yes?' said Litmus, like he was hopeful.

'Yes,' said Mark.

'Hey, what's with IPE air screening everything, why doesn't she, he, it, just talk at us?'

'I asked that once. She said "Well, you are a lot smarter than big people Alito. Grown-ups need long explanations. I screen the right words for each person. For some people I have to use lots of words. For you, lots of the time, I used to use just one, like food, or bed, or stop annoying your father. Food, for a royal court lady, would translate to "this evening's sustenance will commence with a platter of finely…" and go on for about seven screens, until your dinner was cold and no longer nice". We found a better reason though, IPE and me. When we had a meeting on board, we needed all the politicians and military people to know different things, so the air screening was good, and then one day we realised they didn't think IPE was listening, just because IPE didn't talk. We learn lots of true things because of that. That is the best reason. If you never talk, people think you never listen, but IPE hears everything. One day she did talk at me. She screamed "Alito Magnificus, if you don't stop that, I will be really, really angry". I did, but then I giggled and said "Bit late then, hey", because she was really really angry already? It was so funny.'

'Good one Bunny Bum,' said Mark, feeling sorry for IPE – there would have been times when Litmus was just plain horrible to be around.

SOMETHING IS COMING

Mark was back inside the protection of the Telemetrene sphere, because Litmus had ordered it, saying 'Don't push your luck. Magnificci things take time to get their best, and I saw from your sparkly colour in the battle that you're not finished being made yet. Rainbow colours aren't supposed to happen in your sparkleness'.

Commander Yorker was coming over the hull surface of the remains of the Mandelbrot, with two space helmets in her hands.

Litmus put his space helmet on like it was a game, and stood like he was modelling it, pleased with himself. The telemetrene sphere let the other helmet come through, and then Commander Yorker's hand, so the rest of her came inside its safe environment too.

'Welcome back Staffer Planetti,' she said as she took her helmet off, 'It's good to see your roughnut face again. You're a size smaller than your Geneheritage friend? I forgot how young you are.'

Mark had no answer to that. Commander Yorker finished looking at him, and went on talking.

'I'm here because we could see you two were having a conversation, but we're not getting a signal. I don't know how you do it, but our microphones need atmosphere, and there's news.'

'What news?' asked Litmus from outside.

'There is a master ship sneaking up on us, weapons trained. Their outer armour seems to be missing, but we have no defences, and no ship mounted offensive weapons left. I've ordered my crew back into the hull. I'm hoping you two have an answer for this.'

'Yes,' said Litmus, 'When they get here, I will ripped their weapons off, and throwed them away. You will be hided with Planetboy in our sphere, and give me advice on which bits.'

'We have a plan,' said Commander Yorker, like she was laughing at herself for having trouble coping with Litmus.

'They are transmitting orders,' she said next, concentrating on what was going on, her own issues instantly pushed aside.

'Maked it so I can hear, and I am the only one to do answers to them. I want that,' said Litmus.

'As you will,' said Commander Yorker, 'Here they come, right in front of us. That motley green dull colouring is really good camouflage in the dark. I haven't seen them use that before.'

"This is the Capitalisto master ship Xenophobia. You have three hundred thousand litres of water on board. You will surrender all of it."

'We have a lot less than half that,' said Commander Yorker, for Litmus and Mark to hear, 'and we need it for my crew to survive.'

'They are counting your crew as water for them,' said Litmus, 'I know, because I remember this badness from their first time wrecking everything, when I was small.'

You're still small thought Mark to himself. Still small, but one hundred and eighty years more experienced, even if that experience happened from one hundred and eighty turns at being six for a year. Make that six be seven, Mark corrected his thoughts.

'Now I will speaked them,' ordered Litmus, sounding more like he was five.

'Xenothing, I am Alito, Emprino of the Magnificci. You have made me cranky. I am now going to removed your weapons.'

'They're laughing,' said Commander Yorker to Mark, telling him what communications she was listening to.

The sphere's see through shell twinkled strangely, on the side towards the master ship, but only for a moment. Mark wondered what it had just done, or just protected him from.

'And now they're sounding like a control deck full of squawking chirping chickens. This is the strangest deployment I have ever been on,' said Commander Yorker.

'I asked for a chook bomb. That means Grandpa is all right. My ship is coming,' said Litmus happily, 'IPE has chooked the Xenothing for me.'

Or maybe not, worried Mark – the telemetrene sphere was like the helpod, in that it had more tricks up its technology sleeve than anyone suspected. He began worrying where the Magnificci seeder might be, that it wasn't here already. IPE wouldn't be leaving Litmus alone unless she absolutely had to. He could tell by the way Litmus's helmet was tilted, as he looked across at the sphere, that he had had the same thoughts. Were IPE and the captain all right?

'This won't wait,' warned Commander Yorker.

The Magnificus Royale might have survived its battle with The Great Karoshi, and be right now on its way to help, but the Xenophibia's weapons turret was altering shape. No longer threatening, it was getting ready to fire.

LITMUS THE WRECKER DOES HIS THING

Litmus shot forward, until he was up on top of the huge ship. He reached down, knees bent, a tiny figure standing at the point where the turret housing joined the ship's hull. Getting his little hands in under the edge, he lifted the gun turret aimed at the Mandelbrot like it was a very, very big saucepan lid. Now it sat crooked, with torn metal plates wires and pipes where it was still half joined to the ship.

There were big dents in the ship's hull, where Litmus's feet had been when he was lifting.

'Show me 'nother one?' he offered.

The Xenophobia swivelled a smaller turret around, to aim at Litmus. He ripped that one clean off, and threw it away, even as it was firing at him.

'A warning Alito,' said Commander Yorker, 'If they think they are losing, the officers sneak off in their command module.'

'Leaving their crew to die,' said Mark unhappy.

'No, so they can explode the main ship as a weapon. It would take the Mandelbrot with it, killing all my crew. They don't care if their crew die, because they believe the people at the top are all that's important – it's a greedophile thing. There they go – I can tell from that faint glow coming from behind that ship – they just disconnected from the main hull.'

Litmus shot over and around, behind the Xenophobia, vanishing from view.

'All without a back pack, just flies around wherever he likes. Smart buggers those Magnificci scientists,' said Commander Yorker.

'It's an indestructible being thing – where he is in this universe is up to him,' said Mark, 'so he's not really flying, just deciding to be somewhere different.'

Something was happening over there, behind the Xenophobia, causing explosions of light. What looked like sticks, wires, and little pieces of metal, began flying off into space.

'What is he doing?' wondered Commander Yorker.

'This thing is very strong,' came Litmus's voice through the helmet headsets, 'But I maked some dints already, and I just tooked their motors off. They keep making transmitting aerials stand up, or wires for doing messages fly out, but they're not having them either.'

'Uh-oh,' said Mark.

People in space suits were pouring out of the Xenophobia's hull, and rushing up to the half broken large turret.

'They're trying to get it working,' said Commander Yorker, 'Alito, it's a bloody big cannon. I need to bring my troops out. Can I bring my soldiers out?'

'No. Them ones on the turret thing aren't doing any guns, and they haven't been bad yet,' said Litmus, 'I don't want your soldiers hurt. Planetboy, you do some thinking.'

'Well,' said Mark, 'Maybe having it damaged like that is causing leaks inside their ship, that are killing the crew? They might be working on it to fix that?'

'Nice thought staffer, but they are jerry rigging it to aim at Alito,' said Commander Yorker.

Mark thought about the Magnificci being three hundred years behind in the weapons race. This large turret weapon was the ship's main armament, and maybe it could hurt Litmus. Sometimes happy confidence in your own ability, and in how things were going, came just before sad disaster, especially when you were small.

'I'm not being brave,' sang out Litmus from wherever he was, 'Every time I go to leave they poke out another transmitter thing, like it's what they want to do the most. I have to stay and snap them off. I want that. If that thing shoots at me I will get out of the way, and they will be shooted themselves.'

THE XENOPHOBIA'S CREW

The turret jerked around, wild and rough in its movements. One crew of workers held up their left arms, to say they were finished their repair job. The big barrel aimed down, and down, pointing where Mark and Commander Yorker couldn't see, and then another team's arms went up. More workers were reconnecting massive pipes or wires, putting huge collars around where they were damaged, and then tightening the collars on. That crew's arms went up too.

'Definitely trying to get the thing working, and making good progress by the look of it. That one there,' said Commander Yorker suddenly, 'The one standing by himself next to that fin strut, holding something? What's he doing?

'Ah yes – the crew have no vision outside the hull without the command module's permission. That will be a hand held camera, letting workers back inside the hull see what is going on. Alito, Alito, I have it – the crew are mutinying, trying to destroy the command module before it blows them up. From my experience on fighting ships I am sure of it. That "arms finished" work signal, and the weapons maintenance work done so efficiently, that is Star Alliance. They are a ripping good Space Navy. Were.

This lot have been imprisoned and enslaved. I think all they are waiting for now is you to get out of the way. Move back from the command module and hold your arm up. Left arm Alito, and we'll see.'

Mark wasn't sure Litmus knew his left from his right, but Litmus appeared above the Xenophobia his left arm held high, and the turret fired. It was a frightening weapon, that made the large hull of the Xenophobia rock, as the cannon turret fired a targeted stream of molten poisonous high speed energy vomit.

'Yes!!' said Commander Yorker, when the mess of something destroyed went in all directions, 'Finally I am some use in this team. We should celebrate.'

COMMANDER YORKER'S PLAN

Commander Yorker's words were still echoing in Mark's thoughts. Celebrate? People died thought Mark, and they mightn't all have been bad even. What about whoever was being the pilot of the command module? He or she probably didn't have a choice, and was just there doing their job. Celebrating wasn't right, not in war. It was desperately sad whoever won, and whoever lost, because people got to miss, forever, the people they needed in their lives, people from both sides.

'Not in the mood to cheer, staffer?' said Commander Yorker looking at Mark.

'No. War sucks. And people in charge who cause it suck the most,' said Mark.

Commander Yorker didn't have an answer for a moment.

'War will happen, because every society has greedophiles,' she said finally, 'Capitalist, Communist, Socialist, in every "ist" greedophiles cunningly work their way to the top, then steal that world from its people – it's up to the ordinary people not to let them get in charge.'

Litmus had taken his helmet off and wasn't listening. He was busy eating red lollies. He was having to pick the red ones out for eating first, because the lollies were all colours – the Mandelbrot had lost most of its stores, and he had been lucky to get what he got.

The crews of the Mandelbrot and the Xenophobia were helping each other with their repairs, while Mark and Commander Yorker watched.

'How can ordinary people even tell, before it's too late I mean,' said Mark, back on the topic of war and greedophiles.

'The greedophiles are the ones who pay themselves a lot more than everyone else,' said Commander Yorker, 'and think the people making money for them should get paid less, and less, and less. It's easy to spot once you know how.

'I've been doing some thinking about this, because successful Ship of The Line commanders get asked to say nice things about the government, because people trust us, because we have saved the day a few times, and everyone's seen that on the news. I've got a sort of speech ready for that, nearly. Or maybe not a speech, but my plan for how things should go back home, for everyone to have a nice life? This is it.'

She cleared her throat nervously, because she was a fighting ship commander, not a politician clever at public speaking, then she took a breath to start.

'A safe democratic capitalist state only pays its politicians the average wage of its people. The politicians are there to serve, not stuff their bank accounts, and when they retire, they get exactly the same pension as everyone else. That way we know the pensions will be adequate for all our grannies and pops, and for us when we get there.

'Blue Skies One isn't managing that at the moment, but a visit from your Captain Thomas at the end of all this, and they will straighten up and fly right. It's usually rotten business people, people who got rich by taking too much profit for themselves from whatever they did, who want to be politicians.'

'Well I'm not going to use my life up doing that, so they can have the money,' decided Mark, 'Litmus and I are going to fly among the stars bashing up baddies.'

'I thought you didn't approve of war staffer. Bashing up baddies sounds a lot like war to me. Good plan though. If people are going to stay safe at home, someone needs to be prepared to work to keep them that way. Alito the Emprino arriving anywhere and throwing his weight around, that would certainly make the politicians and military idiots reconsider their behaviour. The Magnificci can make your lifeworld star disappear from the sky, and if you really upset that little brat, I personally think he'd be up for it.'

Commander Yorker seemed to like that thought. Now she was distracted, and giving an order to her lieutenant, standing out on the central shell skin of the Mandelbrot, supervising the setting up of the ship for travelling home.

'Lieutenant, get out the safety tow launcher, and mount it on the forrard right shoulder plate. When she appears on the news, I want people to feel proud that the old girl can still fire something.'

'Aye aye Sir.'

Commander Yorker turned to Mark again.

'Makes you wonder how the Democratzia ever thought they could win, taking on the Magnificci. By the way, the Magnificci were the richest of the rich, in all the galaxies. I'm not saying they were necessarily greedophiles, but you are travelling with them now. Use that power wisely, and wherever I am retired to, when I see you in the news I will have happy memories of you.'

'Thanks,' was all Mark could think of to say.

'But first I have to swap what's left of my ship for a new one. I think I will ask to have it named the Extrapolator, and hopefully it will be retrofitted with a few Magnificci tricks up its sleeve, if I can suck up hard enough to Alito and the old captain for that to happen. Your control deck is actually Alito's play room. That IPE thing showed me the real layout of a Magnificci ship's battle deck, and it is amazing. There is almost nothing you couldn't do, in a ship with that much vision, and that much control. I can't wait.'

'Then…where would you go? What would you do with it?' asked Mark.

'I think staffer, finally, this war is winding up. Today was the turning point. We destroyed the only thing capable of stopping Alito and the captain, and they are way past putting up with more political bullshit and threats. Anyone on the wrong side of them from now on is going down, in a big way. Soon as the dust settles from that there's going to be a cushy job – being in the victory fleet – three ships – souped up helpod, flying cucumber, and the Extrapolator, doing public relations visits to everywhere, to inspire people getting their worlds back to normal. Every world we visit, the school children get real time virtual tours inside the vessels, the leaders get a wardroom dinner evening of your Captain Thomas's wisdom, and everyone feels good that something really horrible is over, and they got to meet the people who made that happen for them. After we've done our duty with that, I wouldn't mind being part of your trip out into the unknown, to look for the Magnificci. A ship of The Line can be a useful travelling companion.'

Mark thought about that. All through the galaxies there would be lurking greedophiles, hoping to take control of the new governments rebuilding lifeworlds. Being so small, a helpod and the Magnificus Royale would look easy targets to them, but a thing like the Mandelbrot lurking in the background, a machine designed to cause pain and sadness, that would make them think very hard first. But children would see it too, and Mark didn't think that was a good idea – for kids to have to worry about something like that being out in space somewhere.

'This new ship, this Extrapolator, does it have to be so ugly?' he asked, 'I mean, not ugly, but…but, you know – like the Mandelbrot – threatening nasty, violent evil looking? Kids shouldn't have to see that?'

'Staffer, you are such a sweety. Kids like a bit of pretend death and destruction.'

The Mandelbrot had never looked like it could pretend anything. Mark was just about to point that out, but Commander Yorker started talking first.

'Don't worry your young head – when we do victory parade appearances we drape her in flags, and she looks like a colourful old lady drying her washing.'

The Star Alliance crew were in a hurry to get their ship moving. They were worried the Democratzia would take retribution on the last surviving Star Alliance planet, and they wanted to be back there to save people. And probably do a bit of retribution of their own, thought Mark. A master ship, even without the outer armour plating, and with some Litmus caused weapons damage, was still a powerful destructive machine, and they were now in charge of it. Any Democratzia ships hanging around the last Star Alliance lifeworld were in for a nasty surprise.

Commander Yorker had left the telemetrene sphere. A conference was happening out there, people floating around between the two ships using their helmet radios to communicate, because the Xenophobia's communications systems were locked, for the moment.

Even as they were talking to Commander Yorker, the Xenophobia began to turn, positioning itself for leaving, and they had to rush back inside. They were going home to build a new Star Alliance civilisation, and had to get there while there was still something left to build it from.

FOR OURSELVES, AND FOR EACH OTHER

The Xenophobia vanished into the dark, a large dull blotchy green blob of military hardware.

'Well,' declared Commander Yorker, as she got back into the telemetrene sphere, 'What this weird safety bubble of yours needs is a chair or two, because we're not going anywhere until our lot show up, your ship or the Helpod, to give us a tow. Alito, where the f…, I mean – where is this ship of yours? Are you sure the old captain can fly it by himself?'

Litmus was standing out in space, standing on nothing, like only an Indestructible Being of the Magnificci can, and looking out into the darkness.

'Grandpa left our chair behind,' he said.

'And?' said Commander Yorker, wanting her questions answered.

Commander Yorker tapped at her helmet, to make sure its headset was working, because she hadn't got a reply.

'There they are!' shouted Litmus flinging out a pointing arm, his face excited and hopeful and satisfied, all at the same time.

Even with all your faults, I still have to love you thought Mark. It was the hope and worry and joy of the little creature doing its very best at being alive. Sometimes its very best wasn't very good, but that was just life. Sometimes someone being a minicus near you was really irritating. Right then Mark understood how mothers and fathers, and uncles and aunts, and family friends, and people everywhere, had soft hearts for children. It would take an evil person not to care, for a little creature beginning its best go of its turn in eternity. The more hopeless it was, the more it needed people to care what happened to it. Mark considered IPE's words about that young Axel Thomas, standing on the edge of his childhood, looking out at everything, and saying goodbye to being a boy, forever.

Litmus was looking across, wanting to share his happy moment. His eyes were saying "I'm really really happy. I want to share that with you?".

It was right then that Mark realised – it's not our physical bodies that need to be indestructible, it's our hearts, and not even the great Magnificci can do that for us – we have to do it the best we can for ourselves, and for each other.

'Grandpa hug,' he yelled loud and silly.

'He is going to get the biggest, baddest one ever,' yelled Litmus back, 'from ME.'

'If you have to live forever,' said Commander Yorker, looking at Litmus being himself, 'that is the way to do it.'

The Magnificus Royale was coming through the deep dark blue of space, a beautiful clean shaped thing. A small ship, but the best thought Mark. Who wanted something huge and ugly covered in weapons, when you could be aboard the last flying ship of The Magnificci, sailing the stars with your friends.

Suddenly everywhere, like snow falling, was the sound of Litmus's voice, over and over, from many moments in his life. It was making the telemetrene sphere shimmer, it was in all the helmet headsets. It was everywhere.

'Um? Is that me?' asked Litmus surprised.

Mark's heart sang with happiness.

'That means the Democratzia are toast,' he shouted, punching up into the air with both fists.

He wanted to jump around in circles like a mad grasshopper, just from relief that all the greed driven sadness had come to an end, and from the good feeling of tomorrow being a new beginning, out from under the shadow of violence, but he couldn't jump around like a mad thing – he was standing with the commanding officer of a ship of The Line.

'And now we celebrate,' commented Commander Yorker to herself, watching Mark.

Finally everything was going right in his life. After this they could go family hunting, for him and Litmus, and then, to go searching the universe for the new lifeworlds of the Magnificci, that would be the best adventure ever, or, maybe the whole Magnificci fleet was out there somewhere, coming back through space, just waiting to be met up with?

He saw with surprise that Commander Yorker had a tear in her eye, and a kind smile on her face, while she was looking at him! She's doing that fondness thing – I'm being treated like I'm a minicus thought Mark.

'Hey, wait up with that,' he said, 'Do I look like a boy made out of shining happiness to you?'

'Not how you look,' said Commander Yorker, 'Just what you are. And get over it staffer, because yes you do.'

The End

www.ingramcontent.com/pod-product-compliance
Lightning Source LLC
Chambersburg PA
CBHW031226020726
47499CB00002B/652